Small Town Siren

Other Books By Lexi Blake

EROTIC ROMANCE

Masters And Mercenaries
The Dom Who Loved Me
The Men With The Golden Cuffs
A Dom is Forever
On Her Master's Secret Service
Sanctum: A Masters and Mercenaries Novella
Love and Let Die
Unconditional: A Masters and Mercenaries Novella
Dungeon Royale
Dungeon Games: A Masters and Mercenaries Novella
A View to a Thrill
Cherished: A Masters and Mercenaries Novella
You Only Love Twice
Luscious: Masters and Mercenaries~Topped
Adored: A Masters and Mercenaries Novella
Master No
Just One Taste: Masters and Mercenaries~Topped 2
From Sanctum with Love
Devoted: A Masters and Mercenaries Novella
Dominance Never Dies
Submission is Not Enough
Master Bits and Mercenary Bites~The Secret Recipes of Topped
Perfectly Paired: Masters and Mercenaries~Topped 3
For His Eyes Only
Arranged: A Masters and Mercenaries Novella
Love Another Day
At Your Service: Masters and Mercenaries~Topped 4
Master Bits and Mercenary Bites~Girls Night
Nobody Does It Better, Coming February 20, 2018
Close Cover, Coming April 10, 2018
Protected, Coming July 31, 2018

Lawless
Ruthless
Satisfaction
Revenge

Small Town Siren
Texas Sirens Book 1

Lexi Blake
writing as
Sophie Oak

Small Town Siren
Texas Sirens Book 1

Published by DLZ Entertainment LLC at Smashwords

Copyright 2018 DLZ Entertainment LLC
Edited by Chloe Vale
ISBN: 978-1-937608-72-9

This is a work of fiction. Names, places, characters and incidents are the product of the author's imagination and are fictitious. Any resemblance to actual persons, living or dead, events or establishments is solely coincidental.

Dedication

For Rich

Foreword

Way back in 2010, I was a nervous author trying to get published. I'm still nervous—about everything—but *Small Town Siren* was published in July of that year. Later, I found Bliss, Colorado and wove the two series together in that way I enjoy. I built a little universe filled with cowboys who liked to share, women who don't mind shooting a son of a bitch, and several small towns that formed the basis for this world. A few years later, for legal reasons, I made the difficult decision to leave behind my original pen name and the worlds I'd built. I moved on and became Lexi Blake. There was this start-up company called McKay-Taggart that I decided to double down on and the rest is my own personal history.

But I never forgot my cowboys—my Jack and my Sam, my Max and my Rye. I didn't forget Willow Fork or Bliss, and in my head, I saw all the ways these babies of mine were tied together. I can't help it. We tend to write what we know and the stories of my childhood came from science fiction and comic books—a place where even the oddest of characters can have ties you never expected. In my head, McKay-Taggart and Texas Sirens, Bliss, CO and Lawless, Thieves and Faery Story all fit together.

Fast forward to 2017 and the joy of being able to finally bring my family together. Over the course of the next year, I'll be revising all the Sophie Oak books to bring them into the Lexi universe—as they always should have been.

Small Town Siren was my first and going back over it has been more of a joy than I would have thought. I sort of cringed at the thought of reediting. What could I have to say about characters who've been around for seven years? Turns out there were a few things I've learned since that first book and I hope it shows in this second edition. What I realized was, while the story itself hasn't changed, there was certainly more to show the reader. So I hope you enjoy some of the new scenes and a fresh take on the small town that started everything for me.

It's good to go home, even more so when you know your *whole* family is waiting for you.

Much love,
Lexi

Sign up for Lexi Blake's newsletter
and be entered to win a $25 gift certificate
to the bookseller of your choice.

Join us for news, fun, and exclusive content
including free short stories.

There's a new contest every month!

Go to www.LexiBlake.net to subscribe.

Prologue

Willow Fork, Texas
20 years before

Abigail Moore held her plain white T-shirt up just under her breasts as she stared at herself in the mirror, trying to see any sign of the change to her body. Shouldn't she be able to see some kind of alteration? After all, her whole damn life had changed with a single pee.

Pregnant. She was pregnant and Adam was dead, and what the hell was she going to do?

She let the T-shirt drop. There was zero change to her body yet, but she could see it in her face. Seventeen years old. She was seventeen and her life was over. Everything they'd said about her was true. She was reckless and stupid and she was going to pay the price.

She heard the door to the trailer open and braced herself. Her mother was home. It was time to tell her mother that she had screwed everything up.

Abby wiped away her tears. She had a high school diploma and roughly three hundred dollars from her summer job saved up. She could work through the pregnancy and try to start community college classes after she had the baby.

She would go slow. Slow but steady.

It would be easier to tell her mother about the baby if she had a plan. It was a shitty plan that mostly involved hoping and praying everything went okay, but it was something of a plan.

Bright smile. She would convince Momma that everything was going to be all right.

The smile died on her face when she realized it wasn't her mother standing there in the living room.

It was Ruby Echols. Adam's mother. She was standing in the middle of the trailer Abby had grown up in wearing one of her best Sunday suits and looking around the place like she was trying not to touch anything.

She wasn't alone. The sheriff was standing with her. Behind her, really. The sheriff was in full uniform, his hat on his head and that Colt at his side in view.

"I'm sorry, dear," Ruby said, her voice calm and even, as though she was here to talk about the church charity function. "I knocked, but no one came to the door."

Because Abby had been crying in the bathroom. "I didn't hear you. My mom isn't here. She's still at work."

Abby glanced at the clock. Her mom wouldn't be home for another half hour. Her stomach twisted. Ruby would likely know that. Abby had come to understand that Ruby Echols knew absolutely everything that went on in Willow Fork.

A serpentine smile curled up Ruby's lips. "Oh, when she comes home is up to you, dear."

God, Adam had hated his mother. *Don't look her in the eyes*, he would say. *You might turn to stone. I can't wait until we blow this town, baby. We're leaving and never looking back.*

Adam Echols. So beautiful. So reckless.

She would never love another man. How could she? Adam had been the love of her life and now she had to face it all alone.

"What does that mean? And you, Sheriff Lyle? Are you suddenly interested in enforcing the trailer park home owner's association codes?" She wouldn't put it past them.

Since she'd started dating Adam, Ruby Echols had done everything in her power to make Abby's life miserable. She'd made sure the only grocery store in town wouldn't sell her anything. Abby had to drive forty miles to find a fast food place that would hire her. She'd gotten more tickets for traffic violations than she could keep up with. It wouldn't surprise her at all if the sheriff started ticketing her for not keeping the grass a certain height.

"Don't you turn that smart mouth on me, missy," he growled her way. "I'll have you in a jail cell and I promise you won't like it."

She turned her chin up. "You can't arrest me. I haven't done anything wrong."

He stared her down. "I think I can come up with something."

Ruby held a hand up. "I don't think that will be necessary today, Sheriff. I think Miss Moore will prove not to be a problem after today. Tell me something, Abigail. Was the test positive?"

She felt her eyes widen. "What?"

"The pregnancy test you had that whore friend of yours buy for you this morning. Was it positive?"

Her hands started to shake. God, she'd just found out about her baby. Mere moments before she'd been considering all her options and now fear rushed through her system as icy cold as the stream that ran on the outskirts of town. "That's none of your business."

"It doesn't have to be," Ruby said, her tone entirely too reasonable for this conversation.

"What is that supposed to mean?"

"It means that you can make this easy on yourself or it can be hard on everyone." She clutched her bag in one hand, patting her helmet of icy blonde hair with the other. "You can leave this town and never come back and your mother will continue to have a job and a pension and a home, or you can decide to stay and she will lose all of those things. Right now her employer is waiting to hear from me. If I call before five, he'll fire her today. Imagine that, Abigail. Your poor, uneducated mother trying to find another job that pays even half as well. And she's a diabetic. I'm afraid her health care will go."

The thought turned her stomach. "She didn't do anything to you."

"Oh, but she did. She gave birth to the slut who killed my son."

Abby could argue that Adam had done that himself. Adam had

been the one who'd driven away in the middle of a thunderstorm. She'd begged him not to, but it wouldn't make a difference to the Echols family. Everything was Abby's fault.

Ruby wasn't finished. "In addition to your mother suffering if you don't leave this town, I promise if I see you walking around here with a bastard in your belly, I'll come after it. I won't love it. I won't consider it mine. I'll make sure that child knows every single day what a whore its momma was. You really should have taken me up on my former offer."

Her former offer had been five thousand dollars if Abby would leave Adam and never see him again. Abby had turned her down flat.

"And if I leave?" It took everything she had not to run back to the bathroom and throw up. How was this happening? How was Adam dead and gone and his child growing inside her? How was her world falling apart?

She'd fallen in love with a boy. That was her only crime.

"Like I said, I don't want that bastard. I'm not even certain it's Adam's. Probably not given that everyone knows you spread your legs for half the county."

She hadn't. She'd given herself to Adam because she'd loved him, but Abby knew it didn't matter.

And she knew one thing. All that crying in the bathroom and trying to figure out what to do about her pregnancy had been silly. She knew now. All it had taken was Ruby Echols's threat to make her understand she was going to be a mother.

She would never let anyone hurt her child.

"I need a few days to settle things."

Ruby shook her head, though that helmet of hers moved not a centimeter. "You leave today. You have ten minutes to pack, not that there's anything in this hellhole that's likely worth having. I've got an envelope containing a bus ticket to Dallas and one thousand dollars. The bus leaves in thirty minutes. You're either on it or I'll start paperwork to ensure that baby in your belly comes home with me."

"But my mom." Her head was whirling. How could this be happening? Maybe this was all one long bad dream. She would wake up and Adam would be alive and they would go off to Austin for college.

"Leave her a note, dear. She can't be surprised. After all, you're the town whore. Her life is going to be so much easier without you around," Ruby promised. "Now hurry. This is a one-time offer that goes away if that bus leaves without you."

She wanted to stay and fight. She wanted to tell that bitch to fuck herself.

The Echols family ruled this town. They owned most of the businesses and the bank. Every charity in town depended on their goodwill.

If she fought, she would lose.

Abby turned and went to pack her things.

Thirty minutes later, she looked out the window of the Greyhound bus that would take her to Dallas. She'd already decided that once she was there, she would take another to Fort Worth. Her aunt lived there. She would show up on her Aunt Rita's doorstep and promise to pay her back for the help Abby needed.

She was going to college and then she would see what the world had in store for her baby.

She would never give up.

As she rolled out of Willow Fork, she vowed not to come home again.

She put her hand on her belly. "All right, baby. Let's go see the world."

Willow Fork, Texas
Ten years later

Jack Barnes looked out over the spread he'd spent every dime he had on. Ten thousand acres of prime Texas ranch. It was quiet in the early morning light, a fog rolling in over the land.

In a few hours it wouldn't be so quiet. In a few hours they would receive eight hundred head of prime cattle and then they

17

would be in for it.

Jack took a sip of the coffee he'd made, noting how it steamed against the cool morning air.

God, he hoped he knew what he was doing. Life had been easier in Dallas, but he thought he could see where that lifestyle was going to take them. Him and Sam. He couldn't lose Sam. His best friend.

So here he was. Barnes and Fleetwood. Cattle ranchers. Organic cattle ranchers.

"Hey, Jack," a familiar voice said.

Sam walked out, his golden hair hidden under a beat-to-hell Stetson he'd found at a garage sale.

"Morning," Jack said, turning back to the land. He couldn't quite take his eyes off it. His. It was all his.

No. Theirs. It was his and Sam's.

"How was your night?" Jack asked.

Sam's shoulders drooped a bit. "I don't know. It was weird. The town is very closed off. Did you know they don't even sell beer at the grocery stores?"

"We'll have to stock up then," he offered. He put a hand on his best friend's shoulder. "Don't worry about it. I doubt you're going to have time to think about beer for the next few weeks. We'll be working way too hard getting this place ready to go."

A smile lit Sam's face, reminding Jack so much of the kid he'd first met in foster care. "We have a cattle ranch, Jack."

Damn straight they did, and that look on Sam's face was exactly why he'd taken them out of Dallas.

"We do indeed," Jack agreed. "You ready for this?"

Sam hustled off the stairs and moved toward the stables. He held his arms out as though embracing the world around him. "To be a cowboy? Hell, Jack, I was born to do this. I'm going to ride the fence line one last time before our babies get here. Wouldn't want to lose one."

They'd been training for this for months. Julian had found them a mentor, though they'd both worked as ranch hands before. They knew how to work a herd, but running a business was new.

He had to make this work. He'd gambled everything on this land and this ranch.

Their ranch.

Jack set the mug down and hustled after Sam.

Couldn't let his friend have all the fun, after all.

Jack breathed in the early morning air and promised that he would conquer Willow Fork, Texas.

This was going to be his kingdom.

Chapter One

Willow Fork
Present Day

Sam pulled up behind the old sedan that was parked in front of
Christa Wade's three-bedroom ranch house. She lived in town, a
few blocks off of the square where her diner was located. The front
yard was littered with kids' bikes, proving this was probably the
place where all the kiddos liked to spend their afternoon.

He could believe that. Christa was a nice lady and her husband
Mike was just about his best friend, outside of Jack, of course.

His cell phone trilled and Sam picked it up. "Hey, Jack."

"Hey, when you grab the order from the hardware store, could
you run by the grocer? Benita says we're out of olive oil. She's
texting you a list."

"Sure thing." He wasn't sure what they would do without
Benita Wells. She'd been their housekeeper since two weeks after
they'd moved into the ranch house and figured out that while they
were pretty good with cattle, neither one of them could cook for shit.
They'd put an ad out but one of the ranch hands had come forward,
offering for his wife to take the job while they looked for a
permanent solution.

Benita was the solution and now her husband was their

foreman.

"Tell her I'll be back well before din… Holy shit."

Sam stopped, the phone suddenly not important at all as that crap-ass sedan's door opened up and the single most luscious thing he'd ever seen in his life stepped out.

She had vibrant auburn hair that ran like a waterfall down her back. So much hair. And that wasn't the only thing that hot honey had been blessed with. She wore a V-necked T-shirt and jeans that clung to her body the way he clung to a cold beer after a long day.

She bounced out of the car, proving those amazing breasts were real.

He could feel them in his hands, practically see her nipples tightening under his gaze.

Lust hit him hard and fast and in a way he'd never really known before. Not that he hadn't wanted a woman at first sight before. Hell, men were wired that way, but this one…oh, this one was damn near perfect.

"Sam!"

Damn it. He picked the phone back up. "Sorry, Jack. I'm going to have to call you back. I'll get the oil. Hey, why am I going to the grocery store for oil? I can get some from Mike. He's gotta have a couple of quarts in his garage."

He kind of halfway listened to Jack as he watched the luscious redhead run into Christa Wade's arms. Those could be his arms. The world seemed to slow and she did that *Baywatch* bounce of a run. He could see himself as Christa, opening his arms and welcoming her into them. Sure, Christa kissed her sweet cheek and he would have his tongue halfway down her throat, but it was somewhat the same. Except that he would also pick that pretty girl up and haul her into the bedroom for some sweet, sweet double penetration, and he was fairly certain Christa wasn't planning to do that.

"Sam!"

Why did he have a phone in the first place? "Yeah, Jack?"

"Are you drunk or did you see a woman?"

He felt his lips curl. At least Jack knew him well. "The most gorgeous woman I've ever seen. She seems to be some sort of friend of Christa's since they're doing that thing when women friends haven't seen each other in a long time."

"Were they doing that thing where they jump up and down and their boobs touch?" Jack asked.

He prayed he wasn't drooling. They were still hugging, but they'd both bent backward a bit so they could talk to each other. Redhead had the most gorgeous lips. She smiled and the whole fucking world seemed to light up.

"Yep."

"Okay, you need to take a deep breath. How about you go to the hardware store now and come back to Christa's later?" Jack suggested. "Or perhaps skip Christa's altogether. We don't have to have her out to dinner. It's probably better that we don't. We've got a shit ton of work to do. We don't have time to socialize."

Damn it. If he left it to Jack, they wouldn't have a damn social life at all. They would spend all their time with cows and people who worked for them. Jack was a workaholic. "Nope. I'm going to talk to her."

"Do you even know who 'her' is?"

"Doesn't matter." He was going in. She was probably some friend of Christa's from out of town and she would likely be married because if some man hadn't claimed that woman, the universe was out of alignment.

"Sam, think about this," Jack warned. "You remember what happened last time."

He felt his eyes roll. Jack often took things way too seriously. "Last time I nearly got my ass kicked by someone's husband. But it all turned out okay. We ended the discussion with a round of beers or two." Or ten. "And she wasn't half as gorgeous as this one. This one would be worth a beating. I'll get the oil that's not motor oil. I promise. Bye, Jack."

He hung up because there was no talking him out of meeting her. Jack would try to be all logical and stuff, but Sam preferred to let his dick take over in cases like this.

He slid out of his truck. The good news was he'd taken a shower before coming into town. He was sweet smelling and ready to take down a lady or two. He pointedly slammed the truck door, trying to get the attention of the women.

They paid him absolutely no mind.

"I can't believe you're here," Christa was saying. "I thought it would never happen. You're standing on my lawn."

"It was never your lawn I had a problem with," Red said.

Red had a husky voice that went straight to his cock. Damn. He needed to get a grip or he would scare her off.

Christa hugged her tight again. "I missed you. I know we talk all the time, but I missed you."

Whoa. There was only one person in the world Christa Wade would talk to like that. "Abigail Moore?"

She was a legend in these parts. Ever since he and Jack had moved here, they'd heard stories of her wild teen days. Her adventures were toasted in bars and whispered about in the churches of the town. Even twenty years later there were still members of the small town who considered her a siren leading young men to sin. She was a cautionary tale. She was a legend.

Damn straight she was. That woman could lead him into sin any time she liked.

"Sam?" Christa took a step back, wiping at her eyes. "Hey, what are you doing here?"

A kernel of guilt sparked. He'd interrupted something important, but it was quelled by getting his first real look at Abby Moore as the redhead turned toward him, an amused look on her face.

"Looks like my reputation precedes me," she said with a shake of her head. "That one is not originally from Willow Fork. I know because I would remember him."

She had a gorgeous hourglass figure made for fucking. Her hips were womanly, and though she was petite, there was nothing delicate about her. She'd been made to please a man in bed, and Sam didn't see why that man couldn't be him.

As for her reputation that was merely a plus in his mind. Abby must be in her late thirties now, but he had a hard time imagining that she'd been sexier as a teenager.

Christa's head swung slightly between the two of them as though she was trying to figure something out. "Abby, this is Sam Fleetwood. He and his partner, Jack Barnes, moved to Willow Fork

23

about ten years ago. They own what used to be the old Jones spread outside of town."

A laugh huffed out of Abby's mouth. "Well, naturally they do." She shook her head and held out her hand. "Mr. Fleetwood, it's nice to meet you. Please excuse my casual state of dress. I drove straight here from Fort Worth. I have a few boxes I'm going to store in Christa and Mike's garage. My momma's trailer doesn't have much room, you see."

He took her hand in his and a vision of her between him and Jack smashed through his senses. She would be so small between them. They would turn her this way or that, taking turns kissing her and touching her.

He gently squeezed her hand. "Please call me Sam. I'm not one to stand on formalities. And I'd really like to call you Abby."

Her smile wavered, but not in a bad way. No. That high-voltage smile had briefly dimmed, as though she'd become very, very aware of him. It was something Jack had taught him to look for. It was important to read the signs a woman gave off, and Abigail Moore had enjoyed touching his hand. It was over in a second and she was right back to smiling brilliantly. "Abby is my name. And how long have you been with your partner? I think Christa called him Jack."

He reluctantly let her hand go. "Hell, Jack and I have been together so long it's hard to remember a time we weren't."

"That's nice to hear," Abby said. She glanced Christa's way. "How about some coffee and then I'll put this fine young man to work. You look like you can handle some boxes. Only if you have time. The moving van was about thirty minutes behind me."

He needed to get back out to the ranch, but there was no way he wasn't going to stay. "Of course. I'm here to help."

And find a way in because there was no way he was letting that lady go.

* * * *

Abby took the coffee from Christa and wished the world was a fairer place. Here she was for the first time in her adult life without a child or husband to worry about. She was free and clear to have some crazy times and the hottest man she'd ever met in her life was right in front of her.

And naturally he was gay.

The van had already come and gone and she'd watched that hot-as-hell cowboy move her boxes into Christa's garage. He'd done it all without breaking a sweat, which was sad because if he had he might have taken off his shirt.

She was getting to be a dirty old lady. He had to be ten years younger than she was.

She wondered what Sam Fleetwood's partner looked like.

"So, you bought the old Jones spread?" She was curious. She tried not to be. Not about Willow Fork. But years had softened her and she had to admit she'd had her share of good times in this old town. "Did his son not want to run the ranch?"

Christa shook her head as she joined Abby on the couch. "Kyle left for college. He's a lawyer in New Orleans now. Mr. Jones had a heart attack and couldn't work anymore. He died two years back."

There was the tragedy of the small town. Too many young people left and there was no one to run the traditional businesses. The Jones spread had been a small cattle ranch that had struggled the whole time she'd been growing up. It was a hard life. "I'm sorry to hear that."

Even though old man Jones had been one of the men to stand behind Ruby Echols. Abby had tried to get a job at one of the few restaurants in town, and she'd been told Jones wouldn't sell his beef to anyone who employed her.

She took a long sip of coffee, trying to let the old worries go. Her mom needed her and twenty years had passed. It would be different this time around. It had to be since she was sitting here in ultra-conservative Willow Fork talking to a gay cowboy.

When she thought about it, it was kind of amazing.

If only he weren't the first man in forever who made her hormones perk up and sing.

"But Jack and Sam have reinvigorated the whole ranch," Christa said with a smile. "They rebuilt those nasty old stables."

"Hey, our horses deserve the best," Sam said with a sunny smile.

Oh, that's what he was. Sunshine. He seemed so light and fun. A breath of fresh air after years of clouds. She was going with the flow. So what if he wasn't crazy-mad affair material. He was fun and she could use a friend.

She would be here for a few months, most likely. If she could have some fun, it would make the time pass more quickly while she decided what to do with the rest of her life.

Her baby girl was grown. She was moving to Austin to go to college. It was time to start a new chapter in her life.

"What brings you back to Willow Fork, Abby?" Sam asked politely.

"My mom recently had surgery," she explained. "I'm a registered nurse so I'm going to help her through the worst parts. She's coming out of the hospital tomorrow. She's a fighter. She'll be on her feet in no time at all."

Her momma. It was going to be odd to live with her mom after all this time.

"A nurse?" Sam asked.

"Abby's a terrific nurse," Christa explained. "Graduated top of her class and went straight for the good stuff."

That made her laugh. "She means straight for the crazy stuff. I worked as a trauma nurse for years at John Peter Smith in downtown Fort Worth. Oh, I could tell you some stories."

Sam leaned forward. "I want to hear them all."

Such a sweetheart.

The door rattled as someone pounded a fist on it.

"Well, aren't we busy today?" Christa stood up. "I think it must have gotten around town that Mike made a brisket for supper."

Christa stepped out of the living room to open the door.

"I think we'll have to welcome you properly to town, Abby," Sam began. "You'll have to visit us at the ranch. I was coming here to invite Christa and Mike out to dinner next week. We're having a barbecue for some friends and our hands. We'd love to have you."

She felt her whole body flush at the idea of him having her. Yep, she was going to have to watch it so she didn't make a fool of herself around this golden god of a man. "I'll check my very busy schedule."

"You do that," he replied with a steady smile.

"Sam," a deep voice began.

Abby looked up and felt her jaw damn near drop open. Standing in the middle of Christa's frilly living room was Sam's exact opposite. Where Sam was sunny and light, this man was dark and decadent.

Like one of the characters in her favorite romance novels had walked off the pages.

Six foot two, with jet-black hair and eyes the color of emeralds. Abby hoped she wasn't drooling.

Sam sat back in his chair, crossing one leg over the other. "Jack, meet Abigail Moore. Abby, sweetheart, this is my partner, Jack Barnes."

Jack Barnes turned toward her, his eyes narrowed, and for a moment she wondered what she'd done to piss this man off. For a second it was as if she was seventeen again and she was up against the judgmental authorities of the town. Except he would be even harder to stand up to. This was a man who would get what he wanted, and if he wanted her out of town, she would go or he would ensure that she regretted it.

And then it was gone as though that dark look had never existed. His whole face softened and he held out a hand.

"Ms. Abigail, forgive me for the intrusion. I thought Sam was causing trouble where he shouldn't," he admitted.

"Trouble?" She couldn't imagine Sam causing trouble, though admittedly she'd only recently met him. He seemed super sweet. If he came into her ER, she would immediately put him in the easy-patient category.

Not so Jack Barnes. He would be stubborn as hell if he thought he wasn't getting the right care.

"Sometimes Sam forgets where he's supposed to be," Jack said with a frown.

"Sometimes Sam finds a new place that he's excited to be in," Sam returned smoothly. "Sometimes Jack forgets what it means to be spontaneous and to have fun."

"Sometimes Sam forgets he's got a job to do," Jack replied.

"Oh, I never forget that Jack. It's just sometimes you don't like

27

how I do my job," Sam replied with a silky smile.

Wow, they had some issues. She stood up, hating the fact that she'd already caused trouble. "Mr. Barnes, please let me apologize. I asked Sam to help me with moving some boxes and then Christa offered him some iced tea. It's my fault if he's late to work."

Jack Barnes looked her over. "Yes, I can see that."

Sam didn't miss a beat. "Abby is from Fort Worth. She's a nurse and unfortunately she lost her husband a few years back. She's been on her own since then. She's in town for a few months to help her momma recover from surgery. You can see why I offered her some help with her boxes. She's not going back to Fort Worth. She's not sure where she's going next."

"I'm in transition." She didn't know why but she felt a need to explain herself to the dark-haired man. "I think it's time for a change, but I haven't figured out what that means yet."

He shook his head and released a long breath. When he looked back up, he was charming and held out a hand. "Ms. Abigail, please forgive my temper. We've had two hands down with the flu and I'm on edge, but I should never take that out on a lady. I'm glad Sam could help. Please feel free to call on either one of us if you need anything at all."

His hand enveloped hers as she took it. He covered her with his other hand, encircling her with warmth. She had to remember to breathe for a moment. He was so big and…solid. That was the word.

This was a man she could count on if he liked her. This was a man who would do anything *for* someone he cared about and anything *to* his enemies.

And it was very obvious he was jealous of his boyfriend's time.

"Thank you for that, Mr. Barnes," she replied, gently removing her hand. "But I think you'll find I'm a very independent woman. Boxes aside. I'm here for a few weeks, month and a half tops, and I intend to be very quiet about my stay. I doubt you'll even notice I'm here."

"I don't think noticing you is going to be a problem," he replied.

She flashed him what she hoped was a carefree smile. "Well, I better get on over to my momma's place. Christa, I'll take you up on that job while I'm here. I can start tomorrow if you've got a shift in the morning. Mom doesn't come home until tomorrow night."

Christa hugged her tight. "I'll have a uniform waiting and ready. I love it. You and me against the world. It's high school all over again."

Sam stood up, frowning. "Maybe I should follow you over to your mom's. In case you need any help."

She shook her head and grabbed her purse. "No, but thank you so much." She glanced up at Jack, trying to let him know she wasn't going to come between him and Sam. She'd been happy to make a friend. The last thing she needed was to cause trouble. "Like I said, I'm very independent. Y'all have a good night."

Abby stepped outside before she could start a fight between them. She was sure Mr. Jack Barnes had heard the rumors about her and hustled over to save his boyfriend from getting mired in her problems. She couldn't blame him.

Well, she could, but it wouldn't change a thing. She'd meant what she said. She was here for a brief time and then she would move on again.

Because the last thing she would do was stay in this nasty old town. No matter how hot the cowboys were.

She got into her sedan and was grateful when the damn thing turned over.

Head held high, she drove away, not looking back once. That was a lesson she'd learned the hard way.

Chapter Two

"Did you have to run her off, Jack?" Christa crossed her arms over her chest and gave him a frown that could have frozen fire. "That is my best friend in the world. I don't care what you've heard about her, if you can't be civil to her in my home, maybe you're not welcome here."

Whoa. Jack put his hands up. He had obviously been misunderstood. "Chris, I meant no disrespect, and you know I don't listen to gossip. I thought Sam was about to get into another shitload of trouble, and you know he's on thin ice with the sheriff after the last bar brawl. I had no idea he was talking about your best friend."

"Talking about her?" Christa looked between him and Sam. "I thought you came over here to drop off an invite to the barbecue."

Sam was frowning his way. "I did and then I saw her. I was talking to Jack and explained that I needed a few minutes to say hello. I was being neighborly."

Christa's eyes narrowed. "You were being horny. I don't think it's a good idea. Abby's been through a lot. The last thing she needs is the two of you humping her leg and making a spectacle of her around town."

"I would never hump her leg," Jack replied sardonically. Though, damn, he'd hump plenty of other parts of her. She was the

30

single most gorgeous woman he'd seen in forever. He understood why Sam had gone crazy, but he wasn't thinking. "How long has she been a widow?"

"A few years now," Christa admitted. Her shoulders had finally relaxed. "It's not that you two aren't great guys…"

It was simply they were two men with somewhat perverse needs. That was what he understood and Sam did not. "I understand."

"If we're great guys, then why didn't we ask her out?" Sam rarely gave up.

Christa looked utterly miserable. "It's not that I don't think you should. Honestly, if you could keep it all quiet, I would tell you to go for it, but Abby's been burned by this town before."

"I don't give a damn what the town thinks," Sam began.

"But she will," Jack finished for him. "And she does. Her momma lives here. Hell, Sam, how many women do you know who are happy to date two men at the same time? There's a reason they don't do it. It's considered perverted."

"Well, of course it is. It wouldn't be fun if it wasn't perverted," Sam replied. His eyes held an implied "duh."

"Did she seem like the kind of woman who does things for kicks?" Jack asked. "Who has a sexual bucket list?"

Sam frowned.

"You know people who have sexual bucket lists?" Christa asked.

"Yeah, I do. I know them because Sam and me, well, we help them check off the ménage portion of that list." He utterly hated the fact that here he was playing the bad guy again. "It's not going to happen with her. You need to leave her alone, Sam. She's here to take care of her mother. Let her do that in peace."

Something died in Sam's eyes, a little light. When he smiled this time there was no joy behind it. "Sure thing, Jack. You're right. She wouldn't want to have anything to do with us. Not if she knew the truth. Christa, it was good to see you. I'll go run my errands and see you back at the house, Jack."

"Sam," Jack said, unwilling to let him go without some kind of offer to make things better. "We'll head up to Dallas in a week or two. We'll spend some time in The Club."

This was all his fault when he thought about it. He'd gotten wrapped up in work and they'd missed their last two planned trips into Dallas. There was a club there that catered to men like him and Sam. They needed a good weekend of indulgent sex to get their heads straight. He wouldn't let it go so long next time. It would be kind of like setting an appointment to change the oil in their cars, routine maintenance. If they got regular, rocking-good sex, maybe Sam would settle down and stop going after women like Abigail Moore.

"Sure thing," Sam said. "I'll look forward to it."

He strode out of the house and Jack's stomach sank.

"There's a club?" Christa asked.

"It's nothing for you to worry about," he replied. A nasty thought hit him. Christa and Mike were the only people in town who knew for sure about their "proclivities." Well, besides the women they'd fooled around with, but he thought he'd managed to keep it mostly to rumors. But what if it bothered her? "Unless you would rather we stayed away from you and Mike altogether."

She rolled her eyes. Had she been in the lifestyle, she would have made a glorious brat. "I'm so shocked, Jack." She sobered a bit. "I didn't mean to hurt Sam like that. Abby's been gone for twenty years. We've kept in touch. She's my best friend, but I'm not a hundred percent sure she's ready for any of this. Don't take it wrong, Jack. Believe me. I want her to stay here, and if she fell madly in love with the two of you…"

He held a hand up. "Stop right there, Chris. I'm too old to believe I'm going to magically fall in love with someone. I will admit that she is one fine-looking lady, but I can't see myself falling in love with anyone. If anything, I suspect Sam is going to be the one who'll get married. If the woman he loves is on the open-minded side, perhaps we can work something out, but I don't expect more than sex."

"That sounds sad," Christa said.

"I'm a realist." He had to be. One of them had to be. He left, following Sam and hoping his best friend in the world could forgive him.

* * * *

Two days later, Sam eased into the booth at Christa's Café with a brighter outlook on things.

"You get to look at the reports?" Jack asked, pulling out a newspaper.

Once or twice a week they came into town and had breakfast at Christa's. There was always some errand they needed to run. Today they were picking up feed. Jack said it forced them to socialize, but what he really meant by that was it forced Jack to socialize. Sam socialized plenty.

He glanced around the café. Yeah, he'd socialized with a couple of the women here, but for the most part he managed to stay friendly with them.

Ah, there was the one he didn't want to be friendly with. Well, he did, but he wanted it to go way further than friendly.

Abby Moore stepped out of the kitchen and she was wearing one of the short pink dresses Christa's waitresses all wore, though she filled that sucker out way better than the teenagers Christa hired. He had zero interest in those babies. He wanted a woman, and the perfect one had just walked out.

"Sam? You listening to me?"

He smiled. "Yep. I read the reports. The cattle are healthy and happy and exceptionally eager to get sold and made into hamburgers."

The herd this year was in excellent health, with most of them at prime weight to be sold in the next few months, but then he didn't need a report to tell him that.

Jack followed his line of sight and went still. That was interesting. There were times when Sam could read his partner like a book and this was one of them.

Jack didn't want Abby? Bullshit.

He'd seen the way Jack reacted to her, how he'd covered her small hand with both of his. He'd watched Jack go from pissed off to sad when he realized what kind of woman Abby was. Hell, he even knew why Jack had come running. Normally Sam had terrible taste in women. Well, that was what Jack would say. The truth was he had excellent taste in women. It was simply discretion and Jack's pickiness he lacked. If there wasn't a fabulous woman waiting around on a Friday night to go home with him, he'd take the mean one home because it wasn't like he was planning on having a pleasant conversation with her. Sex was easy.

What he wanted to try with Abigail Moore…now that was going to be a bit trickier.

Because he had conversed with her. Because despite his very clever ruse the other day, he'd walked straight out to his truck, gone about his errands, and then happened to find himself at her sad single-wide trailer. He'd wanted to make sure she was safe. He hadn't spent more than thirty minutes talking to her, but he'd called later on and that had led to a much more detailed conversation and now, two days later, he'd spent roughly four hours on the phone with her.

Oh, he liked her quite a bit.

"Seriously? I thought we had this conversation, Sam."

Sam let his eyes go wide. "What are you talking about? We eat here every time we come into town." He huffed a little. "Are you saying I can't get my waffles because you don't like the waitress?"

Jack sat back, setting the newspaper down. "It's not that I don't like her."

"You don't even know her so how could you dislike her?"

"She seems very nice."

"I think she's lonely. Have you noticed how some of the people won't talk to her?"

Christa stopped at their table with a pot of coffee in her hand. She filled their mugs. "Hey, boys. Abby will be with you both in a moment. Unless you want another waitress."

Jack looked around the diner. "Why are we the only ones in this section?"

Christa sighed. "It's what I like to call 'church lady' day. At this time of day, it's all women who meet for the church or the public school. They plan events and activities. They don't much like Abby, but she can use the money and it'll pick up come lunchtime. The highway workers don't give a crap who brings them their burgers."

Abby seemed to realize she had customers and smoothed down her tiny skirt that could easily be flipped up so he could have access to her pussy. She looked slightly flustered as she tried to find her notepad. She gave him a bright smile and then it seemed to dim as she saw Jack.

He was going to have to be charming enough for both of them until Jack got his head out of his ass and realized that the world wasn't all dark and dim. The man brooded too much.

"Why does she need the job here anyway? I thought she was a nurse," Jack said, obviously unable to take his eyes off her.

He was probably thinking about that pink skirt, too. And the wealth of beauty that lay under it. Though he would bet Jack was thinking about her pretty ass.

"Her husband's cancer treatment was very expensive. Even the co-payments nearly wiped her out. Not that she had much to start with. She paid her own way through school and raised her daughter by herself. She has enough savings to get Lexi through four years of school and for a down payment on a small house or condo. She can use some spending money until she can find work again."

Jack's hands made fists on the table and he moved them under. "We've got a hospital."

"They told Abby they didn't need her services, but they would call her if a position opened up. Small towns work in mysterious ways," Christa said as Abby joined them. "So, Abby is going to help you boys out today. Have a good breakfast."

Abby had a smile on her face that didn't quite reach her eyes, as though she wasn't certain of her welcome. "Hello, Sam. Mr. Barnes."

"It's Jack, Abigail. You can call me Jack." Jack's hands made a reappearance, reaching for his coffee. "You are looking lovely today."

Score one for his freaking team. All he needed was to poke that place in Jack that couldn't stand not lifting up the underdog. In this case, they would be lifting her up and setting her right back down on one of their dicks.

She flushed slightly. "Thank you. It's been a while since I wore a waitress uniform. Now, what can I get you two for breakfast?"

35

"What do you like here?" Jack asked as though he hadn't ordered the same damn thing for the last ten years. "I've heard the waffles are pretty good."

Abby grinned. "They are. They're excellent. Of course, everything is. Christa's mom used to run this place and Christa still uses most of her recipes."

She was off, talking about how she and Christa used to play in the kitchens when they were kids.

When they left, Sam noted the overly large tip Jack left.

It was only a matter of time.

He had to be patient. A wee bit manipulative.

His best friend had taught him that. Sam went about his day with a spring in his step. This was going to work out. He knew it was.

Chapter Three

Abby sniffled as she tried to figure out how to get the cracked board off the stairs that led up to the tiny trailer she'd grown up in. The stairs probably hadn't been properly taken care of since her father died. They'd been tricky to maneuver even back when she'd lived here.

She took a deep breath and tried to remind herself why she was here. Her mom needed her. When she didn't need her, Abby would head straight for Austin to see how she liked the city.

Her baby sure seemed to like it. Lexi was thriving in college. That had to be enough.

The unmistakable sound of heavy tires crunching on the gravel road brought Abby's head up and she got off her knees. There was no way she was having this conversation on her knees.

"Hello, Ken," she said, recognizing her old high school classmate despite the fact that he was wearing a deputy uniform instead of a football jersey. He'd been the best running back in the area until he'd blown out his knee in his sophomore year at LSU.

Maybe he'd seen her struggling and this was a friendly call. So far she'd been lucky. With the exception of the Thursday morning brunch club refusing to sit in her section, she hadn't felt unwelcome.

The community around her mom had given her a warm welcome, but given Ken's frown, she thought her luck might be about to change.

"Ms. Moore," he began and then sighed. "Hey, Abby. Damn, you look good. Have you aged a day since high school?"

She'd so aged. His voice had softened, but she noted he wasn't moving any closer to her. No welcome-home hugs. "You look good, too, Ken. What are you doing out this way?"

His face flushed, another sure sign this wasn't going to go well. He was silent for a moment. When he spoke again, she got his hard lawman voice. "How long do you think you'll be staying here, Abby?"

"As long my momma needs me." She wasn't seventeen years old and desperate. She couldn't be bought off for a thousand bucks and the promise of being left alone.

"Do you have any idea how long that will be?" He stepped toward her.

She held her ground. "She had surgery. I'm going to be here probably six weeks. Maybe eight."

"That's a long time," he said with a frown. "Shouldn't she have a nurse? Why hasn't her insurance brought in a professional?"

How little they knew about her. "I assure you there's no one they could bring in who could do the job better than me. I'm a registered nurse with fifteen years of service under my belt. My degrees have degrees, Ken. Do you know how I managed that? I managed to get my degree while raising a child alone and working thirty hours a week to support us. So you tell your boss Ruby Echols that the girl she shipped away is not the woman who came back."

His jaw tightened and she knew she'd rubbed him the wrong way. She talked to doctors like that all the time and they rolled their eyes and usually did what she told them to because those men were perfectly confident in themselves. That was what she'd learned. It took confidence to be able to listen to other people. Ken looked hard and mean as he stepped into her space.

"My boss is the sheriff of this county and you better not forget that, little girl," he began.

She heard the sound of another car coming down the road, but she knew she couldn't count on anyone to save her. Not from the law. She kept her eyes on the deputy. "Like I said, I'll be here until my mother is on her feet again."

He loomed over her. "And like I said, your momma needs a professional, someone who isn't related to her."

"You mean someone who doesn't make Ruby Echols mad."

He stopped, his eyes looking down at her. "You know it strikes me that we could work something out, Abby. That old lady doesn't have to know you're still here. Not if you promise to stay in this trailer. Hell, I wouldn't even leave you alone. I'd come and visit you."

She could bet he would. She fought back tears. Damn but would this ever stop? She wasn't safe here.

He stared down at her. "What do you say, Abby? You want to stay here, you gotta pay the price."

"Is there a problem, Deputy?" A hard voice broke through her fear.

Abby looked over and Jack Barnes was standing in her momma's tiny, well-kept yard. He was big and solid and she kind of wanted to run over and throw herself into his arms.

She didn't, but she wasn't sure if she'd ever been more grateful to see a man than she was to see Jack.

Ken glanced over at Jack and took a step back. "Now, Mr. Barnes, I was discussing a situation with Abby here. Get back into your truck and move along."

"Is that what he's doing, Abigail?" Jack asked. "Is he having a normal discussion with you? A consensual discussion?"

She had two choices. She could keep the peace or she could throw herself behind that big, broad body and let him protect her. Would she be getting him in trouble? Would she be making Jack Barnes's life worse for stopping to help her out?

"Abigail..." His deep voice broke through the questions running through her mind. "I want to know what's happening. Do you understand me? I don't want some bullshit because you think we should avoid conflict."

Ken turned toward him. "Mr. Barnes, there's zero reason for you to be here."

"Except that I want to know what's happening with Abigail," he replied, his voice steady.

There was a moment when she wasn't sure what was going to happen, when she worried she was about to get Jack Barnes into serious trouble. And then Ken stepped back, his shoulders coming down and his whole demeanor changing in a second.

"Nothing at all, Mr. Barnes," Ken said. "Just checking in on an old friend. Abby, good to see you. Think about what I said."

She stared at him, not giving him a single word. He didn't deserve one. She stood there with her stupid hammer in her hand and wondered why the hell she'd thought this could work.

Jack moved in, taking Ken's spot, though he turned his back to her, watching Ken as he got into his car. He was a big bulwark between her and the cop. He crossed his arms over his chest as he watched the deputy drive away.

Abby took a deep breath.

Jack turned to her. "You all right?"

She nodded.

"But he wasn't being pleasant, was he?"

She felt tears pierce her eyes. Shame, that old nasty friend, flushed through her. She managed to shake her head.

Jack Barnes stepped in, crowding her, but not the way Ken had. Somehow she knew she could back away and he would let her go. He wasn't trying to take something from her. He was trying to give, to give her comfort, to let her know she wasn't alone. His hands came up and he used his thumbs to brush away her tears.

"You call me if he comes around again. You get in the house and lock the door and call me, you understand?" Jack's voice was low, deep and solid.

"Yes, sir," she replied.

His jaw tightened and for a second she could swear she saw a flash of something hot in those green eyes of his. "Damn it, Abigail. You're killing me."

He turned away and looked down at the porch.

"I was trying to fix it but I couldn't get the board off." It was way easier to talk about the stupid steps than it was what had almost happened.

He held out a hand. "Let me deal with it."

She passed him the hammer because she was done trying for the day. "Can I get you something to drink?"

"I wouldn't turn down some iced tea. Give me ten minutes and I can have this fixed." He got down to one knee and allowed her to step up and into the trailer.

She practically ran to the fridge. Her mom was still asleep, and that was a good thing. Sleep was healing, and it also meant she hadn't witnessed that terrible scene with the deputy.

She stopped at the sink. What the hell would have happened if Jack Barnes hadn't gotten out of his truck and intervened? Would she have been forced to use that damn hammer on the deputy?

She took a deep breath. It had been a very long time since she'd been that intimidated, worried that something very ugly was about to happen to her.

One breath and then another and another, and then she turned and got some ice and poured his tea. All the while she could hear Jack hammering. How was that such a soothing sound?

He was an overwhelmingly large man. He could do anything he wanted to her. It was only her and her momma here, and no one would hear her yelling at this time of day. Yet she felt not an ounce of hesitation as she poured a second glass and walked back out.

He was putting the last of the nails in. "This place is falling apart."

"You're telling me." She handed him the glass and sank down on the steps.

They were barely wide enough that he could sit beside her.

She tried not to think about how nice it felt to have his hips brush hers.

"I don't think I like that deputy," he said, his eyes staring ahead.

"Well, there's something we have in common," she replied.

He drank down his tea and then stood, passing her the glass again. He reached into his pocket and pulled out a business card, handing that to her, too. "Thank you, Abigail. And you remember what I said. You find yourself in this position again and you call me. My cell phone is the second number. I don't care what time it is. Day or night, you call me. You tell them you're calling me. You understand? You tell them Jack Barnes is going to want to have a long talk with any man who tries to hurt you."

She nodded slowly, looking down so he wouldn't see how affected she was by his words.

His hand came out, gently lifting up her chin, and he shook his head.

He sighed and stepped back. "Like I said, you're going to kill me, Abigail. I'll have someone out tomorrow to look at that lock on the door."

She started to argue, but his eyes went dark. "Yes, Jack. Thank you."

He turned and got in his truck and drove off.

And she watched the truck until he turned on to the highway, wishing all the while he would have stayed.

Chapter Four

"Right through there," Christa said, waving a hand toward her garage.

Sam stood in the kitchen while a cheer went up in the living room, letting him know the Longhorns had scored. Christa and Mike's house was full of football fans, and apparently low on indoor fridge space since the hostess was sending him out to the garage.

"I just want a beer. Should I be worried that I'm about to be viciously murdered?" He couldn't tell if Christa was trying to get him to move some stuff around her garage or maybe introduce him to a serial killer who lived in there.

The way he'd been going hard after Abby, it really might be the latter.

Two weeks had passed since the day he'd met Abby and he was fairly certain he was crazy about that woman. She was the one, but he couldn't get Jack to understand that sometimes a woman required proof that two men were better than one.

Jack was maintaining his distance. He was insistent that Abby would be utterly horrified if she realized what they wanted. So he'd allowed Sam to hang out with her alone.

"Yes, through there, and no you will not be murdered, though you might think about murdering me for wasting so much of your time," Christa said, biting her bottom lip. "You have to understand. She's my best friend. I had to make sure she was ready. When I opened that box…well, she's ready. At least in a fictional sense.

Check the box marked books."

Now he was interested. He moved into the garage and found the box Christa was talking about. It was obvious this was one of the boxes Abby had been into. The tape had been removed, making it easy to pull it open and get to the goodness on the inside.

What the hell?

He stared at the box of books, and everything inside him stilled.

Not everything. His cock suddenly wasn't still. That sucker grew to what felt like an impossible length, but once it had reached its limitation, even that stilled in shocked awe at the bounty sitting before him. Sam knew that if his dick had a face, it would probably have the same shocked expression on it as the one attached to his head.

Books. Lots and lots of dirty books. That was not what he'd expected to find. Well, except for the fact that the box had been marked books. But he'd thought she would have like Oprah books.

He was fairly certain *Her Twin Doms* by one Ms. Cherry Sparks didn't have the Oprah seal of approval. Nor did *Their Virgin Fuck Buddy* by one Dakota Cheyenne.

There were numerous books by a woman named Amber Rose that also seemed a bit on the salacious side.

Were they all written by strippers, because he knew a couple of strippers who had those names.

After a moment of looking at the books on the top, he managed to find the strength to see what was beneath.

It just got worse—or in his opinion, better.

"Holy shit," he breathed quietly, since he didn't particularly want anyone to know he was out in the garage pawing through Abby Moore's belongings. He was supposed to be out here grabbing a couple of beers from the fridge. That's what Jack thought he was doing.

But damn, he'd wasted weeks of his time.

If it had all been lust, he would likely have shown up on her doorstep and seduced the lady, but he felt something for her. If this was more than mere lust, then he had to think about Jack. He might be able to screw a woman on his own, but if it became serious with Abby, he would never be able to do that without Jack. He'd made the decision to keep his hands off Abigail Moore until he could bring Jack into the picture.

Thus had begun the roughest two weeks of Sam Fleetwood's life, and considering his childhood, that was saying something. He was caught between a rock and a really, really hard place. He managed to arrange several meetings between the two. They'd all had dinner at Christa's Café on Wednesday night after Abby's shift ended. It had been a simple thing to invite her over, and once Jack had realized she was hungry and likely eating all by herself, he'd been the one to invite her to stay. Sam had been able to wrangle an invitation to the Wades' traditional Saturday football watching, and he'd complained until Jack went with him.

Abby Moore was worth fighting Jack's antisocial tendencies over.

Sam hadn't figured he'd be fighting so hard. Every single time he managed to manipulate Jack into spending time with her, Jack obviously enjoyed it, and then pulled away the minute she got in her car and drove off. Jack had admitted that she was beautiful and loving and sweet, but he'd been burned too many times before. Despite his best arguments, Jack wasn't even willing to approach her about the possibility of dating them because he assumed she would be shocked and appalled at the thought of a relationship with two men. Sam knew the argument. He'd heard it himself many times. It was all right for a night or two, but most women weren't willing to risk community outrage by dating both of them. Jack had been sure Abby wouldn't even consider a covert sexual relationship with them.

Jack had turned into Eeyore on the subject.

Sam grinned as he looked down at the box of books. Jack was going to have to rethink everything once he saw what Abby considered great literature. Sam shook his head at the ridiculous covers on the books. These were women's books? Everyone was naked.

What had she done? Had she typed ménage into the search engine at Amazon and bought everything that came up?

He couldn't help himself. He read the back cover of one and then another and another. Most were about one woman and two

45

men. It was perfectly reasonable in his mind. Despite the salacious covers, they seemed to be about love, and one woman and two men constituted a romance in his world.

Then he got to the really wild stuff.

"What the hell is she thinking?" This particular one seemed to be about a woman servicing five men. Five? Where did one woman put five cocks? A strange sense of outrage flashed through his system. He was a reasonably tolerant man. Hell, he had shared women with his best friend since they were seventeen and the woman across the street introduced them to sex, but now he felt like a prude. The thought of Abby playing around with five damn men annoyed the hell out of him. He could feel his face setting in a stubborn line as he repacked the box. His honey was going to have to be satisfied with the two cocks she was going to get. He wasn't getting into anything wild, like sharing his wife with some stranger. It was him and Jack, and that would have to be enough for his dirty little Abby.

Sweet little Abby. Hopefully curious Abby, because he would bet a lot that these books were as far as Abby had gone into ménage world.

He smiled as he got the beers he'd been sent out here for. A light joy overtook him as he realized Abby wasn't going to be shocked by what they wanted from her. Hell, it was her fantasy. If he was wrong and she'd been in a relationship like it before, then she would know what was coming. He wasn't sure why it hadn't worked out before, but he knew one thing for sure. He and Jack wouldn't screw this up. He popped the cap off his beer, took a long, satisfying swig, and headed back in to start the seduction of a lifetime.

* * * *

Jack tried his hardest to concentrate on the big screen. He shifted on the sofa, aware that his eyes kept moving to the woman curled up on the recliner across the living room. He was sitting in the Wade house surrounded by their friends. When he and Sam had shown up, they'd been introduced to the five or six other guests the Wades had

46

invited, but Jack couldn't remember their names to save his damn life. All he could think about was Abigail Moore.

Everywhere he turned these days, the gorgeous redhead seemed to be there, looking at him with her big, wounded, love-me, protect-me eyes. Lately, when he tried to go to sleep, those eyes haunted him.

The truth was, it was getting harder and harder to resist her, though he wasn't about to tell Sam that.

He sure as hell wasn't about to tell Sam that he'd talked to Barry Houseman, who lived in the trailer across the street from Abigail's mother. Barry lived there with his wife and three kids and every one of them now had Jack's number in case they saw anything that seemed wrong happening across the street.

"Find what you needed?" Christa asked Sam as he walked back into the living room.

Jack and the rest of the group sat watching the Longhorns play. There were chairs and barstools huddled around the big screen. Jack and Sam had staked out the couch early. Mike and Christa cuddled on a love seat. There was a secretive smile on Christa Wade's face. Jack took in the sight of his best friend. Sam practically skipped back in the room, and that set off a warning bell. Sam had been in a shit mood for weeks over Abigail. Now he looked like a kid given the toy he'd wanted for Christmas. He really hoped Abigail hadn't done something to give Sam hope. The last thing he needed was Sam with a broken heart. He'd wander around the ranch like a kicked puppy for months.

"I found everything I could ask for, Chris." Sam's grin told Jack he was in trouble. "I really appreciate the heads-up."

From across the room, Abigail smiled curiously. His insides clenched. Damn, but that was one fine-looking woman. Maybe he could handle it if she was simply gorgeous and had a banging body, but her smile was so warm he wanted to bask in it. She was soft and sweet and everything feminine.

She was exactly the kind of woman he needed to stay away from.

"Heads-up?" Abigail gave the group a laugh.

Sam's grins could be infectious. Sometimes he wondered if

47

he'd ever smiled before he met Sam. Sometimes it felt like they were two halves of a whole person—Jack the serious half, while Sam was all about the light. It put Jack in the position of older brother, though the two were only three months apart in age.

"I was looking for some beer, sweetheart." Sam winked.

"You're always looking for some beer." Her lips curled up, and she shook her head with an affectionate giggle as she turned her attention back to the game.

Damn but he liked seeing her smile. Seeing her scared and lonely had sent a hole into him that he hadn't quite managed to fill up yet.

Sam sank onto the couch next to him and a cold beer was pressed into his hand. Abigail started talking to the town's high school football coach. Jack knocked back a long drink as he gave his partner a pitying look. He wasn't going to let himself fall for Abigail. It would be an easy thing to do, but he was in control of his emotions. He wasn't falling for a woman after two dinners, a couple of football games, and that one time Sam convinced him to see a movie then picked her up along the way.

Jack's eyes went straight to the redhead like a moth to the flame. There weren't many women like Abigail. She was smart and funny. Her take on the world challenged him. He'd learned more about politics from her in the few weeks he'd known her than he had in years of browsing through the papers. In addition to working at a hospital, she volunteered at a homeless shelter and had raised a daughter. She'd also been married for ten years, and just two years ago had lost her husband to cancer.

Jack sighed. He didn't care what the town gossips said. She was a lovely, respectable woman. She would be shocked by what he and Sam wanted to do to her. She would run screaming the other way if she had a hint of how badly he wanted her trapped between him and the man he loved like a brother. Jack felt his eyes glaze over as he thought about it. She would be small in between their big bodies. Sam would immediately go for that sweet pussy of hers. He couldn't help it. Sam loved to eat pussy. Jack would be free to tease her lips with the hard head of his dick. He would tell her exactly what he wanted and how deep he wanted her to take him. He would explain, and she would comply. She would do everything he asked her because she would learn to trust him. He would take damn good care of her in and out of their bed.

She would never have to change a tire again or deal with a crooked plumber the way she had last week. The trailer she was staying in was falling apart around her. Jack wanted nothing more than to get her the hell out of there. She deserved a beautiful house with lots of space. One where she didn't have to worry about asshole deputies intimidating her.

That was the kind of relationship Jack wanted deep down. He wanted a woman he and Sam could take care of. He was bigger and stronger, so he should be the one to take care of the heavy lifting. He should make life easy for her because she would make it worth living for him. In exchange, she would take care of them. She would tell them when they weren't properly dressed for an event and force them into suits and ties occasionally. She would watch their beer intake.

She would fuss over them.

She would also suck his cock. That was a given. Sex was a big part of what he wanted from Abigail. He wanted nothing more than to come in from a hard day's work and sink his dick into some warm, wet place on her body. If there was a spanking involved, then that made the day better. Jack liked to be in charge. The thought of dominating Abigail made his cock strain against the fly of his jeans.

Yes, Sir.

He could still see her standing there in her front yard. She'd looked up at him like he was some kind of damn hero for intervening between her and the deputy. She'd called him Sir and couldn't have any idea what that meant to him.

He came out of his daydream and shifted, hoping no one noticed his raging hard-on. No such luck. Sam was obviously trying hard not to laugh out loud at him.

Jack took a long, cold swig of beer and stared mulishly at the TV screen. He didn't even know the score. That woman had ruined the football season for him. All he could think about was sex when she was around.

"Your turn." Sam pointed to his empty beer.

"That was fast." Maybe he should start watching Sam's beer intake.

"I was thirsty," Sam drawled. "Still am. Beer's in the garage."

Jack sighed and stood up. Hell, he was almost empty, too. "I'll be right back."

Sam pulled on his shirtsleeve as he walked by. Jack leaned over. Sam whispered low enough that Jack strained to hear him, but the message was clear. "Check out the box marked books."

Why the hell would he be interested in a box of books? Still, there was something in Sam's eyes that made him pick up the pace.

He opened the door to the garage and quickly found the box Sam had talked about. Abby had left a good number of her boxes in Christa's garage since her mom's single-wide left no space for storage. Jack's jaw dropped when he opened the box.

He picked up book after book. All romances. Most of them ménage, but there was also a bunch of books about Doms and their submissives. He sat down in the middle of the garage and thumbed through a couple, trying to figure out what Abigail saw in these books. They were a window into her soul. Was she interested in sex, curious about the pleasures ménage could bring her? Or was it something more.

He picked up a book by a woman named Amber Rose and read the ending.

Jackie looked down at the twin rings on her finger and her heart was full. She had no idea why she needed Heath and Cass the way she did, but only those two men could truly fill her soul. Her Doms. Her husbands. Her men.

Jack closed the book.

Abigail Moore had sealed her fate. She might not know it, but she was staying in Willow Fork on a permanent basis. She would be staying with him and Sam. Jack took a long moment to think. He wasn't a man to act immediately. He was a man who appreciated a plan. Sam might not like it, but he was taking over this courtship.

Jack smiled, but if Abigail could have seen it, she might have run. Jack felt his heart rate speed up in anticipation.

He'd met his mate, and he had no intention of letting her go now.

Chapter Five

"Well, look at that. Your friends are here." Christa grinned as she rang up a customer. "And they're sitting in your section. I wonder what that means."

"Maybe it means they're hungry." Abby stared as Jack and Sam slid into a booth. Sure enough, it was in her section. Abby glanced around Christa's Café. This late in the afternoon there wasn't a lot of traffic. She counted two people at the counter and another small group in the section Christa was working. It would be hours before the dinner rush. By then, she and Christa would be back at her place, their long shifts over for the day.

Christa looked pointedly at the cowboys who had been haunting Abby's dreams for the last month. "They're hungry, all right. Those boys have been hungry for a month."

What had changed in the last week? She couldn't put her finger on it. Ever since that day when they had sat in Christa's living room and watched the Longhorns play, something had changed between them. Before that day, it had been Sam who called on her, with Jack only making the occasional appearance. Suddenly, Jack was everywhere. In the last week, she'd been out with the two of them almost every night she wasn't working. On the nights she was working, they would show up at the café and insist on escorting her home. It was weird. And wonderful. The last week she'd felt protected.

It was the first time since she'd come back to Willow Fork that she'd felt truly safe.

Abby pulled out her order pad and smoothed down the pink skirt of the uniform she was wearing. When she looked up, Sam was studying the menu, but Jack's eyes were squarely on her.

They were two glorious slabs of masculinity. They both wore tight jeans and western shirts, but the similarities stopped there. Sam was smiling and jovial. Jack was more thoughtful. Abby couldn't stop dreaming about them. It was just her luck that the minute she decided to live a little, she ran into the two most gorgeous cowboys she'd ever seen and they were gay. It was disappointing, but it certainly made her comfortable around them. Well, it made her comfortable around Sam. Sam was the light-hearted, friendly one. Jack, truth be told, scared her a little. He was intense, and she always felt like he was watching her every move, waiting for her to step out of line.

Then he went and blew the whole bad guy image by fixing her mom's porch steps and saving her from the deputy. He'd told her to call him if anything else needed fixing.

She hadn't, of course. It was a friendly gesture, nothing more. She'd been thrilled he stopped to fix the steps, but she knew she was on her own. It wasn't the easiest place to be, but she'd done it before.

Abby smiled as a mental picture of her husband flashed through her brain. Ben had been kind to both her and Lexi. He'd been everything she could have hoped for in a husband. The sex might not have been the hottest, but he would have dealt with that nasty old Caleb Nevins who'd tried to swindle her over her mother's clogged pipes. Jack had heard her complaining about Caleb overcharging her at the café and not two hours later, she had a refund check in her hand. Jack Barnes certainly knew how to handle the occasional con artist, and she had no doubt it was Jack and not some magical change in Caleb's heart.

But until last Saturday, Jack had been very careful not to touch her physically. Sam touched her casually all the time. He was always there to help her out of her car or give her a friendly hug. When they sat on the couch to watch the game on the weekend, he would casually sling an arm around her shoulder, but Abby knew it was just Sam being Sam. He was a tactile person, and Abby didn't mind. If she'd been more secure, she would have slipped her hand into Sam's sometime simply for the comfort of warm skin against hers. It had been a very long time since a man had held her.

Last Saturday afternoon, though, Jack had been the one to pull her out of her chair and lead her to the couch while they were watching the game. He'd said he wanted her to have a better view of the television, but she'd been able to see fine. Nevertheless, she had quickly found herself between the two big men, and they hadn't seemed concerned with things like personal space. Jack had casually rested his hand around the back of the couch, lightly touching her shoulders. His eyes held no small hint of challenge when she looked at him. It was as if he was claiming some right to touch her and daring her to deny him. Abby might have been able to stand up and tell him off if she hadn't seen that part of Jack that was horribly vulnerable. It was there in his eyes when he looked at her. He was waiting for her to reject him. Besides, she had told herself when she settled against him, she didn't want to reject his affection. Jack might be gay, but he was a stunningly gorgeous man. He and Sam must be lacking in female friends out in this small, narrow-minded town. Abby had lots of gay friends, and they tended to be very affectionate.

Still, it hadn't stopped the longing she felt as she took Jack up on his offer and let her head rest against his broad shoulder. Jack's arm curled around her, and when she felt Sam pulling her feet into his lap, she didn't protest, just sighed and enjoyed being close to another human being.

This last week she'd spent a lot of time between them, she suddenly realized. Every chance they had, they moved her to the middle. She sat between them in Jack's big truck when they drove to Tyler to see a movie. She'd been in the middle when they watched TV at her mom's place. Everywhere they had gone in the last week, she'd had a hunky cowboy on either side of her.

"Do you want me to take that table, Abby?" Christa's voice pulled Abby out of her thoughts.

Abby winked at her friend. She took out a pen. "Nope. I can handle those two. I bet they want burgers." It was all they ever ordered. Sure enough, two minutes and a lot of playful flirting later, Abby placed their orders.

Christa cocked a single eyebrow. "You sure they aren't bugging you? I like them, but I can run them out if you want me to. I'm quite handy with a broom when it comes to pests."

Abby sighed. "No. I like the fact that they make sure to sit in my section. It's good to make some friends. I'm flustered. Those are two gorgeous men, after all."

Christa's ponytail bobbed, reminding Abby of what she looked like at sixteen. "Well, we can talk about them all night tonight. It'll be like a slumber party when we were teens. Right down to the cheap bottle of wine I used to sneak out of mama's liquor cabinet and eighties music."

"Why not?" This was the night a nurse came and stayed with her mother to give Abby time off. She had packed an overnight bag and would spend the night in Christa's guest bedroom. It served two purposes, this slumber party. It gave her time with her friend and a willing man to change the oil in her car. Mike was probably already hard at work on her junker.

It was the most she could hope for in this town, to have a nice, slightly drunk night and sleep in a comfy bed for once. Now she wished she'd packed her vibrator. The damn cowboys had her flustered and horny. Abby smiled a little. At least her books were at Christa's. She could sneak out into the garage, open her box of books, and lose herself in some hot romance. Those books were the only romance she'd indulged in for a very long time. It must be why she was so fascinated by Jack and Sam. They would be horrified if they knew she had fantasized about them last night. They were the fuel for her masturbation. Jack Barnes, Sam Fleetwood, and a pack of double-A batteries. That was all she needed to get going.

Christa gave her a hug. "I know I've said it a million times, but I'm so glad you're here. I can't tell you how much I've missed you. The yearly trip to visit you and Lexi in Fort Worth isn't the same as having you here full time."

Abby looked into her friend's pretty face. She missed Christa, too. Unfortunately, some things never changed. "Don't get used to it. I have to move on. If there's one thing being back here has taught me, it's that Willow Fork doesn't change. I've gotten pulled over three times by the sheriff. So far it's been warnings, but eventually he'll start giving me tickets for everything under the sun. I think the only reason he hasn't done it yet is that he knows my mom needs me. I've promised him I'll be gone as soon as she's on her feet again."

Christa's black ponytail swung righteously. "I am going to have such a talk with Len James. How dare he harass you like that?"

Abby sighed. This was why she hadn't mentioned the deputy at all. She appreciated her friend's indignation, but it wouldn't get her anywhere. She'd sealed her fate twenty years ago by having the audacity to fall for the richest boy in town. The Echols family had made it plain how they still felt. They didn't want anything to do with her or her daughter.

They had missed out. Lexi was everything a mom could want from a daughter. She had Adam's good looks and Abby's force of will. It was an amazing combination. Abby had never been prouder than the day her daughter started college. Her job wasn't exactly over as a mom, but the really tough work was done. Alexis was in her freshman year of college, and her future looked bright. It was time for Abby to figure out what to do with the rest of her life.

"Don't give Lenny hell, Chris." Abby gave her a sad smile, thinking of the sheriff. He'd been a nice guy in high school. When he'd gone into a government job here in Willow Fork, he had come under the iron fist of the Echols family. It was just Ruby and her younger son, Walter, now. Hal, the patriarch of the family, had passed on last year according to her mother. Still, Ruby wielded her influence with all the subtlety of a pit bull. "He feels bad enough as it is. What do you expect him to do? He's an elected official. Nobody gets elected in this town without Echols's money backing them."

Christa took a deep breath. "Maybe it's time that changed. Those assholes have run this town for way too long. Now Walter is talking about running for state senate. They don't need any more power than they already have."

Abby searched her friend's face. "Have they been giving you trouble about me helping out at the café?"

"No." Christa's voice was flat. There was an arrogant look on her face. She was a small-business owner who knew how good her product was. "My restaurant is the only one in town that serves a decent breakfast. I haven't seen anything but an uptick in business since you started taking shifts."

"They're curious to see how I turned out," Abby said with a self-deprecating laugh. Despite the church ladies' weekly brunch, she'd found most of the working-class part of town was more than interested in her. Many had been shocked to discover she'd worked her way through nursing school. She'd managed it all on her own and still sent some money back every month to help her mother out. Abby had rapidly discovered a world beyond Hal and Ruby Echols's dominion. It had been a world that Abby conquered in her own small way.

"Or it could be that Sam and Jack suddenly started eating every meal here hoping to catch a glimpse of you. I bet their housekeeper is thrilled with all her free time, lately." Christa looked over the counter to where Sam and Jack were sitting and talking. Sam laughed heartily. He was really something else. Sam Fleetwood was a testament to the fact that the universe was good to some people. He was broadly built, with strong shoulders and a chest that must look lovely without the encumbrance of a shirt. His golden blond hair curled even in its short style, and his handsome face spoke of a man who laughed easily. He was the opposite of his brooding friend. Jack looked like sin on a stick, and he was…well, he wasn't paying any attention to Sam now.

Jack was watching her, and not like before. Abby's breath caught. There was no wariness in his dark green eyes. He was watching her with the eyes of a hungry predator. He didn't even try to hide it. He let loose with a slow smile Abby felt in her toes. It was a smile that promised a wealth of dirty fun.

Abby looked to Christa suddenly. Her heart was pounding at the invitation in Jack's eyes. "What the hell is wrong with Jack? He's looking at me like I'm a perfectly cut filet and he's been on vegetarian rations for a month."

"Wow, he's not even subtle, is he?" Christa looked at the big, gorgeous cowboy with a sort of amused fascination. "Guess that's what he needs Sam for."

She turned to her friend and whispered behind her hand. "I'm sure he needs Sam for a lot more interesting things than his subtlety. I'll be honest, Chris, those two make me crazy. I would give a lot to be able to watch them make love. It would feed my fantasies for years."

Christa's mouth hung open for a long moment. She stared at Abby and then glanced back at the men, her voice going low. "Seriously? Oh, Abby, we have should talked before now. You honestly think they're gay?"

Abby kept hers at a whisper, too, so the men sitting at the counter eating lunch wouldn't hear her. "There's nothing wrong with it." It was shocking that her best friend was homophobic. It wasn't something she'd expected. Had she outed the two men when they'd been trying so hard to fit in? She was the last person who wanted to cause them trouble. She knew how hard it was to fit into a small town. "I could be wrong, of course. It's perfectly reasonable for two men to be roommates in their thirties. I'm sorry I said anything."

Christa rolled her eyes and snorted. "I couldn't care less what they do in the bedroom, though I suspect it's much more interesting than you think from some of the stories I've heard. I like the hell out of Sam, and I think Jack Barnes is an honorable man. I want you to be happy. You need to cut loose and live a little. Ben died two years ago, and Adam a long time before that. It's time for Abby Moore to find herself again."

"What is that supposed to mean?" Abby asked.

"It means watch out, you got an order up. This is a place of business, after all, not some gossip station." Christa waved her finger with an imperious snap she softened with a wink. "Go forth. Those men need beef. And keep a damn open mind."

What exactly was she supposed to be open minded about? Tray in hand, she approached the table. She gave them her sauciest smile, hoping she hadn't hurt their reputations. "Here you go, boys. Two burgers, one with bacon and cheese, one plain and medium rare."

Sam looked ready to demolish his burger. "You're a priceless jewel. I can't believe how hungry I am."

"I can." Jack's voice was a low growl.

Abby had the sudden feeling he might not be talking about food. She flushed under his gaze. "I'll go refill your Cokes."

The minute she turned, she hit a slippery spot on the floor and her sneakers slid.

Sam's arms came up around her to keep her from falling back. She wondered when he had gotten behind her. He moved fast. Jack was there, too. He took the tray from her and held her hand in his.

"Careful there, darlin'." Sam's slow drawl was soft and sweet to her ears. "We don't want you to fall. But don't worry too much about it, Abby girl. Jack and I'll catch you if you go down."

"You will?" Even to her ears she sounded breathy and surprised.

"I promise." Jack's hands securely held hers.

"So do I," Sam interjected with a happy smile.

She nodded, not sure what to do. When she'd fallen back into Sam, she was pretty sure she'd felt the hard press of an erection against her backside. That was crazy. It was probably his wallet or something else in his pocket.

She would not look down to get visual confirmation. Nope. She was keeping her eyes firmly on his face. The last thing she needed was to get caught checking out their packages to see if they were ready for delivery.

"I'll try to stay on my feet, boys," she promised.

Jack's hands were warm and surrounded hers. It made her wonder what it would feel like to have those big hands all over her body. It was impossible not to imagine that callused hand cupping her as he pulled her into the hard strength of his body.

"You all right now?" Jack pulled her away from Sam so that she was steady on her own.

"I'm fine. I'll get those Cokes," Abby said shakily, her every nerve ending on high alert. She was standing between the two most gorgeous men she'd ever seen, and it was too much like a fantasy.

58

She needed to pull herself firmly back into reality. She was thirty-seven years old and a mom. She wasn't seventeen anymore with a gloriously firm body. Her boobs sagged, and while she tried to stay fit, she'd put on a few pounds. The boys were playing around. She had to keep her head on straight.

She had to remember, at all times, where she was. This wasn't Fort Worth, where people mostly lived and let live. This was Willow Fork.

Yes, just for a moment she'd forgotten that. This was Willow Fork and maybe they weren't as nice as they seemed. It happened from time to time that she made the mistake of trusting the wrong people. Jack and Sam had been in Willow Fork for ten years. They were pretty firmly entrenched in the community, which meant they'd probably spent time with the Echols clan.

If she started parading around with these men, it would prove to everyone in the county that she hadn't changed. The threats from the sheriff and his deputy hadn't worked. Maybe Ruby Echols had come up with another plan. Humiliate her. Make her look like a whore in the eyes of the town.

Why else would two of the best-looking men she'd ever met suddenly change their relationship with her? Why go from perfectly platonic to sending her heated looks when she knew she wasn't their type at all?

The thought sent an ache through her.

"What's wrong?" Jack's hand tightened on hers. "You looked very sad for a minute. What happened?"

"I'm fine." She moved firmly out of their reach. It was time to stop playing and be realistic. She was older than them. If they wanted female friends, they needed someone their own age. Otherwise, she looked like she was begging for something they would never give her. She would look pathetic, and that was exactly where Ruby Echols wanted her. "I'll be back in a minute with your drinks."

She walked away to join Christa at the counter. That was one trap she would never fall into again.

* * * *

Jack watched Abigail's fine ass sway as she walked away from them.

"What just happened?" Sam slid back into the booth, his eyes tight with obvious worry.

"I don't know." Jack's gaze never left his rapidly retreating prey even as he took his place across from Sam. He looked down at his burger. It didn't look as good as it had before. "She was responding to us. She practically purred when I held her hand. I would have sworn she was aroused."

"Maybe you come on too strong, Jack." Sam sounded bitter.

"Oh, I come on too strong?" Jack rolled his eyes. "Seriously, Sam. You think I wasn't watching you last Saturday? You nearly sucked her toes into your mouth when we were sitting on the couch. Don't think I didn't see that. You are the most orally fixated person I have ever met. You have to put everything in your mouth."

"Well, blame my mama," Sam shot back. "I wasn't breastfed. It had an effect. We need to try harder. This whole courtship thing isn't working."

Abigail was talking to Christa behind the counter. Jack would have given a lot to be in on that conversation. The two women whispered, and Christa laughed lightly. Something had happened to make her suddenly wary. She had enjoyed their attentions for the past week. His plan had been working. From the moment he realized she might be amenable to a ménage, he'd been carefully preparing her for it. She was a serious woman, and he intended to treat her right. They were taking it slow, allowing her to get used to being between the two of them. She had been ready to move on to kissing, and he intended to do that tonight. He and Sam were going to talk her into coming out to the ranch to watch a movie and then they would kiss her. Sam had argued for doing a hell of a lot more than that, but Jack was sticking to his courting plan. He wanted everything out on the table before they took her to bed. They would talk about what a relationship could be like between the three of them. He might have to rethink that plan. Now she was afraid.

"You don't think Christa warned her off of us, do you?" He really hoped that wasn't true. They had a good business relationship

60

with the café owner. Beyond that, Sam considered her husband a friend. Mike Wade was Sam's drinking buddy. He'd hate to see that go away.

Sam snorted. "Damn, Jack, who do you think told me to open that box of books? Christa told me where to find them and everything."

Jack was relieved, but it didn't solve the core problem. "I think we should pull back and give her some space."

"Screw that." Sam looked a little desperate. "It's been a month. I can't take another night. This whole dating thing is crazy. Can't we fuck her now and date her later?"

"No, Sam. You asked me to give this a chance, and I'm giving it the best chance I can. She's not a one-night stand," Jack said firmly. "She's nervous now. We need to set this on the right footing. We need to let her know we're going to treat her like a lady. Let's ask her out to the ranch. We'll have a nice meal and show her around. She'll see how serious we can be."

Sam looked disappointed, but he rarely argued. "All right. I'll follow your lead, but damn, Jack, don't take too long. I'm likely to die of sexual frustration."

Abigail walked back up, two drinks in her hand. She placed them on the table. "Is everything all right with the order?"

He hated the flat, professional voice she was using. There had to be a way to get her back to the vivacious woman she normally was. "This burger better be good, darlin'. I won't have my product being mistreated."

Curiosity flashed in her hazel eyes.

Sam took the ball and ran with it. "This burger here is 100% organic beef. It's the best you can buy."

"Really?" She looked down at the burgers. "Christa buys your beef?"

"Straight off the Barnes-Fleetwood Ranch," Sam said with a smile. "We're becoming quite big. When we started, we barely had a couple hundred head of cattle. Now we run several thousand and have a bunch of ranch hands helping us out. We have a packaging plant, too."

"We're still smalltime, and I like it that way." Jack could talk about business. "If we get much bigger, we'll have to hire more hands and deal with more people. The quality will go down, too. There's a reason organic ranching is hard."

Her eyes sparkled with interest. "So you don't give the cattle antibiotics?"

"No, unless they're actually sick, of course." Sam slathered his bun with ketchup. "We won't let an animal go without if she needs it, but we don't proactively dose our herd. We take care of them. They're grain fed."

"Yes, I've read about that," she replied, her head shaking. "Those big ranches feed them protein and sometimes they feed them other cows. It sounds horrible."

"It's a way for them to cut corners," Jack explained. "It's cheap. The public wants cheap beef, so they use the parts they can't sell to feed their herd. It's easier to keep the cattle in pens than to let them roam and feed naturally. It's why we'll have to stay small and local."

"So you don't pen up your cattle?" Abigail pushed a stray strand of hair behind her ear.

Sam popped a French fry in his mouth. "We're old-school cowboys, darlin'. We let the herd wander our spread. When we bring them in, we do it on horseback."

Jack shook his head slightly. Sam did like being a cowboy. "One day I'd like to try to add a dairy farm. I think we could sell to the local stores and even feed into Dallas–Fort Worth."

Abigail smiled shyly. "That's sounds like a good plan. I like the fact that you take care of your cattle."

"Jack and I personally give each heifer a kiss good night," Sam interjected, causing her to laugh. "You should come out to the ranch sometime. You would find it interesting. I'll take you riding. We've got some gentle mares."

"It has been a long time since I was in the saddle."

Jack bit back a groan at the thought of riding Abigail. Sam was right. This dating thing was going to kill them both. "You'll like our horses. We take care of them, too. We take damn fine care of everything that belongs to us."

Sam looked up at her. "How about you come out to the ranch

tonight? We could show you around and take you riding, and then we can have dinner, maybe watch a movie."

A bubbly laugh came from her mouth, her face flushing. "Well, Sam, you make that almost sound like a date."

"Then I wasn't trying hard enough, darlin'," Sam said with a serious expression on his face.

"You're asking me on a date?" She looked between them, her confusion plain to Jack.

"I apparently wasn't doing a good job. Yes, Abigail Moore, we would like to ask you on a date. Will you go out with us?" Sam seemed as confused as Abby. "What does she think we've been doing for the last week, Jack?"

"I don't know." Jack turned to her. Maybe he'd been too subtle. "Abigail, what do you call it when a man takes a woman out, picks her up, pays for everything, and then politely takes her home?"

She gnawed on her bottom lip. Her gaze shifted between the two men. "I thought we were being friends. Like Will and Grace, if you two were both Wills. A lot of gay men like hanging out with women."

"What?" That came out way louder than he'd intended and suddenly everybody in the café was watching their table. In all the scenarios that ran through his brain, Abigail thinking she was auditioning to be their Grace hadn't come up.

Sam seemed unperturbed. His blue eyes were lit with laughter. "Jack, I believe she thinks we're gay."

Jack stood up suddenly. It was obvious she was under a misconception that he intended to remedy. "Darlin', I have never been accused of not enjoying a woman. While I don't have any problem with a person's sexuality, I don't swing that way. I haven't been spending time with you hoping you'll give me the name of your hairdresser. I've been spending time with you to try to get you into bed."

Sam could barely talk for his laughter. "Well, if we're gay, Jack, at least I'm the pretty one."

Her hands twisted around her notepad, crushing it slightly. "It's a perfectly reasonable assumption. You two are unmarried, successful men who spend almost every moment together with no visible female in either of your lives. I'm sorry if I offended you. If it helps, I thought you made a very attractive couple."

"Damn it, that does not help, Abigail," Jack said.

"Abby, we're not gay." Sam slid out of the bench to face her.

"I'm getting that now." Her eyes were wide.

"But we do like to share." Sam patted Abby on the back almost sympathetically.

Her mouth formed a perfect *O* before she turned and fled. She was running by the time she entered the ladies' room.

Sam stared after her. "Guess that whole dating thing is over."

Jack felt his eyes narrow. Everyone was watching, but he had no intention of backing down. He'd tried to take things slow. He'd tried to be a gentleman. That was over. If she thought he was backing down, she had better think again. "Time for a new plan, Sam."

He strode toward the women's bathroom.

"Hallelujah!" Sam's shout rang throughout the small room like a battle cry.

Chapter Six

Abby stared at herself in the mirror, the quiet of the ladies' room almost deafening. What the hell had happened? She'd been dating two men and hadn't even known it? And Jack Barnes was wrong about dating. A date ended in kissing. She hadn't even been kissed.

The door to the women's room slammed open. Abby practically jumped, ready to beg whoever was walking through to give her some privacy. Jack filled the doorway with his presence.

"You can't come in here, Jack." She smoothed down her uniform and swept back her hair, trying to retain as much dignity as she could.

"Why not, darlin'? I am going to admit that I'm not a man who tends to let things like social conventions keep me out of a place I really want to be in." Jack walked right up to her. The man really wasn't big on personal space.

Sam walked in and closed the door. He leaned with his back against it. One boot rested negligently against the painted pink door.

"Sam, tell him he can't come into the women's room."

"You're the one who chose the venue for this particular conversation, Abigail." There was nothing vaguely resembling a joke in Jack's voice now. Abby looked to Sam for help.

Sam shook his head. He was grinning like an idiot. "Hell no, honey. You're gonna have to learn that when Jack gets that hard edge to his voice, he means business. Besides, I'm happy with the way things went. Thank you, baby. You made this so much easier. Jack was talking about dating you and treating you like a lady. That was gonna take forever. It's much simpler this way."

"What's simpler?" Abby was unable to keep the trepidation out of her voice.

"Taking you home, taking you to bed, and showing you where you belong," Sam replied with a wink.

"Where do I belong?" Abby couldn't take her eyes off Jack. There was a simple smile on his face that held a wealth of arrogance. He'd been serious. He really had been playing the gentleman. Abby got the feeling she was about to get a full dose of Jack Barnes, and damned if she wasn't looking forward to it.

"Always between me and Sam." Jack reached out and put his hands on her shoulders, his expression intense. "Tell me you don't want us, Abby, and I'll walk away right now. I won't bother you again."

"Don't give her ultimatums." Sam sounded a bit desperate. "I thought we'd give her a taste before we forced her to make a decision. Baby, why don't you let us play around a little? I promise you'll want us."

She looked up into Jack's forest-green eyes. They were very serious as he stared at her. His hand came up to cup her face. He forced her to look at him and Abby felt his will. It should scare the crap out of her, but she found it amazingly sexy. This was a man who would always keep his promises, no matter what it cost him.

"She already wants us." Jack brushed his thumb across her mouth. It was all she could do to not open her mouth and suck his thumb in. "She just needs to admit it. Can you tell me you haven't spent the last few weeks thinking about this? Thinking about you and me and Sam coming together in bed?"

"No," she said. Jack's eyes flared, and she felt compelled to continue. "I have thought about it, but I'm scared."

The time for honesty was here. She could run, and they would probably accept her decision. She could give in and enjoy the sex

66

and walk away. Or she could ask for what she wanted. She could be brave and tell them what she needed and what she was scared of. If she did that and it all fell apart, then she would have to forgive herself. She'd learned that one of the great joys of maturing was learning how to forgive herself.

"What are you scared of?" A deep crease appeared in Sam's forehead. He walked up to her and leaned forward. "Honey, we want to take care of you. We don't want to hurt you."

She felt tears pricking at the edge of her eyes. Everything in her was screaming for that to be true. She wanted them. She craved them.

"You could be lying to me. You could want to make me look bad." She could hear her teenaged self in the statement. She felt every bit as vulnerable as she had then. The last month she'd spent with these two disparately different men had been one of the best of her life. Every evening they'd spent together over the last month had made her want them more. More than once, she'd fantasized about them sweeping into the diner and carrying her away. Lately, when things went wrong, her first thought was to call Jack. Now that her fantasy seemed to be coming true, she didn't trust fate.

Jack's hands came out and soothingly rubbed the back of her neck. He hadn't stopped touching her once. "Sweetheart, why would you say something like that? Why would we want to make you look bad?"

"Because the Echols family wants me out of town." Her heart soared when she saw the complete confusion on their faces. They couldn't make that up.

"Are you talking about that crazy old biddy who runs the church socials?" Jack seemed to struggle to place a name with a face. "She always looks at me funny."

"Ruby. That's her name." Sam frowned. "She's real unpleasant to me. Why would we do anything for her? For that matter, why would she care that you're in town?"

Hope swelled inside her. They really weren't gay, and they really weren't working for Ruby Echols. If that was true, then she had to assume they wanted her. It suddenly didn't matter that they were in a bathroom in a public place. She couldn't wait to feel their mouths pressed to hers. It wasn't forever. The universe didn't work that way, but she could have this moment. She could have a few weeks with them.

"It doesn't matter. Kiss me."

"Which one?" Sam asked.

Abby continued to smile, looking from gorgeous man to gorgeous man. "It doesn't matter, but one of you should kiss me."

Jack's eyes never left her face. "Sam, take care of that door. We wouldn't want anyone walking in."

Sam cursed and bemoaned his fate, but he walked back and took his previous position.

Jack took Abby's face in both his hands. "I'm completely crazy about you, Abigail Moore." He leaned over and finally, after what seemed to Abby like a lifetime of wanting, pressed his mouth to hers.

Abby felt helpless against the onslaught of desire that rocketed through her as Jack took her mouth. He plundered it, his tongue gently forcing its way in and dancing strongly around hers. She held on to his lean waist for dear life as he slanted over her mouth again and again. He poured his will into her and everything inside her responded. She felt that kiss in her pussy and already she was slick and warm. Jack's hands reached up and pulled at the band that held up her hair. He set it free and pulled back to look at the mane of auburn locks he'd unleashed.

"You're so fucking gorgeous," Jack breathed almost reverently as he stroked her hair. In that moment, with Jack's green eyes looking at her like she was some goddess he was worshipping, Abby felt gorgeous.

"Why don't we take this home, people?" Sam's voice was tight. Abby looked back at Sam, and his blue eyes were dark with passion.

He wanted to go home so he could join in. He wanted to have his turn. The thought should have turned her off, but all it did was get her hotter.

Jack's lips turned up in a lazy smile. "You'll have to forgive Sam, darlin'. He's always so impatient. Always has been." Jack suddenly lifted her up and set her on the counter. He looked back at his friend with great affection. "Do you have any idea how many times I've told him that anticipation is the best part?"

Jack's hands pushed up the skirt of her uniform.

"Anticipation is damn frustrating, Jack. And I've been anticipating for weeks," Sam complained.

Even from her vantage point, she could see the erection tenting Sam's jeans.

"Jack? Maybe Sam's right. People will know something's going on in here."

"Hush," Jack ordered. His tongue traced the shell of her ear. Abby sighed and let her head fall forward against his shoulder. It felt so good she suddenly didn't care if the whole town knew as long as Jack didn't stop. His long fingers teased their way into her panties, and she heard a low chuckle come from deep within his chest.

"Oh, Sam is going to love you, darling," he whispered wickedly in her ear. He gently parted her pussy. His middle finger began to circle her clit.

"Oh, god, Jack," Abby panted. She couldn't help it. She pushed back against his hand, wanting to force it lower. She wanted his fingers deep inside her.

"You want to come, Abigail?" Jack's voice was hard and sexy against her ear.

"Yes," she breathed.

"Should I let her come, Sam?"

"I don't know, Jack," Sam replied, his voice husky. "She did think we were gay."

Jack's fingers moved down and dipped into her soaking wet pussy. Abby cried out. He pushed in one and then two fingers. "I think we'll have to forgive her for that. Let's make it plain from here on out exactly how much we want her."

He moved suddenly and with power. Jack lifted her up. Her back was against the wall, and he moved between her thighs.

"Wrap your legs around me. Follow my lead. This part is all about you. This part is lovely and sweet and it's for you." Jack pushed against her, placing the hard ridge of his erection right against her clit. "Can you follow my instructions?"

"Yes." She squirmed against his jean-clad erection. There was only his jeans and her cotton panties between them now. He felt so good against her.

"Yes, Jack," he corrected. "You say my name when I'm fucking you."

Sam's face was taut. She could see him plainly over Jack's shoulder. "Damn it, Jack, you're killing me here. Finish her off. I want to watch her come."

"Please, Jack." Her need was so urgent. She was ready to explode. She could do it if he would rub her clit once. That was all she needed. She was so close. "Please, it's been so long."

"Then ride me, baby." He pushed up against her.

She was caught between the hard wall and an even harder Jack. He kissed her deeply while he stroked her up and down his cock.

"How long has it been, baby?" He never broke the rhythm of his thrusting hips.

Jack had been right. There was something sweet about this. They could have been teenagers stealing pleasure. "Four years," Abby practically cried.

She heard Sam and Jack's shock, but she wasn't concerned with that right then. She tightened her legs around Jack. She was so close. It was right there. "Please."

"Hush now." Jack gently nipped her ear, sending electricity through her. "I'll take care of you."

His palms wrapped around the globes of her ass, and he pushed up one last time. His big erection slid over her clit.

Abby sobbed when she came.

She was shaking lightly as she came down from the high. Jack transferred her back to the counter. He kissed her gently. His hands pushed back inside her panties.

"You are so wet, darlin'." Jack continued to lightly caress her pussy, sending her into spasms as he hit her still-sensitive clit. She was boneless against him, and he seemed to revel in it.

"I got the first kiss." Jack pulled his hand out of her, and she protested the loss. He wasn't listening. He held his wet fingers out. "You want the first taste?"

Sam's eyes glazed over. Without hesitation, he left his post to join them. He looked at Jack's callused fingers coated in her cream.

"You know I do." Sam's voice was almost guttural. He leaned

over with no self-consciousness and sucked those creamy fingers into his mouth. He licked her arousal off Jack's fingers. She felt herself getting wet all over again. "Oh, god, she's so sweet."

Jack looked at her. He leaned over and kissed her briefly. "No more games, Abigail. We want you to come home with us tonight. We want you with us. Think about it. That was a small taste of what we can do for you, but understand, we want you for more than sex. We're serious about you. If you can't say the same, then stay here. We'll be waiting in the truck."

He dropped one last kiss on her mouth and then the damn man strode out the door. She watched him go with great regret.

Sam shrugged. "He's serious. He really won't bother you again if you don't come with us. Don't worry, Abby. I'm not like Jack. I'll bother you until you're so sick of me you give in." Sam took her head in his hands and pressed his lips to hers in an almost innocent kiss. "Make it easy on me. Come home with us."

Sam left, too. She had to think about it.

For roughly two seconds.

She was out the door, running to catch up. There was no way she was letting them go now.

There was a knowing smile on Jack's lips as he paid the tab. He winked up at Christa. "Abby's shift is ending early tonight."

"It is?" Christa looked at her, her brows rising.

"It is." Jack sounded sure of himself now. He took her hand and Abby followed him.

And felt herself blushing as she walked out to the truck.

The ride back to the Barnes-Fleetwood Ranch seemed to take forever. Abby sat between Jack and Sam in Jack's enormous black truck. Her hands were folded in her lap. She was sure she looked very prim and proper and not at all like a woman who had recently ridden a man to orgasm in a bathroom. She felt a smile curl her lips up. It was good to feel naughty.

Jack made it easy on her. He talked about everyday things, calming her and making her feel like this was all normal.

"There it is." Pride was plain in Sam's voice as he pointed out the ranch house. It was big, with a wide porch and bay windows. In the distance, Abby could see a big barn and a smaller house. Despite the fact that she'd grown up in Willow Fork, she'd never been out to the Jones spread. Mr. Jones hadn't been particularly sociable, and his son had been a few years behind her in school.

"It's huge." She studied the big ranch house. It looked to be in excellent shape, with a large wraparound porch and neatly kept yard. The driveway had been upgraded to smooth concrete, but she could see where a gravel road led back toward the barn.

"It's a good house. It has great bones. It was one of the reasons we decided to settle here." Jack brought the truck to a stop.

She was still dazed when Sam hopped out of the truck. He reached back in to help her out.

"I'm so happy you're here, Abby." There was a satisfied smile on Sam's face.

Jack got out and went to unlock the front door.

"I am, too." Though now certain problems were popping up. She'd run out of the diner awfully fast. "I probably should have grabbed my bag from Christa's place. And gotten my car. My car is at Christa's, too. I could go get it and come back."

"I'll take care of everything in the morning." Jack opened the door. "Trust me to take care of you."

Sam took her hand and led her swiftly through a long hallway. She got a vague impression of a house that needed a woman's touch. The house was older, but Jack was right. It had good bones. Sam opened the door to the bedroom. Jack turned on the light behind them while Sam picked her up and then set her gently on the king-sized bed. Sam pulled his clothes off, throwing them in a pile on the floor by the bed. Jack stood over her, looking down with a smile playing on his sensual lips. It was the happiest she could remember seeing Jack since the first time she met him. Her heart filled when she realized she had put that smile on his face.

"I'm going to watch for a while, darlin'." Jack leaned over to kiss her. He played lightly with her mouth before stepping back with a rueful grin. "I think Sam has some things he would really like to do to you."

"Damn straight," Sam said, and Abby's eyes widened as she got her first good look at him. He was beautiful. His body was rock hard. He had long legs and strong arms. His chest was cut and tapered perfectly to his lean waist and then there was…

"Wow." Her words came out as a breathy giggle. She looked at Sam's enormous cock. Long and thick, he was beautiful everywhere.

"That's what all the girls say. Take off her clothes, Sam." Jack watched the scene with heavily-lidded eyes. Abby could see his dick straining against his jeans. He seemed to be built on the same monstrous proportions as his friend.

"Anything you say, boss," Sam drawled. He hauled her into an upright position. His hands moved quickly as he unbuttoned the front of her uniform, pushing it aside and exposing her breasts. He whistled as he stared down at her breasts, barely held in place by a lace demi-cup bra. "Damn, now that is perfect."

Abby knew she should be feeling self-conscious, but she was still a bit drunk from the first real man-given orgasm she'd had in four years. It gave her a confidence she hadn't felt in forever. She pulled her arms out of the sleeves and eased out of the uniform. She reached around the back of her bra and quickly twisted the clasp loose. She tossed the bra away, wanting more than anything to feel Sam's hands on her. She lay back on the big bed.

It was hard to feel self-conscious when Sam looked like he was going to drool. Abby smiled at him. His hands came out to cup her breasts.

"See, these pretty things are begging for me to suck on them." Sam looked utterly fascinated.

"Get the rest of her clothes off first, Sam," Jack said quietly, but it was a tone that brooked no disobedience.

Sam nodded, obviously used to following orders. Jack pulled up a chair and sank gracefully down. He unfastened his fly, but he didn't pull out his cock. A lazy predator who knew he'd get his fill.

"You are beautiful, Abigail." Sam looked at her with lust in his eyes.

"Right back at ya, Sam," she managed with a husky laugh. Her hands were still shaking a tiny bit, and she wondered if it was the cold or the fact that she was finally playing out her deepest fantasy.

She wasn't sure why she was so stuck on the idea of being loved by two men. Perhaps it was because both the men in her life that she'd cared about had died and the thought of loving and then being alone again left her hollow. Or perhaps it was simply the way the writers she read made it sound—being surrounded by warmth and pleasure, two men who put her first, who needed her so much they were willing to share…it was a fantasy, but for tonight she intended to revel in it.

Sam's warm hands ran up her legs to her hips, where he hooked his thumbs under her bikini panties and dragged them down and off. He swore as he revealed her pussy.

"I told you," Jack said with a knowing grin. He looked at her, and she began to get the idea that this was where Jack felt comfortable. He was in control. Despite the fact that he wasn't the one on the bed with her, he was still calling the shots, and that did something for her. Utterly self-assured and confident, Jack watched Sam salivating over her naked body. Jack's eyes lit up as he looked her over. He leaned forward and palmed her breast, sending a flash of heat through her. "Sam has a thing about pretty, naked pussies. I think he's finally found his heart's desire."

"Ohhh," Abby moaned as Sam's fingers ran up the slit of her pussy. It made her very happy she'd kept up her grooming routine during her long dry spell.

"It's perfect. It looks like a hot, ripe peach, and I love peaches." Sam climbed onto the bed and settled between her legs.

She couldn't breathe. He was so close. It had been forever since she'd been this turned on, her every nerve alight with desire. She wanted them, wanted them in a way she hadn't wanted anything in a long while. It was like someone had flipped a switch and her black and white world had suddenly shifted to vibrant color. Sam hooked her knees over his shoulders, and she felt the heat of his mouth hovering over her, teasing and tempting her.

"Jack?"

She heard Sam ask the question, a plea in his voice.

"Go on, Samuel." Jack gave the order. "Eat that sweet pussy."

"With pleasure."

She bit back a scream as Sam ran his tongue through the full length of her pussy. She felt herself cream as he settled in to torment her. He kissed, licked, and loved her with his tongue and lips.

"Oh, god, Sam," she ground out as she wound her hands in his curly hair. Sam responded by parting her with his fingers and fucking her with his tongue.

She caught Jack's gaze as he seemed to be watching her, studying her response.

"It's his real talent. He considers it his life's work." Jack had finally pulled his cock out, and he sat there with his legs spread. His big, beautiful dick jutted out from the *V* of his thighs, and he stroked it up and down while he watched them. The purple crown and the drop of cream topping it held her attention even as Sam continued his slow devouring of her.

Jack's eyes heated up, going from his normally cool emerald to a warm green. He stroked himself again but swiped his thumb over the head of his cock, sweeping off the pre-cum. He leaned forward and put his finger to her mouth.

"Taste me," he demanded.

She sucked his thumb into her mouth and tasted the salty essence of Jack Barnes. She sucked off every bit of that drop and longed for more. Jack pulled his thumb out and kissed her, tangling their tongues briefly before pulling away again. He winked at her and then moved lower.

Her back arched off the bed as Jack captured a nipple in his mouth and sucked. Sam continued his assault. His mouth moved to her swollen clitoris, tonguing it as he thrust his fingers into her pussy.

"Oh, oh, I'm gonna come again." It was building inside, rising like a wave that threatened to overwhelm her.

"Come on my mouth, baby," Sam urged her. "Come all over my mouth. I'll lick it all up."

"I think I might try that, too." Jack growled, and he moved down her body. Like they'd done it a thousand times before, Sam replaced his fingers with his strong tongue, and she felt the heat of Jack's mouth working her clit hard. She looked at the two heads working in time and felt her womb spasm as the orgasm raced through her. Her head fell back, and she let the sensation roll over her body in delicious waves of ecstasy. She stroked Jack's soft black hair as she fell back to Earth.

He and Sam licked and sucked for a while longer, doing exactly what Sam promised, trying to suck up all her cream. They teased and tormented her until she didn't think she could take any more. Finally, Jack moved up to kiss her lips, and she opened like a flower for him. She was completely willing to do whatever these two men wanted. While Jack explored her mouth, Sam stayed between her legs. He seemed to be endlessly fascinated with her taste and smell and feel.

"Did you like that, baby?" Jack's voice was low and husky in her ear.

"You know I did, Jack," she said. "That was the best orgasm of my entire life. Thank you. Thank you, Sam."

She felt him smile against her pussy. "You're welcome, darlin'. Just so you know, I am willing to work for food."

"I'll remember that." She laughed and for the first time in a long time, truly relaxed.

* * * *

Jack's cock was harder than he could ever remember it being, but he had more to prove to Abigail than the fact that he could get a raging erection. He took a deep breath and stood up. Quickly, he pulled his clothes off and lay back down beside her, putting a possessive hand over her belly.

This time was different. He'd known it would be if they could simply get her into bed. He'd known sleeping with Abigail would mean something different than the encounters they'd had before. This time was more than sex. Seeing her in his big bed felt right, but he also was smart enough to know the fight wasn't over yet.

This was a woman who had no intentions of hanging around. He needed to find a way to make her want to stay because he had no intentions of some short-term affair.

He was a careful man and he didn't jump into anything long term easily, but weeks of knowing her, pursuing her, had taught him one thing. He wanted her, and that wasn't a feeling that would be assuaged in a few weeks. He was beginning to think he might need a lifetime with this woman.

Jack slowed down despite the throb in his cock. He had a couple of questions. Besides, Sam was still doing his thing. He'd moved up and started to nuzzle her magnificent tits. Jack cuddled up to the left side of her and kissed her mouth again. He was never going to get used to how he felt when he kissed her.

Electric. Alive. So fucking possessive he could barely stand it.

She moved restlessly as Sam laved her nipples.

"Why four years, baby?" Jack brushed her pretty red hair back.

Her voice was breathless, but she answered him immediately. "Too much going on. Ben was sick, and then I was mourning. I had a teenage daughter to raise. I didn't have time, but if I had, I wouldn't have found anything like this."

"So you haven't had a relationship like this before." Despite those hot books of hers, he would have bet his life she hadn't actually tried ménage. "We're your first."

And for damn sure your last.

"Why would you think I've done this before?" Her hazel eyes were wide.

Sam looked up from tonguing her nipples. "Baby, all the books you read are about ménage. It's a reasonable assumption you might have tried it before."

Her face flushed, eyes going wide with obvious horror. "How do you know about my books?"

Sam came up on her right side, and she was caught between them. "Darlin', I found that box of dirty books in Christa's garage."

Abigail tried to sit up, but Jack had her pinned down with a hand on her belly and a leg over hers. She gave Sam a stern look. "You went through my things?"

Sam's face was completely unrepentant. He laughed deep in his throat as he nuzzled her neck and his fingers played with her nipples. "Just your books, but if the rest of your stuff is half as hot as those books, I'll inspect all of it."

Abby looked like she wanted to protest. It was definitely time to distract her. He ran his tongue along the shell of her ear. Sam joined in, palming her breasts.

"Do you want to check out my vibrator, too?" The question popped out of Abigail's mouth and she turned a bright red.

"Yes," Sam replied quickly. "I would very much like to see your vibrator and any other sex toys you have."

"And all your lingerie." Oh, she was fun to tease. He loved how her whole body flushed the sweetest pink when she was embarrassed. "I bet her vibrator is one of those little things. Women always buy vibrators too small. We should get her a butterfly."

Sam's eyes lit up. "A strap-on with a remote control. We could make her wear it when she works at the café, and we could turn it on when she's pouring coffee and watch her come."

"Whoa—" Abigail held her hands up. "I don't think Christa would appreciate the lawsuit that would come when I spill coffee into someone's lap because Sam dialed up my clitoral stimulation."

Jack put a finger over her lips. It was time to get serious. "Hush, now. Sam won't be trying anything crazy, yet. Now, sweetheart, I need to know something." His hand trailed down, and he traced a teasing design across her pussy. He loved the feel of her soft skin. He needed to make a few things plain before they continued. "Do you know what we want to do to you?"

She took a deep breath before replying. "You want to have…make love to me?"

Good girl for switching those words around. They were getting somewhere. "At the same time."

Sam's hand slid under her backside to cup her ass. "One in your sweet pussy, and the other fucking that tight ass of yours. We want to fill you up."

"Sweetheart, have you ever had a man take you anally?" Jack thought he knew the answer to the question, but he wanted to be sure.

Abigail chewed her bottom lip softly as she shook her head. "I've read about it, of course. It never came up in real life. I know I have a bad reputation, but I didn't actually earn it. There was only Adam and then Ben. Adam and I talked about it, but we never did it. As for Ben, well, it wasn't his style. I'm not opposed to it, but it scares me a little."

Sam cradled her against his chest. "Shh, it's all right. We're not demanding that tonight. We'll get you ready for us."

"Sam's right," Jack cooed in her ear. "We have all the time in the world to prepare you for that. Tonight, though, we'll take turns. Sam, get the condoms."

Sam groaned a little but kissed her forehead and slid out of bed. Jack took full advantage, pulling Abby close, rolling his body over hers. He didn't try to keep his weight off of her and she didn't protest. Yes, this was what he needed. He needed her softness against him, all her warmth and feminine sweetness beneath him. She wrapped her arms around his neck and kissed him with everything she had. His tongue delved in her mouth, seeking to fuse them together.

His dick was so hard he could pound nails with it. Patience. He needed some as he parted her legs.

She was so small and delicate compared to him. He sat up suddenly as Sam passed him a condom. Jack looked down at the erotic sight of Abigail spread out for his pleasure. She was gorgeous and soft and so fuckable he couldn't stand it anymore. He tore the condom open and rolled it over his cock.

He found his place at her core and moved inside her.

"God," Jack moaned as he began thrusting in short bursts, trying to work his dick into her incredibly small pussy. "You're so tight, baby. You feel so good."

Her voice was shaky, deep in her throat. "I think you were right about my vibrator. It was definitely too small."

"Hush, baby. I'll go slow. You'll see that we fit together fine." He didn't let up but he was gentle.

Sam moved in beside her. His hands began smoothing back her hair. "It's all right, baby. You're so beautiful. I wanted you the minute I saw you. I took one look and said I am gonna make that woman mine."

Abigail relaxed as Sam talked to her and his hands caressed her breasts. Jack's patience paid off as he managed to thrust in to the base of his cock. He held himself still over her, waiting for her to adjust. After a moment, she moaned. Her fingers dug into his shoulders, an insistent plea.

"It feels good, Jack." Her eyes were half closed, and a dreamy smile came to her lips.

"That's right," Sam said happily. "Give yourself to us. We'll make you feel so good."

Her hot pussy was a vise around his cock. He needed to move. "Wrap your legs around me."

She wrapped her legs around his waist as he started to thrust and twist his hips. He sought the perfect angle to make her fly.

"Oh, Jack," she cried out.

He looked into her eyes. She was close. It was a good thing, too, because his balls were starting to draw up. He nodded to Sam to let him know he was close. Sam's talented fingers tugged on her nipples. Abby's head fell back as she came. Jack picked up the pace, content he'd taken care of her and could seek his own release. He spread her legs apart, hooking her knees over his elbows, leaving her completely exposed. He thrust forward, and he could feel his tight balls against her ass. He pulled back and thrust again. His body tensed, and he exploded inside her. He continued to thrust until he emptied himself, then fell forward into her arms. His chest heaved like he'd run a race. He breathed in her smell.

He wrapped his arms around her waist, hugging her as he laid his head on her chest. She felt perfect there. He kissed her breast reverently and felt one of Abigail's hands tangle in his hair. He saw she was doing the same to Sam, and he was perfectly satisfied that they hadn't scared her off. She'd liked everything they had done to her so far.

But he knew damn well tomorrow would start the fight to keep her all over again.

After a moment's sweet rest, Jack rolled off her and she protested the loss of his warmth.

The minute he got up to dispose of the condom, Sam was on top of her. Jack laughed at the speed with which his partner took over. He was on top of her before she knew what was happening.

"My turn." Sam had the smile of an eager puppy.

"I'm in trouble." She laughed as her arms wound around Sam's waist.

Weren't they all?

Chapter Seven

Sam's head came up as he heard the door slam. He sat up in bed and immediately looked for Abby.

All night he'd been warm and happy. Normally he slept in his own room. He didn't complain, but he honestly didn't like sleeping alone. The night before, he'd slept like a baby, curled up against her, knowing that Jack was on the other side.

Where had that woman gone?

He yawned and stretched, every muscle singing as he moved toward the window. She was probably in the bathroom. There was a thought. She would want to take a nice long shower, and he could help her with that. A vision of Abby all soapy and warm made his dick come back to life.

Then he knew that wasn't going to happen because he saw Abby on the porch, her purse in hand.

"Damn it." He went for his jeans because the housekeeper and the hands would be wandering around at this time of day. "She's running, Jack."

He poked his partner's back. Jack was asleep on his stomach and didn't look too concerned that Abby was making a break for it.

Sam looked down at the bed they'd shared with the glorious

redhead. He looked at the clock. It was a little past seven. It was way too early to be up on a Sunday.

"I'm going after her." Sam wasn't sure where she thought she was going. "What is she thinking? We're miles from town."

Jack stirred at the sound but waved him off and pulled a pillow over his head to drown out the noise. Sam zipped up his jeans and reached for a shirt. He came up with Jack's, but that didn't matter. Where were his boots? He couldn't go running after her barefoot. "That highway is dangerous. There's no place for her to walk. She could get run over, damn it."

"She isn't walking," Jack grumbled.

Sam heard the distinct sound of a car door slamming. He went back to the window, this time jerking the curtains open so he could see the whole of the yard. Jack groaned as light flooded the room. Abby was in Jack's truck. It purred to life and he knew he was too late. Sam sat down on the bed as the truck screamed out of the driveway.

She was gone. She'd left. Without even saying good-bye.

Jack's head came up as he heard the truck's gears strip. He smiled a little. "I swear if she wrecks my truck, I am gonna paddle her bottom raw."

He didn't get Jack's calm demeanor. He was panicked, but Jack simply yawned and settled back down, pulling the quilt over his body. What the hell was happening this morning? He'd been sure Jack had been as crazy about Abby as he was. Last night had been the best sex of his life, but what if it hadn't been the same for Jack? Sam had spent the last five weeks of his life chasing after Abigail every free minute he had. He thought after last night that the relationship was settled. It looked like he was wrong.

"What the hell are you panicking over?" Jack's eyes were sleepy as he yawned and rested his head in his hand.

"I'm not panicking." That was a lie because he kind of was. How could she have left like that? It wasn't like he hadn't had a woman sneak out on him before. Hell, he'd done the same, but he hadn't expected it from her. It hurt. They'd connected and she'd run.

Jack rolled his eyes. "I can feel it from here, and it's disturbing my sleep. Don't worry about Abigail. She'll be back in this bed tonight. She might run, but she won't get very far. She's got a shift at the café starting at nine."

"How do you know that?"

Jack stretched. "Because after you fell asleep she told me she couldn't miss her shift. I explained that we would get her there one way or another," he said with a satisfied grin.

"Then why did she leave without waking us up?"

Jack sat up, his back against the headboard. "Because she's scared. We were overwhelming last night."

"You don't think we hurt her?"

"No. She's scared because she feels something for us," Jack said. "To tell you the truth, I'm happy she ran. I'd be worried if she'd gotten up and fixed breakfast and acted nonchalant. She's a forever kind of girl, and this morning she's worried she had a crazy one-night stand. It was easier to take the truck and expect that we'll come and pick it up from her in a public place than to face us in private."

Sam felt his eyebrows came together in perfect consternation. "But we told her how we feel about her."

"And no man ever lied to a woman like Abigail to get what he wanted?" Jack yawned. "She's no untried girl. She's been through a lot. She doesn't trust us yet, but she will. Right now, she's coming up with a whole bunch of silly reasons that last night happened. She's calling it a one-night stand and thinking it won't happen again. She's doing it all because she's trying to protect herself in case we decide we're done with her. We have to get her thinking straight, and then she won't have anywhere to go except right back to us. I'll get her for us, Sam. You do your good cop routine, and I'll be the big bad boy. No woman can resist it. Have I ever let you down before?"

Sam took a long breath and released the worry. He would trust in his partner. He had ever since the day when he was fifteen and had been placed in a group care home. Jack Barnes had quietly threatened the other boys in the house with egregious bodily harm if one of them touched the young, terrified Sam Fleetwood. Sam had lost his mom and dad, and he'd stuck by Jack ever since. Jack was bigger and tougher than anyone he'd met before or since.

"Not once, Jack," he said with a grateful smile.

Jack's years in foster care had given him street smarts that Sam still didn't possess. He knew what could have happened to him if Jack hadn't been there. He knew because most of it had happened to Jack.

"It's gonna be all right," Jack promised. "Now get some more sleep. Chasing that woman is going to be damn tiring work."

Sam laid back down with a smile on his face because Jack was in charge. He didn't have anything to worry about.

* * * *

Abby answered her cell phone without bothering to look at the number. It was a mistake she made because she was so flustered she wasn't thinking straight.

"You get out of town, you whore!"

She sighed and touched the screen to hang up as she maneuvered Jack's enormous black truck onto the street across from Christa's house. The thing drove like a tank. Those phone calls were becoming more and more frequent. She would have to change her number soon.

Ruby Echols enjoyed calling her far too much.

She couldn't help but think about Adam every time she got one of those calls. It was odd how it all seemed like a dream at times, like something that had happened to another person. At other times the memory was so fresh she could hear his voice, see the way his dark hair had curled around his ears.

She couldn't help but remember how they'd parted. He'd gotten jealous and she'd been sick of having to justify herself over and over again. Their fight had been loud and public. Adam had driven off, swearing they were over. Then he'd gotten drunk and wrapped his car around a tree.

Damn, but she'd been young then. Now she had to wonder if they would have made it. Could they have actually had something long term? Or had she gotten swept up in young love and passion and drama?

Was she getting swept up in the same thing all over again?

She parked Jack's truck and tried not to think about what he'd done to her last night. It was impossible. Her whole body hummed happily, reminding her how well the men had used her. She had needed it. She was single and no longer had an impressionable teenager under her roof. She was free to play around.

Except last night hadn't felt like playing. It felt serious and that worried her. The way they talked to her and held her made her think they were guys she could fall for.

She rested her head down on the steering wheel with a groan. Not going there. She wasn't seventeen and naïve. She was thirty-seven years old. Jack and Sam were younger than she was. She had a certain reputation, and those men required the goodwill of the community to do business here. If the Echols family chose to, they could probably cut off Sam and Jack from vital resources. They could stop their feed supply or screw with their financing at the bank. They would do it, too, just to spite her. Even if she was brave enough to have a crazy relationship with two men, it would hurt them in the end.

She opened the door and jumped down. Jack would ease out of the seat, but she practically needed to pole vault out of the thing. She'd felt so petite when she stood between Jack and Sam. It was their fault. She was a perfectly normal-sized woman, but they were practically giants.

Giants who had taken such sweet care of her last night.

She would have to resist them next time, though. It was for their own good. The night before she hadn't been thinking about anything but her own wants and needs. She owed it to them to protect them. They didn't understand how this town worked. Her friends could accept her all they liked, but without Ruby Echols's support, she was a pariah.

She was getting ready to text Jack and let him know he could pick up his truck at Mike's when she turned the corner onto Christa's street. She would leave the keys with Mike and maybe he and Christa would even drive it back out to them.

Maybe a flirty thank you text would be a good way to leave things between the three of them. After all, men often backed off once they had what they wanted. It would make things far easier on all of them if they did.

Then she got a look at her car. "Damn it."

The plan to take her car to work was blown to hell because someone had spray-painted WHORE across the hood and slashed her tires. Luckily, the car was in the carport, and no one could see the vandalism from the street. Abby took a deep breath and banished the tears that threatened. She had promised Christa she could have Sunday mornings to spend with her family, and she meant to keep that promise. She wouldn't wilt away because some jerk thought it was funny to humiliate her.

She could go to the sheriff, but it wouldn't do any good. He would make an obligatory report and then nothing would be done about it. She would ask Mike for advice later. In the meantime, she would be driving the tank. It served Jack right since he was the one who had insisted on leaving her car behind. If he'd let her drive her own car, it wouldn't have been defaced.

God, she wanted to call Jack. She wanted to call him and cry and throw the whole thing in his lap. He would take care of it and Sam would cuddle her and coddle her until she felt better.

She hopped back into Jack's monster truck and tried to pull away from the street. She closed her eyes when she heard the door scrape against Mike's trailer as she tried to make a too tight U-turn.

Jack was gonna kill her.

Maybe he'd just spank her. It might make her day.

Maybe, she thought as she pulled away from the scene of her crime, it wouldn't hurt to see them one more time.

If they wanted to see her again. No one had to know. If they kept it very, very quiet, she might even manage a couple of nights with them.

She could remember her time with them for the rest of her life. It would be a shield against all the lonely nights to come.

Well, if Jack didn't kill her for wrecking his car.

Two hours later, she smoothed down the skirt of her uniform. It was a pale pink waitress uniform that Christa had all of her waitstaff wear. It was unforgiving, but she wore it anyway. Luckily, Christa also kept a few around in case a waitress spilled something. Abby had been able to change into a fresh one.

The short-order cook shouted out that her order was up, and Abby grabbed the plates of scrambled eggs and pancakes and moved toward Kyle Morgan's table. He sat with his two young boys. Abby had gone to school with Kyle and had heard he'd gone through a divorce a couple of years back. He'd kept custody and seemed to have survived with very little bitterness. He was a regular customer, and she liked talking to him. He smiled at her as she set down his breakfast.

"Thank you, Abby," he said, and both his kids thanked her as well.

"Do you need some more coffee? I think they made a fresh pot."

"I would love some." Kyle's hand covered hers as she turned to grab the coffeepot from the counter. He was handsome, but she'd never thought of him in a man-woman way. He was a friend she hadn't seen in a very long time. "I was wondering. I thought maybe you could come by the house tonight for supper. I was going to grill some steaks. I thought it would be a good way to catch up."

"I'm afraid Abby has plans for tonight," a low voice growled behind her.

She nearly jumped out of her skin. She pulled her hand quickly away from Kyle and wondered why she felt guilty. She hadn't been doing anything wrong. Jack looked like she had, though. At least Sam looked happy to see her.

Kyle's eyes widened. "Does she?"

Sam slapped Kyle on the back. He managed to make the gesture friendly. "She does, indeed." Sam looked at the young boys. "How's the team going?"

The boys smiled and chattered about their baseball games. Kyle looked a bit rueful as his gaze switched between the men. "The team really appreciated the new uniforms and the lighting system is incredible. It's really helped those kids. They love baseball. Now they can play night games since we have the lights. As their coach, I have to say thank you. You've made a huge difference in those kids' lives."

"Glad to help, Kyle." Jack's eyes were still dark.

Sam chatted with the kids, and Kyle leaned forward, directing his attention to Jack. "Is that the way it is, then?"

"It is," Jack replied firmly.

"What is?" Abby didn't understand the masculine byplay. She had the notion that this cryptic conversation was all about her, but neither man was actually looking at her.

Kyle's head fell back and he laughed. "Well, hell, I always did say it would take two men to tame Abigail Elizabeth Moore."

"Kyle Morgan!" Abby looked around the café. Sure enough, people were staring.

"Remember that," Jack said blandly as he took Abby's hand. "I need to talk to Abby about a little thing called grand theft auto. Sherry, take her tables for a bit, will you?"

She found herself being hustled back toward Christa's small office as Sherry, the other waitress, leapt into action. Did everyone jump to do Jack Barnes's bidding when he opened his mouth? Abby was willing to admit he was a strong man, but he needed to understand she wasn't a doormat.

"Don't you push me around." Abby found herself being herded through the door.

She turned to face Jack and forced herself to stand her ground as he looked at her. He really could be intimidating when he wanted. Abby stepped up and went toe-to-toe with him. Unfortunately, it meant she had to crane her neck to look up at him.

She reached up and poked him straight in the chest. "You don't scare me, Jack Barnes."

"I can tell," he said with a sexy smile. His mouth turned down as he got serious. "Maybe you better get a little scared, though, darlin'. Let's go over all the ways you have insulted me today."

"I wasn't insulting you," she protested.

"You left this morning without so much as a kiss good-bye. Do you how much that hurts a man? Sam didn't even get in his cuddling time. He gets cranky without it. Were you using us for sex, Abigail?"

"That's ridiculous." Her hands unconsciously went to his chest and started rubbing soothingly. Now that he was close and they were alone, she was thinking about all sorts of things she'd rather do than fight with him. All the reasons she had given herself earlier seemed far away now that Jack was standing right in front of her. He was here and solid and she wanted to feel good for a few minutes. No one in her life made her feel the way Jack and Sam did. "Of course I didn't do that."

Jack's face could have been carved from granite. "How am I supposed to know that? I worshipped you last night. I told you how I felt. You said nothing, and then this morning you left, stealing my truck in the process."

"I didn't mean to make you worry." Jack was really upset. They had been serious about having her in their lives. Her heart seized at the thought of having them with her all the time.

"Then I walk in to try to talk to you, try to figure out what we did wrong last night..."

"You didn't do anything wrong," she said quickly. "You and Sam were perfect."

"Then why were you making a date with Kyle Morgan?"

"I wasn't making a date with Kyle Morgan." How could he even think such a thing? Getting busy with Kyle Morgan was the furthest thing from her mind. "He wanted to catch up. We went to high school together."

"Don't be naïve, Abby." Jack pulled up a chair and sat down. "He was asking you out. He wants a mama for his kids and a sweet body in his bed. He must have thought he hit the jackpot when you sashayed back into town."

Kyle coached high school football. There was no way he could be seriously contemplating a relationship with her. Walter Echols was on the school board. He might be running for a higher office, but Adam's younger brother would never be so absorbed with his campaign that he couldn't crush one man's career.

"I wasn't going to date Kyle Morgan."

Jack pulled her into his lap, and she steadied herself on his broad shoulders. She was already responding to him. How could she want him again so soon after last night?

"Why wouldn't you go out with him?" Jack asked quietly, his hand tipping her face up to look at him.

"Because I don't want anyone but you and Sam. I haven't since I walked back into town."

Jack's lips curled up a bit. He leaned over and brushed his mouth lightly against hers, leaving her wanting more. His hand played on her knees and threatened to go straight up her skirt.

"Jack, we can't," she whispered. "People might be able to hear."

"Then you'll have to be quiet, won't you, darlin'? I know that will be hard for you. You make a lot of noise, and I love it." Jack had a devilish look on his face. "We still need to figure out how you can make up for stealing my truck."

She had a wicked idea. Jack and Sam made her forget her inhibitions. The truth was no one would come back here. And very few people were in the café to have even seen her walk off with Jack. And hell, half the town still called her a whore under their breaths. Why shouldn't she at least earn their scorn?

But that wasn't what this was about. For a while, she could go wild again. Just for a few more weeks—if she was careful—she could feel young and free again.

She slid off his lap and got to her knees in front of him. Jack's cock immediately responded. She touched the denim of his jeans and felt the long, thick line of his erection. Jack sighed while she gently lowered the zipper. The previous night, the boys had been intent on pleasuring her. Jack had been right to say they worshipped her. They made her feel like a goddess, but she hadn't been required to do more than lay back and enjoy it.

She'd missed actively participating. They hadn't asked her to suck them off, and that had been a mistake. Jack shifted in the chair, pushing his jeans and briefs down. Nope. She hadn't had enough time to appreciate the cock in front of her. Reaching out, she let her fingertips skim the soft skin covering that rock-hard erection.

"Lick the head," he said, his voice low.

She let her tongue reach out to delicately lick the broad purple crown of Jack's cock. He moaned, letting her know how much he liked it. She treated it like a delicious ice cream cone she wanted to savor, curling her tongue around the ridge and sucking the head lightly into her mouth. The tip of her tongue delved gently into the slit, licking the salty confection already forming there. She loved this, genuinely loved sucking cock, pleasuring her partner.

"That's right, darlin'. Damn, your mouth feels good." His hands found her hair, and before she knew it, her ponytail was gone and Jack's fingers were tangled in her long hair. "Take me deeper now."

Abby obliged, loving the feel of his hardness against her tongue. He was all steel and silky skin, and she loved the way his cock jumped when she lightly licked it, as if it was seeking her out. She relaxed her jaw and let him sink deeper into the warm wetness of her mouth.

"God, that feels incredible. Suck harder."

He tightened his grip on her hair and slowly fed her his length. She didn't panic as he filled her, simply breathed through her nose and let her tongue swirl around as much as it could with what little room was left.

"Take it all, darlin'. Swallow me down."

Jack thrust his cock deeper.

"Baby," Jack warned, "baby, you're gonna make me come."

She pushed farther until she could feel the head of his cock touch the back of her throat. Reaching up and caressing his tight sac, she pointedly swallowed around him. Jack groaned and held her head on him as he spurted his semen into her mouth. Her throat worked furiously to suck it all down. It was salty sweet, and she licked it off his dick as he softened inside her.

Jack's hands were gentle in her hair. She looked up at him, and his eyes were so tender. Had any woman ever seen him looking so vulnerable before? Oh, she was in so deep with the both of them. With Jack and Sam. It both terrified and thrilled her. She had thought this feeling long past her. She'd loved her husband. They had been friends first, and then lovers and partners in raising her daughter. If she was honest with herself, she'd married Benjamin as much for Lexi's sake as her own.

What she felt for Jack and Sam had nothing to do with anyone but the three of them.

"Thank you, sweetheart." Jack's voice was deep with sexual satisfaction. He tucked himself back into his briefs and redid the fly of his jeans.

Smiling brightly, she came off her knees and settled herself back on Jack's lap. She held her face up, ready for his kiss. "You're welcome. I hope that makes up for me leaving this morning. I should have stayed and cuddled."

Now that she thought about it, she was upset she'd missed cuddling time. If she kept it quiet, maybe she could manage an affair with the two of them. She had to keep them off the Echols's family radar.

Lightly brushing his lips across hers, Jack's hands went firmly to her waist. "I am properly placated for your very rude exit from our bed this morning."

Quicker than she could think, Abby found herself flipped over and turned across Jack's knee.

"What the hell?" How had he moved so quickly? She wasn't exactly a lightweight, but he'd picked her up and maneuvered her like she weighed nothing at all.

"But there is still the matter of one stolen and damaged truck," Jack announced in that voice Abby was beginning to realize meant business. One big hand caressed her bottom as the other held her down.

"Now, Jack." Abby tried hard not to laugh because that might upset him further. She had no honest fear of him at all. He would never hurt her, and frankly, she was curious. The last few years had been one long, dry spell, and she'd filled in the dreary space with an astonishing amount of erotica. Jack might think she was intimidated, but in truth, she was already getting hot. Sucking him off had made her wet and ready. His hand getting ready to spank her did nothing to change that fact.

Submissive. That was the word for how she was feeling. Submissive and hot and ready. "I'm sorry about the truck. I have depth perception issues."

He flipped the pink skirt of her uniform up to her waist, uncovering the bikini panties she wore.

"These won't do." With a strong jerk, he pulled the panties off her hips and they tangled around her knees, leaving the twin globes of her ass exposed. She couldn't help but wiggle as his hand cupped her mound. His deep chuckle warmed her. "Now, what do we have

92

here? You're already wet, Abigail. I guess I don't have to worry about scaring you off. I am more than willing to let you drive my truck whenever you like, darlin'."

Jack teased her with his long fingers. A moan came from deep inside her. She wasn't trying to get away. Not at all. She wanted to tempt him inside. "I'm even willing to deal with your depth perception issues. But you have to deal with the discipline I will hand out for every ding you put on that fine piece of machinery."

His hand pulled away from her but only for a moment. Then it came down with a hard *thwack* to her ass.

She barely stopped herself from screaming. The spanking stung briefly, and then she felt the heat deep in her pussy. She moaned as he brought his hand down again. Maybe ten times. Maybe more.

She could feel him getting hard again.

"You like this? I like it, too. Your cheeks are a pretty pink. I love that color."

"Do it again." She thrust her butt up. She wondered what it would feel like if he spanked her pussy.

"Maybe later, sweetheart," he said with a chuckle. He leaned over and kissed her ass, one kiss on each cheek. He reached down and pulled her panties off, then set her on her feet.

"What are you doing?" Her entire body flushed with sexual arousal.

He shoved her white panties into his jeans pocket. "I think I'll take these with me. I like the idea of being able to push your skirt up and have my way with you."

"I like it, too." She was getting suspicious that her punishment wasn't over. A sexy spanking was one thing, but leaving her unsatisfied was going to piss her off. "Let's do it now."

Jack patted his stomach. "Oh, darlin', I can't. I was denied my breakfast this morning. I had to spend the whole morning worried sick about you, so I don't have the energy."

"You asshole," Abby spat as he made for the door. "I want my panties back."

Jack pulled them out and waved them. "Spoils of war, baby, spoils of war."

He shut the door behind him, and she thought briefly about

walking out after him and announcing loudly to everyone in the café that Jack Barnes was a terrible tease.

Revenge. She would get some revenge on that man. Right after she'd taken care of herself. Bastard. She was so hot she couldn't think straight, and he was probably sitting out there laughing about it.

"Abby, sweetheart?" Sam's voice was soft as he opened the door and looked her over before closing it and locking it behind him. He stood there with his angelic face, and it was all she could do not to jump him. He looked delicious in a white western shirt and tight blue jeans. "What did that mean old Jack do to you?"

Abby felt herself pouting but couldn't quite stop it. Sam's hands reached out for her, and the look on his face was sweetly lascivious. Jack might deny her, but Sam sure as hell wasn't going to.

"He yelled at me." She heard the hitch in her breath. Emotion welled up inside her. It had been that kind of morning. She had been able to put her car out of her mind, but now it seemed to be crashing in on her. She needed some affection. She should never have left this morning. The world would be a better place if she'd stayed in the comfort of that big bed, safe in between them. "He yelled at me, and he spanked me, and he stole my panties."

Sam looked like he was trying hard not to laugh. "Was that the worst thing he did?"

She shook her head.

"What was the worst thing?"

"He didn't even fuck me," she admitted on a low wail.

Sam pulled her into his arms. "I'm so sorry that mean old Jack did that. He can be downright ruthless sometimes. To be truthful, though, you did steal his truck."

"And I tried to make up for it." She nuzzled his chest and let her arms wind around him. "I gave him a blow job and everything."

"Well, I'll have to step up and take care of you. I can't let Jack get away with something as bad as that."

She went up on her toes and pressed her lips to his. "No, we can't let him get away with it." A thought made her pause. "Sam, we should stop. I don't want to make Jack mad. I don't want to come between the two of you."

He grinned as he looked down at her. "Who do you think high-fived me on my way in here? He didn't have any plans to leave you unsatisfied, baby."

She sighed, and her hands went to his zipper. "I knew there was a reason I liked him."

He leaned down and kissed her passionately, his tongue forcing its way in to play with hers. She hopped up on the desk, thankful Christa was such a neat freak. There was next to nothing on the top. She let her knees fall apart, and Sam immediately invaded. He shoved his pants down to his knees, and his fingers foraged between her legs. He slipped a finger between the slick folds of her pussy, rubbing up and down and circling her swollen clitoris.

"Damn, baby," Sam breathed against her mouth. "Jack did a number on you. You are soaking wet. Did you like your spanking?"

She bit her lip and pressed up against his teasing hand. She needed more. She needed his cock. "I did. Please, Sam."

Sam's blue eyes were dark as he looked at Abby. Abby watched as he quickly sheathed his big cock in a condom. "Please, what? What do you want me to do to you?"

She knew what she wanted, and she wasn't afraid to ask for it. "Fuck me, Sam. Fuck me now, and fuck me hard."

"Yes, ma'am." Sam slammed into her pussy.

He felt so right inside her. She held herself wide for him. He pushed and pushed until he was tightly seated. He didn't need to go easy. Jack had her wet and ready for some rough play.

She moaned and clutched Sam's shoulders as he pounded into her. Her hands slid down his back to tighten on his perfect ass. It clenched and released under her hands, and she fought to pull him in deeper.

"It's feels so good, Sam." Her head fell back.

Sam's hands found her still-sensitive ass, using her rear to hold her tight for his fucking. Her cheeks tingled, reminding her of everything Jack had done to her, and the image made her even hotter. He was sitting out there in the dining room, and he knew exactly what they were doing.

Sam fucked into her pussy like a man on a mission. He pressed into her and rolled his hips so he could slam against her clit with each thrust. Abby pushed back against him, fighting for her orgasm with everything she had. Sam's finger slipped between her cheeks, and he circled her tight anus.

"I can't wait to take you here." Sam groaned, and she felt his finger push inside her rear.

"Sam!" Abby cried out at the surprise sensation.

Sam played with her anus, gently pushing in and out, while she started to come. She panted as she tightened her legs around his waist.

Abby's release was the best feeling in the world. Then it was Sam's turn to moan. He picked up the pace and pounded into her. His finger came out of her ass as she fell back, completely sated, and Sam took his own pleasure. He rocked hard into her, throwing his head back as he stiffened over her when he came. He fell over on top of her. Joy. It was pure joy to have him so close. She kissed his cheek and the strong line of his jaw. When he looked up, he smiled at her.

"If that was punishment, Sam," she began with a grin, "you tell Jack I'm gonna be a very bad girl."

Chapter Eight

Walter Echols valiantly managed to not roll his eyes as his mother joined her small group of friends. Not a one of them was younger than seventy, and he liked to think of them as a school of blue-haired barracudas.

There were five of them, not counting his mother, and they met each week at the First Methodist Church of Willow Fork. Walter wondered why it had ever been called First. It seemed silly since he expected there never would be a second. There was a Presbyterian church on the other side of town, but it was attended by the blue collars of Willow Fork. Sometimes Walter wished he could be counted as one of those hard-working men and women. It wasn't that he didn't enjoy his family's money. He enjoyed a good car and fine dining as much as the next person. But in a small town, money wasn't simply something he enjoyed.

Money defined who he was in Willow Fork, and he had a duty to it.

One of the barracudas broke from the group and began swimming toward him. She was using a walker to do it, but Walter still felt the menace. Even an ancient barracuda still had teeth. They might have been purchased, but they were sharp. This was one of those times when not having money would work in his favor. Hillary Glass slowly worked her way toward him, an indignant gleam in her eye. If he was a regular Joe, he would be free to flee. But he was an Echols, and he had a reputation to uphold.

"Good morning, Mrs. Glass," he said politely as he looked around the fellowship hall. His wife was talking to the pastor. No help there. He reached mentally for something to say. "How is your son, Lyle?"

Walter smiled broadly, proud of himself for pulling that out of thin air.

"Still queer and going to hell," the old lady said with a frown. "That's what happens when you let your son leave a nice place like this and go to college in some godless city."

Oh, yeah. Walter remembered why he didn't normally mention Hillary's son.

Lyle Glass was a flaming homosexual. Funny man. Walter had gone to school with him. Lyle never failed to make his classmates laugh, but he'd been gay long before he'd reached the godless campus of Baylor University. If he recalled correctly, Lyle had moved to Dallas after he finished his undergraduate degree and was working for a large corporation as a manager. Walter would have to look him up the next time he was there. Walter was thirty-five and rapidly discovering this was a time when a man wanted to reconnect with his past. But then, he suspected, the past was exactly what had put the righteous gleam in Hillary Glass's rheumy eyes.

"What are you doing to protect your poor mother from that tramp?" Hillary's voice was loud enough that a few people turned to see what was going on.

"I doubt Abigail Moore is coming after my mama," Walter said evenly.

The thought of Abby actively attempting to hurt his elderly mother was ridiculous. The woman could have had her revenge in a million different ways, yet she hadn't even sued the family for her daughter's support. Adam had died with a trust fund, but Abby hadn't come after it. The truth be told, he'd actually started wondering how he was going to protect Abby from his mama.

Not that he was good at protecting anyone from his mama. Even himself. He loved his wife. Jan was his second wife. He'd been young when he had allowed himself to be shoved into a marriage with the "right" woman. Claire had come from a good, solid family and had been selected by his mother. It had only been a few years after Adam's death, and he'd been willing to do anything to please his parents. They'd been shell-shocked, and so had he. After Walter graduated from college, he'd let his mother shove him into the next step.

Unfortunately, his mother's choice of a perfect wife had left him for another man two years into the marriage. When Walter's mother had tried to come up with another mate, Walter had put his foot down for the first time in his life. Ruby Echols might not have approved of Jan, but ten years and two beautiful kids later, she'd been forced to accept her.

Yes, he loved his wife, but if he'd been single, he would have been all over Abigail Moore like cheese on nachos.

That was one gorgeous woman, even now. He had seen her on a couple of occasions and thought she might even be sexier than she had been then. There was a worldliness about her now that had been absent before. She had confidence that only experience could give a person.

He'd been two years younger than his brother when Hurricane Abby hit, but even at fifteen he'd understood what his big brother saw in the redhead. She was beautiful and loyal. Abby had been funny and always sweet to her boyfriend's kid brother. She'd been wild. She and Adam had lived a fast life for a small town. They'd been caught drinking at the lake on more than one occasion, and if they were in a parked car, everyone knew not to approach it until it stopped rocking and the windows cleared. Walter could still remember how happy his brother had been once he'd told his parents off and promised he would keep seeing Abby even if they disinherited him.

His parents blamed Abby for Adam's wildness, but Walter knew his brother better. Adam had been wild long before he got together with a girl from the wrong side of town.

Now she was back, and twenty years hadn't dimmed his mother's fury.

"That piece of trash being in this town hurts your mother," Hillary complained.

"She's only in town to help her mother get back on her feet." Walter tried to be reasonable, though he'd already attempted the line of logic on his mom and it hadn't worked. "Diane Moore broke her hip a while back and had some surgery. She's been struggling."

He didn't mention that Abigail was a registered nurse. Hillary wouldn't be impressed with her education or experience.

"I don't care about her," Hillary said bluntly. "And neither should you. It's her fault her daughter turned out so vile. You better do something, Walter, or your mother's friends will step in and do it for you."

He heard the click-clack of Hillary's walker as she moved away from him and put his fingers to his temples. Yes, he could feel a migraine coming on. He'd already talked to the sheriff about gently edging Abby out of town. He didn't want to inundate her with tickets, but she needed to know it would be hard to stay here. She'd been plain in her intention to leave once her work here was done. She wasn't shoving her way into the upscale social events of Willow Fork. She worked at her friend's café and helped her mom out. Why his mother couldn't leave be, he had no idea.

He would have to come up with something else to placate her.

Jan looked over at him and smiled as she picked up their little girl and fixed her four-year-old body to the hip his mother had commented was far too large for a true lady. His mother wouldn't know a true lady if one bit her in the ass, and Jan had offered to on several occasions. Walter smiled back and wondered when he was going to be a man. His one foray into rebellion had netted him the best woman he'd ever met. He was currently engaged in his second foray. His mother had been dead set against him running for state senate, but Walter wanted out of town so bad he could taste it. Luckily, his father had been all for it before he died last spring. Walter felt bad for Abby, but he needed his mother's support.

Just this one last time.

Once he got to Austin, all bets were off, he promised himself. But for now, he had to find a way to deal with Abigail Moore.

100

* * * *

After spending a couple of minutes in the bathroom trying to make sure she didn't look like a woman who had performed numerous sexual services for two different men, Abby walked back into the kitchen with her head held high.

She was a professional. She had spent years working in one of the toughest ERs in the state, and she could stare down almost anyone. Working as a nurse in the emergency room had prepared her to handle just about anything. If someone gave her that righteous look she'd come to expect, she would treat them like a drunk on a full moon night at John Peter Smith Hospital.

"You done with your break, hon?" Len Sawyer gave her a knowing smile as she walked into the kitchen.

He settled a massive stack of bacon on a single plate. He'd been Christa's short-order cook for ten years. She'd only met him a month ago, but he seemed to have taken a shine to her. He was an older man who was happily married to a beautician. Karen Sawyer had told Abby to come into her shop any time she liked and she would take care of those troublesome grays. Abby had very much appreciated the thought, but instead used a box at home because she didn't want to put anyone out of business. It was a pain in the butt, but she was also driving to Tyler when she needed anything.

"Yes," she said with a crisp nod. "I'm quite refreshed and ready to go back to work."

Sherry bounced into the kitchen, her ponytail bobbing up and down. She called out an order and then turned to Abby. There was a broad smile on her face. "You have got to tell me how you did that. I have been trying to be the meat in that sandwich for ten years."

"Don't you go being nasty, girl," Len warned.

Sherry looked up, completely guileless. She was twenty-five and had no ambitions beyond making her hair appointment next Monday. "I am not being nasty. Well, maybe I am, but this is girl talk. You don't listen in." Sherry sighed. "Ten years. I understood in the beginning. I was jail bait, but even after I was all legal and stuff, I couldn't get them to date me."

"Them?" Abby was shocked that Sherry knew. It was supposed

to be a closely guarded secret.

"Hon, everyone knows those boys are perverts." Len waved his hand. "I suppose the old church ladies might have cared at one point, but Jack and Sam rebuilt First Presbyterian after that fire a few years back, so they decided to close their mouths. To each their own, I say."

"It's not like they haven't dated." Sherry wrinkled her cute nose. "Those boys haven't been celibate, but they tend to be real picky. Well, Sam's not, but Jack is. They might try to keep it quiet, but this is a small town. Everyone is up in everyone else's business. Those boys made a public declaration of intent regarding you. It'll be all over town by the time the Cowboys game is on."

Her cheeks felt like they were on fire. How was she going to go back out there when everyone knew what she had been doing?

"I'd watch out for Melissa Paul, though," Sherry warned. "She works at the Walmart a town over. She has wanted to get her hooks into Sam Fleetwood for a long time. Sam went out with her about a year ago, but Jack couldn't stand her, which tells me he has good taste. Sam broke it off, and she's been acting like a scalded cat ever since."

"Sam dated someone without Jack?"

Len nodded as he cracked eggs into a bowl. "Sam is the one who dates. Jack joins them later, if you know what I mean. I just about fell on the floor when he told Kyle Morgan he was serious about you and you were his girlfriend."

Abby's jaw dropped. "He said what?"

Sherry's face lit up. She loved juicy gossip. "Kyle Morgan's boys asked if you were Jack's girl, and he said yes. He even smiled when he did it. I didn't know his face worked that way. Usually Jack is *grrrr*, and dark and broody. He likes to have a badass reputation."

"Then the man shouldn't rescue every stray dog he finds." Len laughed as he flipped a pancake. "It was hard to stay terrified when I saw him stop that big truck of his to move a turtle out of the road. Let me tell you, Abby, it didn't take long before the women of this town figured out Jack Barnes was a sucker for a hard luck story. That man has fixed more leaks, roofs, and cars than any one should have. He doesn't date the way Sam does because he doesn't have the time."

"But he does it all with a frown on his face," Sherry observed. "I suppose he thinks that keeps his image up." She stared out the window to the dining room. "Gotta go. The natives are restless."

She walked off, a fresh pot of coffee in her hand.

"He's a good man." Len pushed the tray toward her. It was full of pancakes and greasy bacon and runny eggs. It was a heart attack waiting to happen. The nurse in Abby wanted to lecture someone. "So is Sam. A woman could do a lot worse."

She noted the table number and stopped in her tracks. "Len, we're going to have to change this order."

The cook looked back curiously as she explained to him what she was going to need. He shook his head like he wasn't so sure this was a good idea, but she had a plan. If Jack Barnes was going to announce she was his girlfriend, he was going to have to learn to deal with what that really meant.

Five minutes later, she reloaded the tray herself and got back to work.

* * * *

Jack stared down at the plate Abigail placed in front of him. There were eggs, Canadian bacon, and a bowl of fruit. There was only one problem with it.

"This is not what we ordered." Jack had been looking forward to a huge breakfast of his usual pancakes, bacon, and fried eggs. He'd worked up an appetite, but it seemed their woman wanted some revenge. His mood took a deep dive. He hadn't expected that.

"It's all you're getting," she said saucily.

Sam poked at the fruit like it was some foreign thing he'd never seen before rather than chunks of pineapple and melon. He looked at Abigail with a desperate expression on his face. "Where are our pancakes? We ordered pancakes. Come on, Abby. I was nice to you. Jack was the mean one who stole your panties. Punish him."

Jack's eyes narrowed on her as she rested her hand on her hip and appeared ready for a fight, which he was willing to give her. "Take this back, Abigail. Bring us what we ordered."

She shook her head. "I don't think so. There are no more pancakes for you here."

Jack slid out of the booth and stood over her. Now everyone in the café was watching. "Are you telling me we are no longer welcome in this establishment?"

Sam stood behind her and put his hands on her shoulders, almost as if he was ready to pull her out of Jack's line of fire if he had to. "I'm sure that's not what she meant, Jack."

She rolled her pretty hazel eyes. "I'm not kicking you out. Why would I do that? I'm telling you that if I'm your girlfriend, I have certain rights. You've taken certain rights and privileges concerning me, and I think I should do the same with you."

"What privilege is it you're looking for, Abigail?"

She didn't seem the least bit intimidated by him as she poked him straight in his chest. "I am claiming the privilege of keeping you alive through tomorrow." She leaned in and kept her voice low. "Do you have any idea how much lard Len uses? I had to make the egg white omelets myself because he said it was a sin to waste the yolk. If that is the way you eat every day, then you're a heart attack waiting to happen. I see it every day. Don't think a thirty-year-old man can't have a heart attack."

"But we work on a ranch all day," Sam argued. "We need a lot of calories."

"Calories are fine as long as they come from a good source," she said practically. "You need good, low-fat protein and complex carbohydrates."

Every muscle in Jack's body stilled for a moment. He looked into Abigail's eyes, searching for the truth. "Are you telling me you changed our order because you're worried about us? Not because you want to get back at me?"

The confusion in her eyes was all he needed. He felt his gut unclench as he realized she was fussing over them.

"Why would I do that? What would I need revenge for? I will get my panties back, though, Jack." The last part was whispered with a purely feminine promise of retribution, and it caused him to laugh long and hard.

He sat down again, picked up his fork and dug in, giving Sam an encouraging smile.

"It'll be fine, Sam." Abigail winked at them. "You'll find you can survive perfectly well on relatively healthy food. People do it all the time."

Sam eased into the booth and frowned at the plate. "Who eats fruit for breakfast?"

"People who want to live." She turned to check on another customer, but Jack's hand reached out and held her.

"We have a date tonight," he reminded her. She hadn't actually said yes when they asked her out the day before, but she'd fucked them a couple of times since then, so it seemed a reasonable bet. "We'll pick you up at seven."

Abigail sighed and put a hand over the one holding her arm, stroking him as though trying to soothe him. "I can't leave my mom. I'm sorry. Believe me when I say there's nothing I would rather do than see the two of you again."

Sam grinned. "I think you'll find your mama is playing bingo at the Presbyterian church tonight with her friend Sylvia."

"But Mom can't drive and Sylvia won't be able to support her if she needs help."

"That's why one of our ranch hands and his wife are going along with them." Jack had already solved that problem. "Juan and his wife are very fond of bingo." They were also fond of the bonuses Jack handed out and had fallen all over themselves to be helpful. "Your mom knows them from church. She's very excited about getting out of the house."

"I bet she is," Abby said in a low drawl. "Are you going to go over and help her with her hair, Jack?"

"If that's what it takes." He had the confidence of a man who knew he had all the exits guarded. "Seven o'clock. We'll go into town. Somewhere nice."

She seemed to brighten at that and nodded. "Seven it is, then. I'll be ready, and I think I'll wear a dress…and maybe some heels."

She gave them what he was starting to think of as her siren smile. It never failed to get him excited. As she walked away, he felt somewhat responsible for the bounce in her step.

Sam stared at his partner. "Are you really going to eat that?"

105

"Every bite," he swore. "Maybe you've had enough people who gave a shit about you in your life, but I haven't. She made this herself, and I'll be damned if I don't eat it, despite the fact that Canadian bacon is far inferior to honest-to-goodness American bacon. You're going to eat it, too. It might hurt her feelings if you don't."

"Fine." Sam tried the melon. "At least I have dinner to look forward to. Promise me she won't get up from our table at the steak house and take over the kitchens to make us something healthy."

"I promise nothing. That woman is a force of nature."

Sam nodded. "That was smart of you to set up a fun night for her mom."

"It's all about breaking down the stop signs she's going to put up." He was a firm believer in plowing through obstacles. He never tried to go around something when he could smash through. "She wants us. She's a little scared. We need to treat her like a fractious mare."

Sam's eyes lit up with mirth. "Yeah, I get what you're saying. We need to sneak up on her real quiet-like, and then, when she's calm and stuff, we jump her, force a saddle on her, and ride that baby until she can't imagine a time we weren't on top of her."

"Exactly," Jack agreed as his phone rang. He pulled it out and checked the number. It was familiar so he answered. "Hello, Christa, how are you doing this morning? Are you checking to make sure Abby got to work? I assure you she is one hundred percent here and giving us both hell. Whoa…what do you mean? They wrote what? Tell Mike not to have it towed yet. I want to see it for myself. We'll be there in half an hour."

"Eat fast, Sam."

"What's up?" Sam took a drink of coffee.

"Looks like someone in this town doesn't see how sweet our Abigail is," Jack said in a low growl that let everyone who heard it know there was going to be trouble.

Chapter Nine

"I love you," Abby said into the phone.

"I love you, too, Mom," her daughter replied. "I just worry about you being in that town. I hope you're finding something to do there."

Abby felt herself blush. "Absolutely, baby. I'm finding plenty to keep me busy. I'll talk to you tomorrow."

When she likely wouldn't tell her precious baby girl what she was really doing in Willow Fork. Jack and Sam. Yep. She'd been doing two hot cowboys, and she would very likely do them both again tonight if all went well.

She hung up with her daughter and went back to looking at herself in the mirror, trying to get her makeup just right.

"You look beautiful, Abigail," a soft voice said behind her. "But then, you always were. Even as a child, I knew you would be a beautiful woman someday."

Abby turned from the slightly warped mirror in the tiny bathroom and smiled at her mother. The trailer was small, and there was only the one bathroom. Her mother leaned against the doorway. "You look like you're feeling better."

Diane Moore was a handsome sixty-year-old woman. Her hair

was the same auburn color as Abigail's, though she'd stopped dealing with grays years before and now they had mostly taken over. She was dressed in a charcoal gray pantsuit that was slightly too big for her. Diane had joked that falling off the porch and breaking her hip had done wonders for her figure.

"I've had a very good therapist." Her mom winked at her. Abby had taken her to and from the rehab facility and diligently made sure she did every exercise.

"You look pretty yourself, Mama." Abby gave her a careful hug.

She patted her graying hair. "Well, Abigail, you never know who you might meet playing bingo." Her mother crossed her arms and suddenly looked serious. "Are those old biddies leaving you alone?"

She didn't want to think about them tonight. "Don't worry about it. I can handle them."

"You shouldn't have to. I should have taken care of it back then." Her mother looked so sad that Abby turned and reached out to her. "I should never have let you leave."

"I didn't give you a choice. You know I couldn't stay. There were too many bad memories. You would have lost your job and your pension for nothing."

"How dare that Ruby Echols think you weren't good enough for her son? I'm glad she didn't have anything to do with raising Lexi."

Thinking of her daughter made her smile. If there was one thing she didn't regret it was raising Lexi outside of Willow Fork. She'd thrived in Fort Worth and she would conquer Austin. Her baby could be anything she wanted to be. "I am, too. Now stop talking about people who don't matter. I have a date tonight."

"Are the boys picking you up in that tank of Jack's?" her mom asked as she turned back to the mirror and applied some gloss to her lips.

Abby winced. Jack's truck was already in the shop. Sam had picked her up from work earlier in the afternoon. He'd used their time alone together to get her all hot and bothered again with an impromptu make-out session.

"I think we'll have to use Sam's Jeep. I kind of put a dent in the truck." Her mother frowned, and Abby suddenly felt like a teen again. She crossed her arms defensively over her chest. "I had to get to work. He can't blame me. Well, he did, but let me tell you that man's bark is way worse than his bite. Underneath that rough exterior, he's a big old teddy bear."

"I doubt that seriously." Her mom sounded incredulous. "Oh, he might be around you, but make no mistake that Jack Barnes is one dangerous man. He grew up real rough."

Abby turned around, lip-gloss suddenly way less interesting than what her mother was saying. "I know his mom died when he was young."

Christa had told her that much, but she hadn't known a whole lot more about Jack's history.

"I don't know the whole story. Jack doesn't talk about it, but I know no one claimed him after his mom died. He grew up in foster care, and that's where he met Sam. The first time I met Jack I thought maybe it had damaged him, you know. Sometimes when a person doesn't get enough love as a child they become cold and distant. Jack seemed to be that way."

"He isn't." Abby leaned forward. She wanted her mother to believe. Jack was anything but cold. Even when he tried to keep his distance, he'd been caring. He'd been unsure and scared, she realized now. He hadn't wanted to get close until he had been sure she wouldn't reject him out of hand.

"Everyone knows that." Her mother patted her hand. "But don't make the mistake of thinking because he's gentle with you that he can't take care of himself. When those boys first bought that ranch, there were people in town who treated them badly. Their lifestyle was odd, to say the least. It didn't seem to bother Jack, but it made Sam upset when people treated him like dirt. Do you remember Frank's?"

Abby nodded. "I sure do. It used to be the only bar in town. I remember they had some strict rules. No liquor could be served after midnight, even on a Saturday, and there was no dancing and no loud music."

The town had restrictions, and though Frank's was a private club, it had to follow the rules.

"They refused Sam a membership," her mom said. "The only place in town where he could get a beer and they wouldn't let him in the front door because Frank Webb thought he was gay."

"Asshole." Sam was so social. It would bother him to be closed out. "I'm glad they went out of business. What a jerk."

Her mother's face was practically gleeful. "They went out of business exactly six months after they told Sam he wasn't welcome. Two weeks after they tossed Sam out on his butt, The Barn opened up. It was on some land in an unincorporated part of the county, so the rules didn't apply. Is it so surprising that everyone in town flocked to a place where they could drink and dance and listen to whatever music they wanted, however loud they wanted it?"

"That was a very happy coincidence." She should check out the honky-tonk. It sounded like fun. Christa and Mike were regulars. She bet Sam could dance. Conversely, she would probably have to coax Jack to take a turn on the floor with her. It would be worth it to have those big arms around her as they swayed to the music.

"Coincidence? Whose land do you think it was on, baby girl? Jack Barnes called some friends of his, and he gave them the seed money and the land to open the place on. He crushed Frank Webb. I'm telling you this not because I think you should be wary of the man. I want you to understand that he takes care of his own."

A hundred questions popped through Abby's mind. "It makes you wonder. How does a boy with no family and no connections end up with a huge spread? How much do you think he and Sam spent on the ranch?"

"All I know is sometime between turning eighteen and being basically homeless after he aged out of the group home he lived in, and when he and Sam started Barnes-Fleetwood five years later, they came up with roughly five million dollars. I heard Bernard, the city treasurer, talking about it, and that's what he figured it cost to start up their business. I doubt they earned it flipping burgers." There was a knock on the door. Her mom leaned over and kissed her cheek. "That's my ride now. You have a good time tonight, Abigail. You let those boys take care of you. I won't wait up, honey."

"Okay, Mama. Have fun." She watched her mother disappear down the narrow hall. As she finished getting ready for her date, her mind whirled with the possibilities of the night to come.

* * * *

Jack's jaw dropped when Abby opened the creaky door to her mama's run-down single-wide. Nothing that gorgeous should have been in a sad trailer. She deserved to be walking down a grand staircase, making an entrance worthy of a princess.

"Damn, you're going to give every man in the county a heart attack." A low whistle came out of Sam's mouth.

"Do you like?" She twirled so they got a good view.

Jack took in the sight of her in an emerald green dress that clung to her delicious curves and showed off her creamy, ivory skin. Her auburn hair hung past her shoulders in soft curls that made him want to thrust his fingers in and feel the silky softness of the locks. He loved the fact that she had curves. It made her soft and feminine, and it took his breath away that such a lovely creature wanted him. And there was no doubt in his mind that she wanted him. It was there in her hazel eyes as she looked at him. He had to take a deep breath.

Dear god, he was really, deeply in love for the first time in his life. It was amazing and scary and made his gut twist in a knot at the thought of losing her.

When he and Sam had talked about finding a woman to marry, he'd thought Sam would fall in love and he'd go along for the ride. He would need to like the woman, of course, and he had intended to be good friends with her, but he hadn't expected for his heart to seize every time she smiled at him or his knees to feel weak when she took his hand. He even liked it when she gave him hell. He wondered for the first time what she would look like in a wedding dress.

"Hey," she said softly, looking up at him with gentle eyes as she smoothed down the fabric of his dress shirt. "What's wrong, Jack?"

He pulled her close and breathed in the sweet scent of her hair. She always smelled like peaches. He'd started to crave the fruit.

"Nothing's wrong." He wasn't lying. Everything was perfect.

Sam came around the other side, and he hugged her from the back. Abigail sighed and leaned against him, obviously loving the way they surrounded her. Sam looked over her shoulder solemnly at Jack. Sam knew. He'd known all along that this woman was theirs.

"You look stunning." Sam laid a gentle kiss on her shoulder.

"There won't be a man in town tonight that will be able to keep his eyes off you." Jack frowned at the thought. She looked really amazing. There was no question Abigail was the most beautiful woman this town had probably ever seen. She was sexy as hell, and her sophisticated dress bespoke years of big city living. "Maybe you should put on a sweater."

She threw her head back and laughed. "Not on your life. I will not cover up this work of art with a staid, old sweater. I assure you, the people around here have seen a cocktail dress before."

"Not the way you fill it out, they haven't." He was already thinking about how he was going to handle covetous eyes. He would stare them all down. He could handle it if all they did was look, but the first hand that touched was likely to get ripped off.

Even in heels, she had to go up on her toes to press her lips against his.

"You like the way I fill it out?" The question was husky and did all sorts of things to his cock.

"I love the way you fill out everything, darlin'." All of his previous thoughts were lost in that haze of lust that seemed to follow Abigail around. He let his hands roam the curve of her hips as he deepened the kiss, tasting the mint of her mouth and groaning as her tongue reached out to his.

"Hey, I want in on that action, baby." All too soon, Sam was turning her head toward him and taking her mouth with his own.

Jack didn't feel a surge of jealousy as Sam's mouth slanted over Abigail's. Watching his best friend with their woman just made Jack hot. He let his hands find her amazing breasts, slipping his palm up and cupping them through the green satin of her dress, satisfied with the way the nipples pebbled for him. All he had to do was push the bodice down and he could have them in his mouth. If he pushed the dress up, he could go down on his knees and taste her sweet pussy. He liked the dress even more. She should wear dresses more often. They were awfully convenient.

"Hey, someone said something about feeding me." She pulled

away from Sam, her tone light and teasing. "This is our first official date, misters. I will not have it be said that I'm easy."

Sam grinned down at her. "You might not be easy, baby, but I assure you I am hard."

Abigail kissed him affectionately on the cheek as she righted her dress and grabbed her purse. "You're always hard. I'm coming to rely on the fact." She grabbed Jack's tie and smoothed it down. "You look too good tonight to stay in. You're not distracting me. I want my night out."

"Whoa, there!" Sam struck a pose. "I would like to point out that I am the good-looking one in this partnership. And the charming one."

"And the sarcastic one," she finished for him as she opened the door. "And Jack is the dark, sexy, broody one who steals women's panties."

"Just yours." He didn't want her to think he routinely engaged in panty theft. It was something special he did just for her.

"Well, I found a way around your tendencies toward absconding with my underthings. I'm not wearing any." With that and a happy laugh, she ran toward the Jeep.

Sam immediately ran after her, asking if she was serious, and Jack stood there with a smile on his face. His best friend in the world was chasing their future wife around a tree, swearing he was going to get his hand up her skirt to see if she was lying. All the warmth in the world waited for him. All he had to do was step out the door and he could be a part of it.

He hesitated. All the warmth was out there, but there was risk involved. It wasn't simply that Abby could leave them or change her mind or fall in love with someone else.

She could die. It happened all the time. His own mother had died when he was six years old, leaving him all alone in the world. Sam's parents had died. Abigail's husband had passed on. It was inevitable that he would have to deal with it. Abby would die someday and so would Sam. Jack didn't know how he would ever be able to recover if that happened, but what choice did he have? The way he looked at it, he could take the risk or walk away.

Jack walked through the door. In the end, there was no choice at all to be made. He loved them. That was what mattered.

"Leave Abby alone, Sam," Jack commanded as he made sure the door was locked. "We'll find out soon enough what's under that dress. I promise. Let's feed her because she'll need the energy."

* * * *

Abby shivered, even in the warm interior of the car. Sam kissed her throat and moved up to her ear. They were cuddled up in the back of the Jeep while Jack drove. Sam was taking advantage of his "alone time," as he called it, to make out while they made the hour-long drive to town. She wasn't sure she'd be able to last for sixty minutes of Sam's exquisite torture while they drove into Tyler. They had only been driving for ten minutes and she was ready to push him down and jump on top of him.

It would ruin her dress, though. She didn't want to walk around in a dress that was obviously wrinkled from use.

"Hey, you two, hop out and let them know we're here," Jack ordered from the front seat as the Jeep rolled to a stop.

She was aware that he'd watched them through the rearview mirror, and she'd caught him smiling at her. The car was stopped in front of an austere-looking building she knew only too well.

Sam was already opening the car door and getting out before she'd fully processed what was happening.

"Delbert's?"

She was a little dazed at the prospect. Delbert's Steak House was one of two nice restaurants in Willow Fork, though The Treasure Cove hadn't been around as long. Delbert's was the place for the wealthy people in town to be seen and the poor people to aspire to go. It was exactly the type of place she meant to avoid.

"Yes, it's the nicest place in town." There was a satisfied look on Jack's face. "Nothing but the best for you."

He looked so happy with himself and earnest that she found herself letting Sam ease her out of the car. Sam gave Jack a salute to let him know he would follow orders, and the Jeep pulled off to go around the building to park.

"Come on, sweetheart." Sam took her hand to lead her into the building. "We're a couple of minutes early. Let's get you warm and we can wait for Jack in the bar."

She stopped under the elegant green awning. It was lit with pretty twinkle lights. "I thought we were going into Tyler. You said we were going into town."

Sam frowned but squeezed her hand. "I suppose that is what you would think. Sorry, Jack and I live outside of Willow Fork. We call it town. I've heard people here talk about going into town, though. I suppose they do mean Tyler. Is there something wrong?"

She stared at the frosted glass of the door. It was a Sunday night. It might not be too crowded. Back when she was growing up here, Sunday night had been an important church and family night. It was possible there might not be trouble. She didn't want to wreck her first fancy date with them by having to explain she wasn't welcome in most of Willow Fork's fine establishments. It might put a damper on the mood. It also might make them think twice about seeing her. If they really understood what an outcast she was with the important people in Willow Fork, it might force them to face the fact she could hurt their business.

"No," she forced out with a too-bright smile. It had been over twenty years, after all. It might be perfectly fine. "I was surprised. Delbert's didn't have a bar the last time I was here."

Sam held the door open for her. "I expect things have changed over the years, sweetheart. Both Delbert's and The Treasure Cove became private clubs about eight years ago. I like to think of it as progress. Now there are two whole places in town where you can get beer. I'm going to start lobbying the city council to let us buy it at the grocery store. I have to buy in bulk when we go into Dallas."

"I'm sure that's inconvenient for you." She looked around the place. She had only been in here once, and that had been her sixteenth birthday. Her father had told her it was a special occasion, and they'd all gotten dressed in their Sunday best. It had been a wonderful night.

He died a month later.

The place hadn't changed much. There was new carpet on the floor, but she caught a glimpse of the crisp white linen on the tables and the single rose and candle in the middle of each. That was the same. The lobby area still had antique couches for people to sit on while waiting for a table. The place was surprisingly full this evening.

As they approached the hostess station, she realized that hadn't changed, either. There was still someone snooty standing there. The hostess was an icy-looking blonde who warmed up considerably once she got a look at Sam.

"Mr. Fleetwood." The young woman had a voice that sort of grated on Abby. Icy Blonde completely ignored her, preferring to grant her chilly smile to Sam. "I saw your name on the reservation list. I made sure to give you and Mr. Barnes the best table in the house."

"I appreciate that." Sam's hand pointedly came to Abby's waist, and he drew her to his side. "We all appreciate it."

Icy Blonde did not notice. It was like Abby didn't exist. She leaned forward and looked around to make sure no one could hear her. "I was thinking we could hook up afterward. I get off at ten. You and I could go back to my place. We can invite Jack, too, if you want."

Sam's ready smile faltered slightly. He pumped that charm right back up though. "I'm afraid I have to pass, Cecelia. I have a girlfriend now, and she might have a problem with it."

"I certainly would, Sam." Abby was surprised at the blatant rudeness of the young blonde. Abby didn't recognize her, but she looked a bit like a girl she'd gone to high school with. Helen Smith had been two years older, and she'd gotten pregnant young, so this was more than likely her daughter. The fact that she was competing for men with girls her daughter's age made her queasy.

"I'm sorry, Sam. I was mistaken. She doesn't seem like your usual type. She's much more…mature." The blonde sneered, finally giving Abby her full attention.

Sam laughed. "Hell, everyone's mature compared to me. At least that's what Jack says. If you're talking about age, she's only five years older than me. Trust me, she's one hundred percent my type."

But maybe she *was* too old for him. Self-doubt and insecurity crept into her brain. What the hell was she thinking? She was older

116

than them. She had a past that could really cost those men a lot. She had no intention of staying in this horrible, small-minded town. Now she wished she'd put on that sweater Jack advised her to wear. The dress that seemed so perfect before now felt cheap. It *was* cheap. She had bought it at a thrift store.

The blonde got back to business with a haughty shrug and told them their table would be ready in five minutes.

Sam glanced around the lobby, obviously putting the whole thing out of his mind. "Hey, that's Dave Klein, Abby. He's our feed supplier. We do a whole lot of business with him. I need to go say hello. You wait here for Jack, all right?"

She nodded, a little shell-shocked. She watched Sam greet a man in a big Stetson with a handshake and stood there feeling ridiculously vulnerable. Everyone was staring at her and talking behind their hands. Gossiping. The town ran on gossip, and not in a good way.

The blonde stared down her nose, and Abby could practically hear her thoughts. She was wondering why anyone would pick an almost forty-year-old mom over someone as firm and young as her. As for the rest of them, they were thinking that Abby Moore had come back into town and immediately taken up with not one, but two men.

She was still living up to her reputation.

Maybe she should tell Jack she wasn't feeling well. It wasn't exactly a lie. Her stomach was in a knot. They would take her home, and then she would do what she should have done in the first place. She would get her mom back on her feet and look for a job in Austin. She could chalk up the whole thing to a crazy midlife crisis and get back to reality.

A deep masculine laugh brought her out of her dark thoughts. Across the lobby, Sam was talking and laughing, his blue eyes full of mirth. He was so beautiful. He made her feel lovely and young. He deserved better than what she would bring him.

Was she ridiculous for falling for them? For wanting more with them?

"Oh, no, no, no," a firm voice said from behind her.

She turned and saw the owner of the restaurant hurrying toward her with a stern look on his face. Luther Delbert was older, but he still looked imposing enough. A thin, tastefully dressed man in a three-piece suit, Luther was every inch the wealthy host of the establishment. There had always been an aristocratic air about him, and now his slender face was pinched with distaste.

"This won't do." He turned to Icy Blonde with a frown. "Who took this woman's reservation?"

Icy Blonde looked briefly satisfied. Her eyes crossed the room as though making sure Sam was occupied. "I certainly didn't, Mr. Delbert. She just walked in."

Abby was about to protest when Luther Delbert hooked her elbow with his right hand and started to pull her toward the door. Her shoes caught on the carpet, and she pitched forward, falling to her knees.

"Get up," Delbert said, his voice low but clear. The man obviously didn't care that everyone was watching now. "Your kind is not welcome here. How you have the gall to walk in here I have no idea, but I won't serve you, do you understand? I would lose the business of the good people of this town."

Suddenly there was a warm hand reaching down to envelope hers.

"Abby? Are you all right?" Concern and confusion marked Sam's handsome face.

She blinked back tears as she let Sam haul her to her feet. Her knees ached where they'd met with the tiled floor and she nodded mutely. What the hell had happened? Humiliation had happened and every person in the restaurant had seen it, bore witness to how unwelcome she was.

"I apologize for the drama, Mr. Fleetwood." Delbert's voice was all smooth and silky now as his professional demeanor took over. "Your table will be ready in a moment. If you don't mind, I'll escort this…lady out. She doesn't have a reservation."

"Oh, I mind." Sam clutched at her hand and looked around at the crowd, a fierce frown on his face. "What the hell is wrong with you people? You don't help a lady when someone assaults her?"

Quiet filled the room and Sam flushed a dull red. Some of the patrons were whispering into their cell phones, others texting away, getting the news out to the town that Abby Moore had caused trouble. Again.

Though he kept holding her hand, it was obvious he was beginning to get the picture. Some of the older patrons turned their backs on her. She tried to step away, wanting to get the focus off of Sam, but he wasn't having it. If anything, he pulled her closer.

"Is there a problem?"

Every head swung to the front of the lobby where Jack Barnes stood in a tailored suit, looking like the devil himself. Sam sighed beside her, and his hand went firmly around her waist.

"Not at all, Mr. Barnes." Delbert wiped the bitter look off his face in favor of a gracious smile. "We're having some trouble with an unwelcome guest, but I'll get it sorted out very quickly. If you and Mr. Fleetwood would care to step into the bar, the first beer is on the house."

"He pushed her down, Jack." Sam's voice was tightly coiled.

Jack's eyes flared briefly at that statement, and then an arctic chill settled in his dark green orbs. She took a deep breath because she was intimidated, and she knew that look wasn't directed at her. Luther Delbert seemed to shrink right before her eyes. The lobby had gone deadly silent as Jack stared at the owner of the nicest place in town.

"She fell," Delbert explained as he seemed to realize there was something going on he failed to understand.

He looked back and forth between Abby, Sam, and Jack as a revelation seemed to slowly dawn on him.

"I guess I'm not used to the heels. I lost my footing." She wanted to get out of there. The debacle had drawn enough attention to them. She could see the feed store owner whispering something to another customer. The words were too low to hear, but she was pretty sure she wouldn't like what he was saying.

She'd known better and now she was going to get them in trouble.

"Because he grabbed you." Sam looked the owner directly in the eye. "You told her you wouldn't serve her or her kind. What the hell is that supposed to mean? What is her *kind*?"

"Sam." Jack's voice was deep and deliberate. "I think Abigail

119

would prefer another place to eat tonight. Why don't you take her out to the car and we'll find something more suitable. I promised to take her someplace classy, and it's obvious I made a mistake by bringing her here."

She couldn't force herself to look at Jack as Sam laced his fingers through hers and started to lead her out. All she could think about was how much this incident might cost him. Sam stopped briefly in front of Jack's enormous frame.

"You gonna take care of this?" Sam's question was low.

"Yes," Jack promised. "I think I would like to have a private discussion with Mr. Delbert."

She walked out, pulled along by Sam. Her feet beat against the tile in a staccato rhythm. Like she was a zombie shuffling along. She supposed Jack was going to stay behind to try to smooth things over. It had to be done. She hated the fact that she'd pulled them into her trouble, but she should have known better. A blessed numbness overtook her as Sam gently maneuvered her toward the parking lot.

Nope, nothing had changed at all.

Chapter Ten

Sam watched Abby laugh as Christa ordered another round of drinks, the bar loud and vibrant around them. The girls were enjoying those pink fruity things the women on TV liked. He didn't care what it was. It was loosening her up, and after the scene at Delbert's, Sam would have given years of his life to put a smile back on her face.

"Tell me you're going to crucify that fucker, Jack," Sam said as his partner sat back down at their table at The Barn. It was hours later, but the rage still simmered close to Sam's surface.

It had taken everything he had to walk Abby out of that place and soothe her wounded pride. He'd gotten her back to the car and then made a few calls while she retouched her makeup. Sam hadn't missed the tears in her eyes. The first call had been to David Sandberg and his wife, Polly. They were old friends of his who ran The Barn. Sam had been explicit in his instructions, and he hadn't been disappointed.

Abby had smiled when she was shown into the small, private dining room at the honky-tonk. It was located in the back of the building and mostly used for storage, but it was quiet, and Polly had done wonders turning it into a romantic space. She'd gone all-out in the twenty minutes she'd had. By the time they'd escorted Abby in, the space had been transformed with an intimate table and pretty tablecloth, china and silver for the place settings, and candles the only illumination in the room. The light made everything soft and gauzy, and he'd watched Abby relax as Polly played the gracious hostess. She had soft music on and glasses of wine ready for them. He and Jack were really more beer drinkers, but they could handle a glass of wine on occasion.

They had carefully avoided the subject of the scene at the steak house after Abby had tried to apologize and Jack quickly shut her down. He let her know that there was nothing to be sorry about. It was their fault for taking her to a place that would treat her like that.

Slowly but surely, she'd started to laugh again as they enjoyed their quiet meal. Sam and Jack told her all about the pitfalls of cattle ranching in the modern age, and Abby told them stories from her life as a trauma nurse.

It had been nice to share a meal with her. He had done it many times over the last month, but this was different because all the cards were on the table.

"I'm gonna kick his ass, you know," Sam stated flatly.

Jack's lips curved into a knowing smile. "You'll do what you need to do, Sam. Make sure to let me know what your alibi is so we can have our stories straight."

Sam nodded. Mike Wade sat down at the table with his second longneck of the night. Sam had been thrilled to see Christa and Mike were at The Barn. Abby could use a girlfriend.

"So the rumors are already all over town." Mike looked over to the bar, his gaze finding his wife and Abby.

"That was fast." He shouldn't be surprised. It was a small town and everyone in that lobby had a cell phone and knew how to use it.

"Oh, I bet it wasn't five minutes after it happened that Christa got the call." Mike took a long swallow of beer. "She's friends with one of the bartenders. Christa said the staff thought Luther would have a heart attack after Jack had his talk with him. The way they told it, the man went white as a sheet and left for home early. What the hell did you say to him?"

"I pointed out a few facts of life he has overlooked up to this point," Jack said evenly. "I explained to him that he had roughly six months' worth of business left, so he should start looking for a new career or move to a new town. He did that sputtering thing. You know, the one where people tell you they don't believe you, or you can't do that. I find that part of these conversations very annoying. I greatly prefer to move on to the part where he realizes I'm going to bury him. Men handle this one of two ways, I've found. They get pissed off or they cry. Luther, it turns out, is a crier."

Mike whistled. "Damn, Jack, what did you tell him you were going to do?"

"Offer The Treasure Cove a thirty percent discount on all our products. Pull our beef out of Delbert's, obviously. I happen to know that the owner of the Cove has had trouble getting a loan to redecorate and expand his selection. He wants to hire a new chef. I believe I feel like investing in a restaurant again. This one turned out well."

"Damn straight." Sam loved it when Jack plotted. Sam would have simply kicked the man's ass, but this was much better.

Of course, he would still kick the man's ass, but Jack's revenge was longer lasting. Sam's would just make him feel better.

"If that doesn't tempt the good people of Willow Fork away, I'll buy the property and kick him out," Jack finished. Like Sam, Jack had ditched the jacket and tie. He watched Abby with an unmistakably possessive gleam in his eyes.

Mike nodded. "Well, I'm with you. I believe in retribution. There are people in this town who more than deserve a little justice coming their way for how they treated Abby. I saw they already towed the car."

"Yeah, her new one will be delivered tomorrow." Sam grinned at the thought of Abby tooling around in her brand-new convertible. He'd ordered it himself when Jack had informed him Abby needed a new car. Sam had chosen a pretty pearl Mercedes. It would look nice with Abby's auburn hair.

"She's going to put up a fight, you know," Jack mused.

"That's half the fun." Sam sat back. He was looking forward to Abby's reaction when she got the car. "She looks awful cute when she's yelling at us."

"That she does." Jack turned to Mike after taking a long swig of cold beer. "This is really all about some boy who died more than twenty years ago? I don't understand what the problem is. From what I've heard, Abigail wasn't even in the car with him."

Mike rolled his eyes and sighed. "Abby and Adam had a big fight that night. Practically the whole town heard it. They said some awful things to each other. You gotta understand, Adam was wild. He ran off, got drunk, and killed himself driving too fast down the highway. One of his friends said he was trying to get to Abby so they could make up. He wouldn't have been on the highway if he hadn't been trying to see Abby. It's ridiculous, but they blamed her. Adam's mama, Ruby, claims Abby changed him. Back then, the Echols family ran this town. I suppose they still do. They used to be the biggest employers in Willow Fork. Ruby's dad ran a textile mill. It closed down shortly after Abby left. It hurt the town, but the Echols family didn't seem to lose much cash."

"Then why does everyone follow their orders?" Sam had noticed a certain portion of the town practically worshipped at the old biddy's feet.

Mike shrugged. "I suppose it's a habit. People want a king. Especially in a small town. I guess that person is usually the town's mayor or the richest family or the biggest employer."

"Two out of three ain't bad," Jack commented with an arrogant smile.

"It's going to have to be. I don't think either one of us wants to be the mayor." Their packaging plant was small, but it still employed more citizens than any other business around.

"No, but the mayor might be more willing to stand up against the Echols family if you and Jack mentioned that you might have plans to expand in the future," Mike mused. "Plans that might not include Willow Fork."

"They might not." Jack's eyes narrowed. "If this town doesn't accept our queen, then this set of kings will take their business and their money and their jobs elsewhere."

Sam exchanged a look with Jack. Sam would go along with whatever needed to be done. It would be hard, but they could do it. He wouldn't have Abby treated like that.

Jack put his beer down. "Mike, will you excuse us for a moment? I need to have a private word with Abby and Sam."

Mike smiled knowingly as Jack stood. "I'll keep the table warm."

Sam's entire body went on red alert at the thought of cornering Abby. He'd been crazy to find out what she was wearing under that skirt. "What's the plan, Jack?"

"Follow my lead," Jack said with a predatory look.

Sam had been following Jack's lead for years. He wasn't about to stop now.

* * * *

"What is this place?" Abby tried to contain the excitement of being alone with Jack and Sam.

Jack used a key to open a door at the top of the stairs. The Barn had, at one point, been an actual barn, Jack had explained over dinner. When they renovated it to make it a bar, they created a second floor for offices and storage.

"Sam sometimes gets plastered." Jack escorted her through the door into the room. "I had the contractors build this room specifically for those times."

It was a small room but well kept. There was a bed and a dresser. Several bottles of water and aspirin were on a bedside table, ready for use. "Are you telling me Sam has a drunk room?"

"Hell, no." Sam's smile was wicked. "The bar is my drunk room. This is my passing out room."

"It's a drive from the bar to our house, and I was worried Sam might decide to take the more direct route right through our land." Jack turned on the light by the bed. "I couldn't take the chance he might plow through our fences or hit the herd."

"I don't always make the best choices when I've had a few," Sam admitted with a negligent shrug.

"Come here." Jack sat down on the bed. He indicated his lap, and she felt her body getting soft and warm.

This was the part of the evening where she'd sworn to herself she would explain that she needed to slow things down…like to a stop. She would be polite, but she needed to end things. It was for their own good. So why was she coming up with a million excuses to put it off?

Earlier, she'd told herself that they had gone to the trouble of changing their plans, so she should enjoy dinner with them. Then she thought it wouldn't hurt to dance with Sam. Just once. Once with Sam and once with Jack. Then she would tell them. Then Christa had shown up. Now she was wondering if she shouldn't chuck the whole idea of leaving them. The truth was she didn't want to. She wanted all of this to be real. She found herself settling onto Jack's lap. His hands went around her waist, and for the first time in hours, she felt safe.

"I need you to tell me why you didn't mention that someone had vandalized your car, sweetheart." Jack's voice had gone dark and deep.

She sat up straight, her whole body on alert at the tone he used. How had he found out about that?

"Abby didn't know about it," Sam protested. "She was driving your truck, Jack."

She flushed because she knew the truth.

"Abigail went by Christa's earlier in the day." Jack looked down at her. "I suppose she meant to trade my truck for her car, but then realized that plan wouldn't work. That's how she got that dent in the truck. It was from Mike's trailer."

Damn, she was in trouble. It was right there in his stare. "I am sorry about that. I know I should have gone on and taken my car anyway, but I was embarrassed, and I didn't have time to get four new tires. They slashed those tires good."

Jack tilted her head up so she was forced to look him in the eyes. "What you should have done was call me. What you should have done was been mad as hell and told me what was going on. She didn't call out for you tonight, did she, Sam?"

Sam's face was grim. "No, she didn't. If she hadn't fallen, I expect Luther would have hustled her out the door without me knowing about it. I was busy talking to the feed store owner."

"You should have shouted out the minute you even thought that son of a bitch was going to lay a hand on you," Jack explained

126

sternly. "I never want to have to hear about you being hurt or humiliated from someone else again. I want to hear it from you because I want to be the first person you call when you need help. It's me or Sam. There's no going it alone."

It looked like they were going to push her into the discussion after all. "I don't think you should get involved in this."

"Wrong answer, sweetheart," Sam said.

Jack's eyes narrowed. "Not get involved?"

She swallowed. Yep, now that intimidating look was turned right on her. "Just in that part, Jack. It's nothing that should worry you. I can handle it." Jack's face was turning a slightly pink color and his right eyebrow started to twitch. "Are you all right? I think you might be having a reaction to the stress, or is that a nervous tick?"

Sam started laughing.

She sent him a dirty look. "Don't you laugh. Stress is a serious problem."

"And I need some stress relief, Abigail." Jack's hands tightened around her waist. "Can you think of anything that might relieve my stress?"

"Exercise." At least he'd asked her a question she could answer honestly. "It's absolutely the best thing for stress."

"Excellent." Jack neatly flipped her over his knee.

"Do you practice that move?" She found herself staring at the floor again. He was really good at it.

"It looks like I will be getting a lot of practice in the near future." Jack pulled the skirt of her dress up, exposing the fact that she had been completely truthful about her lack of undergarments.

Cool air hit her backside. Her heart started to race. She had always thought she might be sexually submissive, but these men were proving it to her.

"I want to make a few things very plain." Jack's voice was a dark seduction. "I want to settle some things between us so there is absolutely no misunderstanding. Do you understand the type of sexual relationship I want with you? That Sam and I want with you?"

It took everything she had not to laugh at him. She was laid out over his knee with her bare ass in the air. He couldn't be less subtle if he tried. "Yes, Jack. You want to top me."

"It is not something I want to play at." Jack's hands caressed her buttocks. She heard him sigh. "I'm in charge in the bedroom. If I hurt you, I want to know because that is not my intention, but I want to experiment. I want to push your limits. I want you to trust us with your pleasure."

"I trust you." All thoughts of leaving them were gone now. She had to find out where this was going. She owed it to herself to see if this was really what she wanted.

Adam had been very dominant. It was what had attracted her to him in the first place, she recognized now. They might not have understood the correct terminology, but they had been headed toward it.

Her relationship with Ben had been completely different. She had subjugated her own needs because she wanted to protect her heart. Ben had been what she needed then, but Jack and Sam…she needed them now more than she'd ever needed anything in her life. She was ready to discover who she was as a woman.

"We'll take good care of you, baby." Sam's voice had gone husky.

A hard hand came down on her ass, the pain a shocking burn that bloomed across her skin and then turned to a sweet heat that sank deep inside her. She moaned and waited for Jack to continue.

"That was for not telling me someone vandalized your car." Jack's hand came down strongly on her other cheek.

She cried out and clutched at Jack's leg. Her pussy was getting ridiculously wet. *Please don't let him walk out like he had before.* She wanted both of them, wanted Jack to fuck her hard while she sucked Sam's cock.

"That was for not telling Sam that some asshole was threatening you." His hand rained down on her, sharp and hard. He gave her another five.

She gritted her teeth, letting the sensation wash over her. It hurt and aroused her all at the same time. Her bottom was hot and sensitive, and she wriggled against his lap, trying to get some relief from the desperate ache lodged in her pussy.

Another sharp slap.

"Stop moving," Jack ordered, and she stilled. She was rewarded with Jack's fingers slowing pushing into her exposed pussy. "When I am disciplining you, you will remain still. If you need it, I'll tie you down." His fingers slid into her wetness as his thumb slipped over her clitoris, and she had to bite her lip to keep from crying out. "Outside of our sex life, I won't completely dominate you. I will protect you and take care of you, but I won't expect you to not be you. I won't order for you in a restaurant or tell you who to be friends with. I want you to have all the things you want. But when we're alone, I want you naked and submissive. I don't think you'll mind, sweetheart. Sam and I will treat you like a princess."

"We want to give you everything you need, everything your heart desires." Abby felt Sam's hand caressing her bottom where Jack had spanked her. His fingers trailed over her cheeks, tracing the sensitive skin. "If you have obnoxious friends, we'll put up with them."

"But here, in the bedroom, I want you to obey me." Jack lifted her up, easing her around.

Sam's strong arms lifted her off Jack's lap, and she found herself on her feet. Jack got up as well. He towered over her. It made Abby feel very petite.

"I want your submission," Jack said solemnly. "Can you give it to me?"

"Yes." She felt Sam relax behind her as she answered. Had he really thought she would refuse?

Jack's smile was slow and satisfied. "I want you to undress me, Abigail."

He stood in front of her, hands at his sides, waiting for her to obey. She eagerly went to the buttons of his shirt, drawing them through and exposing his gorgeous tan chest. "Does Sam top me, too?"

Jack's smile was warmer than she could ever remember. He was in a happy, safe place, she decided. He needed this from her.

"If he likes. But mostly Sam likes to be told what to do, too. He's got a submissive streak like you, darlin'." He glanced back at his partner, who was waiting patiently. "Sam, you can take your clothes off or you can wait for her to undress you."

Abby looked briefly at Sam.

He was tossing his clothes off behind her. "I can get it."

Sam's eager voice made her smile. She carefully unbuttoned Jack's white dress shirt, pulling it from his slacks and pushing it off his strong, broad shoulders. Her skin sang wherever she touched him. Even as she went to the small closet and hung it up neatly, she could feel Jack's quiet satisfaction with her. She did the same thing with his pants. She neatly took care of the rest of his clothes, making sure they were hung up or folded. Sam's were chucked to the floor, and he was eagerly kissing the nape of her neck as she put up Jack's shoes.

"You'll have to get used to Sam." There was great affection in Jack's voice. "He is impetuous, to say the least."

"I think I can handle it." With Jack naked in front of her and Sam naked behind her, she reveled in the feeling of being between them.

"Look up," Jack commanded. "Give me your mouth, sweetheart."

She tilted her head up and gave him what he wanted. Jack's lips touched hers, and she felt his tongue demanding entry. Her mouth softened, allowing him to press her lips apart and sweep inside. His tongue plunged in as he slanted his mouth over hers. Jack held her face in place, and she felt the delicious thrill of Sam's teeth on the back of her neck. Sam's hands trailed down her spine. He grasped the zipper of her dress and slowly lowered it. The dress hit the floor, and she started to step out of her heels.

"No." Jack's hands pulled her bra off. "The shoes stay. Sam, hang up her dress. You might not care that you're walking around wrinkled, but Abigail does."

Sam went to hang up the dress while Jack pulled her into the hard circle of his body. His erection prodded her belly, but he took the time to hug her to him, cuddling them close together. The light sprinkling of hair on his well-muscled chest tickled her nipples as he held her, obviously enjoying the contact. Suddenly, Sam's erection nuzzled her backside as he got in on the action.

"Come on, Jack." Sam's voice was deep. "Cuddling is for after.

I want to fuck."

She felt Jack's deep chuckle against her body. "All right, Sam. Always so impatient. On your knees in front of Sam, sweetheart."

She turned and dropped to her knees. She felt Jack kneel behind her. His warm hands cupped the curve of her hips and ran down her buttocks. Her cheeks were still sensitive from the spanking and she shivered at the sensation.

"Take Sam in your mouth, Abigail."

Sam's blue eyes were deep as he stood before her with his cock in his hand. He stepped forward to tease her lips with the head. "Open for me."

"Go slow," Jack instructed her. "Lick him first and keep your hands off him. Use your mouth."

She did as he asked, balancing on her knees as she leaned forward to delicately lick the head of Sam's dick. She paid close attention to the slit in the head, allowing the tip of her tongue to briefly thrust inside. He was salty and silky on her tongue, and she loved the taste of him.

Sam moaned as she ran her tongue along the underside of his cock. "Fuck, Abby, that feels good. Touch my balls, baby."

For someone who liked to be told what to do, Sam didn't have any trouble barking out orders, Abby thought with a smile.

She briefly turned to look at Jack. He was in charge. Jack nodded his permission. She brought her right hand up to gently roll his sensitive sac. Sam growled with pleasure as she licked up and down his rock-hard length and cupped his balls.

"Feed her your cock, Sam." Jack moved behind her. "Spread your legs, Abby. Whatever I do to you, you don't lose that cock until he comes, understood?"

Jack didn't wait for an answer, which was good, since she found her mouth suddenly full. Sam pressed forward. His hands tangled in her hair, gripping it firmly. He looked down at her, and his face was a mask of lust.

"Do you know what this is doing to me, Abby?" The question was a guttural groan. "The sight of my cock disappearing into that hot mouth of yours is the sexiest thing ever. Take it all in. Relax, baby. You can take me. You can take all of me."

"She'll take all of you," Jack stated. She was glad Jack was so certain because she was struggling a bit. Sam was an awful lot of man. "She'll take all of you, and when you come, she's going to swallow. As for me, I think I'll eat some of this incredibly ripe pussy."

Jack slid underneath her. He lifted his head up slightly, and his tongue slid into her slick slit. Abby cried out around Sam's dick.

"Don't you lose that cock." Jack's fingers slipped into her pussy as his tongue placed firm pressure on the pearl of her clit. "You come all you like, but I'll stop if you lose Sam."

Sam gripped her hair firmly. "She won't lose me. How long before I can come?"

"If you want to come with her, you should fuck that mouth, Sam. Her clit is ready to go off. I give her thirty seconds."

Sam pulled and pushed her head as he fucked her mouth. He worked her hard, but she barely noticed. Jack was sucking her clit between his teeth, his fingers curled deep inside her, and it was all she could do to breathe.

An orgasm shot through her, pulsing like a great wave through her pussy and outward. As Jack continued to lick her, she relaxed and let Sam use her mouth. He thrust in staccato rhythms as his dick seemed to get even bigger.

Sam held her hair and pushed his cock to the back of her throat. When she swallowed around him, he let himself go. She loved how crazy she could make him. He groaned as he came in her mouth. She swallowed as fast as she could, not wanting to miss a drop. She continued to lavish affection on his dick as it softened.

Sam went on his knees and caught her as she started to pitch forward. She fell into his arms as Jack slid out from under her. Sam took her mouth again, this time with his own. His kiss was sweet and grateful, and he played with her tongue for what seemed like the longest time.

Sam held her close as she shook with the aftermath of her orgasm. "That was amazing, baby. I love how you respond to me. You don't hold anything back. Do you know how sexy that is?"

"It isn't hard to go wild with you." The way he was looking at her made her feel beautiful and precious.

"Back on your hands and knees, sweetheart." Jack's deep voice rumbled out the order.

She immediately complied and spread her knees, anticipating Jack's penetration. He was the only one who hadn't come yet. She closed her eyes and waited for the glorious feeling of Jack filling her wet pussy.

"This is going to be a little cold, darlin'."

She bit back a gasp at the feeling of Jack parting the cheeks of her ass and a cold substance being shoved gently up her anus. Yep, she hadn't been expecting that. She shivered slightly as he pressed against her flesh.

"What was that?" Abby asked, even as she figured out the answer for herself.

"It's lubricant." Sam's voice was soothing. "Jack is going to insert a plug, and it's going to stretch you to get you ready. Do you understand?"

She took a deep breath and nodded. The plug touched her and she groaned as it pushed against the super-tight muscles of her sphincter.

Sam murmured to her while stroking her hair. "Just relax."

Easy for him to say. Jack pushed the plug gently forward. Sam wasn't having something shoved up his ass to make way for something even bigger to later be shoved up his ass. Abby concentrated on breathing and letting Jack have his way. Lots of women did this. Many of the women in her books dealt with anal plugs, and they seemed to like them just fine.

"Push back for me, sweetheart," Jack ordered.

Abby groaned as she shoved her ass toward Jack and the plug slipped in. She wriggled at the tightness she felt, but once it pushed past the initial ring of her anus, there wasn't any pain. There was a strange sort of discomfort, but she could probably get used to it.

She felt Jack place a kiss on the small of her back before he got up. Sam held her hand to steady her while she rose to her feet. The plug felt odd, but she was learning that the tight feel could be pleasurable as well. Jack got on the bed on his knees. Her eyes widened at the sight of his big cock curved up along his stomach. It was so hard it looked painful.

Jack sheathed it quickly in a condom, and then Sam was lifting her up, seeming to know instinctively what Jack wanted. She found herself on her hands and knees facing Sam. He stood at the edge of the bed, seemingly ready to watch the action. She felt the heat from Jack's body cover her skin as he came up against her back. Sam leaned down and kissed her gently, and she felt Jack's hands on her hips and his cock seeking entrance.

Jack pushed her slightly forward, pulling down on her hips and pushing up into her pussy. Even as wet as she was from her recent orgasm, she groaned as Jack fought his way in.

"Fuck," Jack groaned. "She's so fucking tight."

He pushed himself in another inch.

She struggled to stay on her knees. She'd never felt so full. It was uncomfortable and thrilling at the same time.

"You're so beautiful, Abby." She could hear Sam's sweet words. "I am so crazy about you. I can't wait until we can share you. Think of it, all three of us together. That's how it should be."

Sam's hands came forward to mold her breasts. His fingers plucked at her nipples. Sam wasn't good at just watching. She'd figured that out rapidly. He dropped to his knees in front of her, trying to join in. Jack found a rhythm, and she started a glorious, slow build toward another peak.

"You feel so good, sweetheart," Jack groaned from behind as he pushed and pulled his way in and out of her body. "You're so perfect for us."

Jack's breathing became labored, and she knew he was getting close. She wasn't, but she was okay with that. Jack had already given her a monster orgasm. She could handle it if she didn't come this time.

Jack wasn't having that. He pulled her up, giving Sam a good view of her pussy. Abby was on her knees, her back nearly flush against Jack's chest. He held her tight, his cock still deeply embedded.

"Stroke her," Jack demanded hoarsely. "I'm gonna come."

Sam was on the bed in a heartbeat. His eager hand quickly parted her slick labia, and the minute he firmly stroked her clit, she went flying. Her fingers dug into Sam's shoulders as she felt the orgasm explode along her every nerve. She sobbed against Sam and pushed back to get every second of sensation. Jack hammered into her as he reached his own orgasm. His low groan was music to her, and she shoved her ass toward him, helping him to go as deep as he could. He finally exploded inside her. Jack fell forward, pushing her into Sam, who laughed as they all tried to fit on the tiny bed. Jack rested against her back as he came out of her body.

"I love you," she heard herself whisper. "I love you both."

Jack stilled behind her, and for the barest moment, she wondered if that had been a terrible mistake. She hadn't meant to say it. God, she hadn't meant to feel it. She shouldn't feel it.

"I love you, too, Abigail," he said, sounding terribly vulnerable.

She knew in that moment that he had never said those words before to any woman. She couldn't take them back. She couldn't.

Maybe it could work.

Sam's smile was sweet as he kissed her forehead. "I loved you the moment I saw you."

She let her head rest on Sam's shoulder and her hand trailed back so her fingers tangled in Jack's hair. She had everything she could have hoped for in that moment, and just then, it seemed like it would be enough.

Chapter Eleven

The big Grandfather clock in the living room chimed the nine o'clock hour, but Ruby Echols wasn't even beginning to think about going to bed. There was no real point in it. She had gone to bed at the traditional hour of ten o'clock for the last month as a matter of principle, but she slept very little. Every single night Ruby lay awake knowing that dirty whore was back in town. How was she supposed to sleep knowing her own sweet son was buried in the ground while the woman who had led him to his death was having a grand old time?

Ever since the moment Abigail Moore sauntered back into town, Ruby's life had been taken over again by the rage that had simmered close to the surface for twenty years. Adam had been her beautiful baby. He was headstrong, but that was to be expected. He was handsome, rich, and smart. Arrogance went hand-in-hand with that. Unfortunately, he also had a man's terrible taste in females.

Had Adam lived, he would have come to his senses. He would never have actually married someone of Abigail's class. He would have realized he had a future that couldn't possibly involve a tramp like that red-haired hussy.

Ruby felt a smile cross her face. Yes. It was all going to be fine.

Adam would attend the finest schools and take his rightful place in proper society. She already had a girl picked out for Adam. Claire Winbourne would make a lovely bride. She was blonde and looked elegant in designer clothing. She wasn't fat like the Moore girl. What men saw in fat women Ruby couldn't understand. She herself had always maintained a proper figure. She ate very little because to be full meant one lacked restraint. It was what a lady did. Adam's wife would be slender and graceful.

She put a hand to her head as the pain came. It flashed through her head and brought her back to the present.

Claire had married Walter, not Adam. Claire couldn't marry Adam because Adam died.

Sometimes she got these things mixed up. Claire had married Walter, and Walter had screwed everything up. Now he was married to some fat girl named Jan who had been a secretary at one time.

"Mother Echols?"

She looked up to see fat Jan in the doorway. Jan Lane Echols was a brunette with large breasts. They made her look trashy, and Ruby had offered to pay for plastic surgery to help her look more like a lady, but Jan refused. Ruby carefully schooled her expression. She had done everything she could to get rid of the gold digger, but it hadn't worked. Now she had to deal with the fact that her granddaughters would grow up to be the sort of women who should be dancing half-naked for tips. The stupid cow hadn't even managed to produce a single son.

"What is it you want, Janice?" Ruby asked evenly.

"I came down to see if you needed anything. I heard the rumors about what happened at Delbert's. I thought it might upset you."

The thought made her smile. She'd gotten the news earlier in the evening and had reveled in the gossip. More than one of her friends had called, all taking great delight in informing her of the whore's dismissal. The fact that the Moore girl had thought she would be welcome in a genteel place like Delbert's boggled the mind. Well, the idiot had never been very smart. The fool had turned down the money she offered her to stay away from Adam.

"It didn't upset me at all. It simply proves that society still works. A person of her character should not be allowed to mingle with the rest of us."

Jan's blue eyes rolled. It was further proof that her daughter-in-law wasn't Echols material. Sarcasm had no place in a properly bred lady. "You need to be careful, Mother Echols. She wasn't alone tonight. She was with Sam Fleetwood and Jack Barnes. You might not approve of their lifestyle, but there is no question you don't want to upset those men."

A brief vision of Jack Barnes entered her head. He was dark and handsome, like Adam. He was broader, but Adam would have been broader, too, had he been allowed to reach maturity. Adam would have taken on a man's build and authority. Sometimes, she got confused and saw Adam when she was looking at Jack Barnes. Ruby waved off the statement, her big diamond ring catching the light. It shouldn't shock her that Abigail Moore was trying to get her hooks into the Barnes fellow. She'd heard he was considered quite the up and comer in the business community.

"They have no place in society." Neither man ever attended socials or the charity balls. They might have money, but they weren't socially powerful.

"Only because they don't want to," Jan replied. "I don't know how serious they are about Abby Moore, but I wouldn't want to get between Jack Barnes and something he wanted. I'm asking you to think about Walter before you do anything to hurt that girl. I wouldn't want Walter's election to get nasty."

"You worry about Walter's campaign." She was against him moving to Austin, but she certainly wouldn't let him fail. Failure wasn't something an Echols did. "And I'll take care of that whore."

Jan started back up the stairs, but turned, her mouth a flat line. "I don't get what your problem with Abby is. I know she had a thing for Adam, but it's been twenty years. Isn't it time to let go of all this anger? People change and she seems perfectly nice. I had lunch at the café with the girls. She was really sweet to them. Everything I've learned about that woman points to how fine a life she's led since she left town."

She stood up, reaching her full five-foot height and feeling rage well within her. "You took my granddaughters to meet the whore who killed their uncle?"

She might not care for the girls, but they carried the Echols name and would not be allowed to sully it.

"Adam was killed in an accident and it was twenty years ago." Jan's mouth firmed, and she crossed her arms stubbornly. "I'm not going to have some twenty-year-old feud hurt Walter's chances of getting elected. The way you treated that girl was shameful then and ridiculous now, and I won't do it. I am not going to pretend she doesn't exist. I intend to ask Ms. Moore if my daughters can meet their cousin. They won't have any more, so I think it's important that they know the family they do have."

The crack of her open hand against Jan's face resounded through the room. Pain bit through her palm, racing up her arm, but she ignored it. She was sixty-eight and knew people considered her physically weak. They didn't understand the strength that a righteous cause could give her.

Walter flew to his wife's side, surprising them both. Walter's arms went around Jan, hugging her to him. "Are you all right, baby?"

Jan pulled away from him and rubbed her reddened cheek. "I've had enough. I never wanted to push this, but I am going to now, Walter. I love you. It's me or her. I don't want her influencing my girls anymore."

"You idiot," she sneered at her daughter-in-law. "A boy never leaves his mother."

Walter was quiet for a moment. "I've been thinking a lot about that lately, Mother. I've been thinking about all the times you held me and lavished your love on me. It didn't take long to go through those memories since they didn't exist. Everything you had was reserved for Adam. Every bit of love you had in your heart was for him, not me. No matter how hard I try, I can't make up for the fact that Adam is dead. I'll be damned if my girls have to live like that, too. Only one person has ever loved me for being me. Mother, if you think I would choose you over Jan, you really have lost your damn mind." He looked to his wife. "Pack up the girls. We'll stay in the motel tonight. I'll find us a place to live tomorrow."

How could he speak to her in such a manner? She watched her youngest child like he was a stranger. Didn't he know his obligations? Hadn't she spent his whole life making sure he understood what he owed his family?

Walter ignored her. He was too busy looking at his fat wife.

"I love you, Jan. I love you. I will always choose you." He finally turned to Ruby. "As for you, Mother, I'll make certain the housekeeper knows to take care of you."

Her whole world shifted. She steadied herself as her son turned to leave. She still had one card to play. "I will cut you off, Walter. I will make sure you don't get a dime."

Walter shook his head. "I'm not the idiot you think I am. I don't need your money, Mother. I have worked my entire adult life, and I know how to save. Daddy made sure I knew how to take care of myself financially. I've made some very savvy investments. Jan and I will do fine. You keep your money. I suspect it will be the only thing you have to keep you warm at night."

With that, he took his wife's hand and walked up the stairs. Ruby Echols sank to the antique divan that had been in her family for generations.

Her head felt heavy. Adam was leaving. Again? That was what Adam had said. He'd stood right here in this living room and said the words.

I don't need your money, Mother. Abby and I will be fine.

Adam was leaving her again and this time he was taking Walter, too. Abigail Moore was the reason she was losing her family. Just tonight Adam had tried to take her to a fancy restaurant. He was going to make fools of them all and that couldn't happen.

She picked up the keys to her car. Abby Moore wasn't going to win this time.

* * * *

The honky-tonk seemed even louder than before after the quiet intimacy of Sam's room. Abby immediately spotted her best friend still sitting at the bar. Christa's left eyebrow was practically in outer space as she walked up to her. It took everything she had not to pat her hair or smooth down her dress self-consciously. Did she look like a woman who had recently had mind-blowing sex with two men? Suddenly, with her body still humming from the recent orgasms, she didn't care.

"You look like the Cheshire Cat, you know." Christa smiled as she slid a frosty cosmo Abby's way.

"Do I?" She took the drink and sighed. "I can't ever think why." The grin on her face wouldn't go away.

"Probably for the same reason I need to hose down my desk from this morning's session," Christa complained good-naturedly.

Embarrassment flushed through her system. "I am so sorry about that."

"No, you're not," Christa replied. "I wouldn't be. So was it Sam or Jack on the desk?"

She gingerly sat down on the barstool, the small butt plug still lodged discreetly where Jack said it would do them all the most good. She leaned over to her best friend and was so happy she had someone to confide in.

"Sam was on the desk. Jack was in the chair."

Christa's mouth hung open for a moment before she shook her head and laughed. "Girl, I am gonna live through you from now on. I want Facebook updates hourly. I can see it now. Abby Moore…is exhausted from doing her two gorgeous men."

She gnawed thoughtfully on her lower lip. "I think I love them, Chris. Hell, I don't think, I know I love them. I'm seriously considering staying in this two-bit town so I can be with them."

Christa's hand went up in victory. "Yes! Another evil plan works. Damn, I'm good. My brain is wasted on this town. Mike is gonna owe me a week's worth of dish duty."

"What do you mean?" She glanced over to where Jack stood talking to Mike. Sam was joining them, his blond hair still slightly damp from the shower. Abby's insides fluttered when she thought about what he'd done to her in the shower.

Christa looked entirely satisfied with herself. Her jet-black ponytail bobbed as she nodded. "Oh, yeah, it was me. I sold you out. I told Sam to rifle through your book collection if he wanted to know the way to your heart, which, by the way, is apparently through your…"

"Christa Marie Wade!" she admonished righteously, then ruined

141

it by grinning. "You hush that filthy mouth of yours. I should be angry with you for giving that away. Girlfriends are supposed to keep quiet about their friend's porn."

"Not in this case," Christa argued. "I saw the way you looked at them. Every time either one of them walked in the room you would go all gooey. Sam followed you around like a puppy, and Jack brooded even worse when you were around. They wouldn't approach you because they didn't believe you would be okay with their lifestyle. Those books let them know you were an open-minded girl. If I hadn't shown Sam, the three of you would still be all about unrequited love. Instead, you're practically glowing. And you owe it all to the fact that I can't keep my nose out of other people's business. If it keeps my best friend in town, then all my plotting was worth it."

Sam eased up behind her barstool. "Oh, Christa, did you confess?"

He lifted his hand to let the bartender know he was ready for another beer, and then his palm settled on her back, warming her.

"I did, indeed." Christa favored Sam with a saucy wink. "It's my weakness as a super villain. I have an undeniable need for credit. I was thrilled to hear that Abby was thinking of staying."

A single brow rose over Sam's eyes at the pronouncement. "Thinking?"

"Well, it's a big decision." She noticed Sam's handsome face had turned mulishly stubborn, and she was beginning to recognize all the signs of Sam getting ready to tattle on her to Jack. She put a hand on his arm. "It's not like I'm planning on leaving anytime soon. I have to make sure my mom is fully healed, and I have to find a job."

"Why would you need a job?" Sam asked a bit too loudly.

She looked over, and sure enough, Jack had heard the exchange. He was staring at them, his green eyes filled with suspicious concern.

What exactly did he expect her to do? Lie around and wait for one or both of them to need some attention? She'd worked all her life and she wasn't going to start selling herself out now. Especially not when there was zero real commitment between the three of them. "Because life requires money. Did you expect that I'd hang around in my mom's trailer for the rest of my life? It's going to take a hell of a lot of money to put my daughter through college."

"You don't trust us to take care of you?" Sam asked, sounding perfectly indignant.

Out of the corner of her eye, she confirmed that now Jack was hurrying toward them.

Like she hadn't heard that one before. Several doctors had offered to "take care of her" before she'd married Ben. They had been quite easy to chase away. Her head was a little buzzy and she felt some of the recklessness of her youth flowing back through her veins tonight. "If you want me to trust you to take care of me, maybe you should think about marrying me."

The minute the words were out, she sobered and realized what she'd done. That wasn't something she should joke about. They weren't flirty doctors looking for a quick hookup. She was about to apologize and take it all back.

"All right," Jack's deep voice said from behind her. "Thursday work for you, sweetheart?"

Christa's eyes were wide and Abby realized she wasn't the only one watching this scene play out.

She turned to Jack, certain her whole body was a nice shade of pink. "Jack, I was only trying to freak out Sam a little. He was being a tad bit overbearing. I wasn't demanding that you marry me."

"She sure as hell was." There was an arrogant grin on Sam's face. "She said she wouldn't be able to trust us if we didn't marry her."

She shook her head. "Don't be ridiculous. I was joking. Besides, you are overlooking the fact that it's illegal to be married to two different men at the same time."

Sam shrugged. "We got it all worked out. We're going to rock-paper-scissors for it."

Jack sighed and shook his head. "No, we are not going to do that. We take this very seriously. I am going to legally marry you. You'll be Abigail Barnes in the eyes of the law, but we expect you to wear Sam's ring, too. I expect you to take him as seriously as you do me."

143

Sam was wearing a dippy grin. She put one hand on her hip. "That's hard sometimes."

"You'll muddle through." Jack leaned over to steal a kiss. "I'll apply for the license tomorrow. It takes three days. We'll move your mother into the guest house."

Her head whirled. "Wait a minute. We've only known each other for a month and a half. You can't railroad me into marriage."

Jack smiled wistfully. "Would it help if you knew I considered it more like I'm gently herding you into marriage?"

"No." She had to laugh at the picture of Jack and Sam treating her like prized cattle. They did love their cattle. "That doesn't make it better." She got serious, thinking about what had happened earlier. "There's a lot I don't think you've considered. Marrying me means something in this town, and not something good."

Jack shook his head. "It's too late, Abby. You said you loved us. You're not going to be able to wiggle out of it now."

"You belong to us," Sam said implacably.

"And you belong here." Christa looked as serious as the men. She reached over and grabbed Abby's hand. "I've missed you. I love you and I'm tired of being apart. This is the time in our life when we get to go crazy again. This is the time when we get to be who we are instead of who we thought we should be. I can't stand the thought of figuring that out without you."

Sam's hand reached out to wipe away the tears she didn't even realize she'd shed. Was she really going to let something that happened twenty years ago cost her all her happiness now? If she did that, then she wasn't the woman she believed herself to be. If she let them run her out of town, she would be going against everything she'd worked to become. The idea of explaining to her daughter that she now was going to have two stepdads was daunting, but at least she knew her mom was all right with it.

Had anything in her life ever felt as good and right as being with these amazing men?

She looked at Jack and Sam and grabbed her joy with both hands. "Thursday sounds great."

The smile that spread across Jack's face was well worth it. He looked happier than she'd ever seen him, and his masculine beauty took her breath away. Jack leaned in and kissed her lightly, but with the promise of so much more. "I love you, Abby-almost-Barnes."

"I love you, too," she said solemnly.

Sam was less circumspect. He hauled her off the barstool and twirled her around before leaning her back for a wildly passionate kiss.

"Damn, Abby, you made us wait long enough." Sam's hands cupped her cheek with a tenderness that took her breath away.

"I made you wait a whole month and a half," Abby pointed out. She couldn't take her eyes off him.

"Like I said, it was too damn long." He smiled over at Jack, but something else seemed to catch his attention. She watched as his face went stark white and he swallowed deeply. His face twisted like he was really trying to think of how to put something to her. "Baby, you know how I explained to you that I don't always make the best decisions when I am inebriated? Here comes one of those bad decisions. Please save me."

He placed her strategically in front of him in a suspiciously shield-like fashion.

"Look what the trash man forgot to pick up." Christa stood up and came to Abby's side.

Abby was aware that Jack had moved onto her barstool. He looked terribly amused as a bleached blonde slinked into the room, wearing a shirt that barely contained her store-bought breasts and jeans that someone had spray-painted on. Her hair had been teased to within an inch of its life, and Abby couldn't tell how old she was under the pound of makeup she was sporting. There wasn't anything wrong with a woman wanting to look good, but this was way, way too much. There was no mistaking the predatory gleam in the blonde's eye as she looked around the bar. Her brown eyes were hard, but they widened when she caught sight of her prey cowering behind another woman. It didn't seem to affect her. She gestured to someone, and yet another peroxide devotee of far too little clothing came out of the woodwork.

"Oh, look. She brought a friend," Christa said with a sarcastic grin. "I do believe she did that for you, Jack."

Jack had the good sense to shudder. "I would hide behind

145

Abigail, too, but Sam is taking up all the space."

The dynamically tacky duo pushed their way across the crowded dance floor, making a beeline for Sam Fleetwood.

"You want to tell me who I'm protecting you from, Sam?" Abby had a guess.

"Melissa Paul." Sam confirmed her suspicion. "She took advantage of me one night while I was drunk out of my mind, and then she had the horrible idea that she was my girlfriend."

"Women get that way when you sleep with them," she murmured.

"Well, they shouldn't." His hands tightened on her shoulders. "I assure you I didn't mention it to her. I could have been stone drunk out of my mind, but the words *I love you* wouldn't have passed my lips. I saved those words for you, baby."

"Uh-huh," she muttered with a resigned sigh. She looked back at her cowering future husband. "Does it bother you that you're currently hiding behind a woman's skirts?"

Jack laughed but Sam looked unrepentant. "No, ma'am. You will find I am very flexible when it comes to your skirts. I will attempt to get into them as often as possible, and when the need arises, I will hide behind them shamelessly."

Abby grinned because he was really heartbreakingly gorgeous. He was going to make her life a joy to live. She would never be bored with these two around. Abby couldn't stop the smile that spread across her face.

She was going to marry them.

"Sam," Melissa Paul breathed in a sultry voice. It was so deep and sexy that she wondered if the woman got paid by the minute to talk on a sex line. "If I didn't know better, I would think you're avoiding me."

"Then you must know something we don't." Christa sounded sassy and confronted the blondes with one hand on her waist. "Because he is definitely trying to avoid you."

There was a huffing sound from the secondary blonde, but Melissa Paul rolled her eyes and focused on Sam. "Can we go somewhere and…talk? Leslie here can keep Jack company. She doesn't mind at all, do you, Leslie?"

The other blonde was slightly unsteady as she took a step toward Jack. "I don't. He looks hot. I don't think he's scary at all. Lissa thinks you're too kinky for her, but that don't scare me none."

She reached out and put a hand on Jack's chest.

That was too much. Abby reached out and forcibly removed the offending hand. "Hands off, honey. This one is mine."

"Maybe he should decide." The blonde was now paying attention to Abby.

Jack was stumbling all over himself to get the words out of his mouth. "Oh, I am one hundred percent hers. Yup, all hers. We're getting married on Thursday."

Abby heard Christa laugh and barely managed to contain her own because Jack looked positively terrified at the idea of having to deal with the horny chick.

Melissa Paul looked infinitely pleased. "So old Jack is marrying the village whore. Good for him. I always knew he didn't mind used goods."

Sam suddenly wasn't cowering anymore. He stood straight up, and Jack was out of his barstool, too. Leslie had the good sense to look afraid, but Melissa didn't have the Darwinian instincts to know she was in trouble. She was still looking coyly at her prey. If she wanted to defuse the situation, she would have to take it in hand. When she thought about it, this was a ridiculous situation to find herself in.

Her throaty gut laugh got everyone's attention. Sam, Jack, and Christa all looked at her like she'd gone the tiniest bit crazy. Abby gestured toward the blonde. She couldn't stop laughing. It was making her cry a little.

"Look at her. She called me a whore. Seriously? Honey, I can see your nipples. Don't be ridiculous." She took a deep breath. "Now, turn around before you make a complete idiot of yourself."

Melissa Paul's head bobbed in outrage. "I'm not the one making a fool of myself. You're some old cougar trying to get her hands on a man who could be her son."

Abby's hands went up in disgust. "What? Did I have him when I was five? I am not that much older than him. What have you done, Sam? Have you slept with every twenty-something blonde in the county?"

Sam looked at her with wide eyes. She was beginning to think of it as his kicked puppy look. "Not every single one. I'm sure there are some I missed, and now I promise my blonde-banging days are over. I swear I haven't slept with a single other person since I met you. I am all about the redhead now."

Abby sent a questioning look back at Jack.

He smiled angelically. "I don't even like blondes. You'll find I've practically been a saint compared to Sam."

"I believe that," Abby said flatly, shaking her head the whole time. She turned back to her younger rival. "Now, you're scaring Sam. Please go away."

Melissa looked between the two men and Abigail, a revelation slowly dawning. "It's true, isn't it? I thought that was some ugly rumor. You two perverts like to share women. Well, hell, Sam, if that's all you need, I can do Jack, I suppose. You don't have to settle for some old chick. I can be kinky, too. Me and Leslie will even do a four-way if you like."

"But I'm the whore." Abby looked to Christa, who had the same look of disgust on her face.

"Damn straight, you're the whore," Melissa shot back. "Everyone knows it."

There was a charge of electricity running through the bar. Everyone was watching them. This could get bad. Christa winked, letting her know she had Abby's back. A strange sense of excitement thrilled through Abby. Her life had been relatively calm for the last couple of years. Christa was right. This was the time to reclaim a little of her crazy youth, and it was definitely time to put the young girls in their place.

"Keep your hands off my man." She wasn't going to back down. "This one's mine, too. I don't know what he did to make you think he wants you, but he doesn't. He's very sorry to have led you on…"

"I didn't…" Sam started, and then smartly shut his mouth at the look on her face.

"…but he is very committed to our relationship," Abby explained firmly. "There will be no more drunken hookups. He's going to curb his drinking so he can make more appropriate choices in the future. Sam is limited to three beers from now on."

"What?" Sam looked around for help from some corner. There was none forthcoming. "Damn it."

"So go find some other man to bother." Abby dismissed the woman with a curt nod of her head.

Melissa Paul obviously wasn't used to being dismissed. She leaned over and shoved a hand into Abby's chest. "Listen here, bitch. I am not letting some old cougar push me around. You can have Jack. I think he's a pervert, anyway, and I'm going to tell everyone in town that he's forcing Sam to sleep with you. Everyone knows Sam depends on Jack for money. I'm going to ruin all of you if I don't get Sam."

Christa gasped. The whole bar seemed to hold its collective breath.

Abby had had far more than enough. Her hand curled into a fist. "You forgot one thing about us cougars. We have claws."

She reared her fist back and punched the younger woman straight in the face.

* * * *

"What the hell are we supposed to do, Jack?" Sam couldn't keep his eyes off the two women.

Abby got Melissa in a chokehold. Leslie had tried to jump into the fray to help her friend, but Christa had given a loud rebel yell and leapt on the smaller woman. They were wrestling on the floor of the bar, tangles of limbs and hair and vicious nails.

It probably shouldn't arouse him, but it did. Well, his Abby taking on Melissa Paul did.

"Watch out for her nails, Abigail!" Sam yelled. He knew how deep they could sink. Not that he was going to mention that to Abby.

Abby and Christa taking on the women who'd come for him and Jack had caused a chain reaction. Many of the women in the bar seemed to think a taboo had been broken and had thrown themselves into the new norm with a malicious glee. Three other girl fights had broken out, and it was hair-pulling, nail-scratching chaos.

149

"We do nothing." Jack took a long drink. "That woman is defending your honor and you're going to let her. Besides, Abigail's winning. Our little honey is downright mean. You had best follow that three-beer dictate of hers or she'll pile drive you. Where the hell did she learn that move?"

Melissa pulled out of the hold and reached out to snatch at Abby's hair. Abby yelped, but then kicked out perfectly with her heel and Melissa went flying.

Sam watched his future wife pull another female up by her hair. A warmth flooded him. She was really pretty when she was fighting.

"And think about it, Sam," Jack continued. He was watching Abby with a content grin. "She's doing all of it with a plug up her ass."

Sam's breath caught. Jack was right. "She is one hell of a woman."

"And she's all ours," Jack said with a satisfaction Sam couldn't mistake.

He turned to the man sitting next to him, pointing toward where Abby had Melissa down for the count. "We're going to marry her."

The cowboy's eyes widened. "Brave man."

In the distance, Sam heard a familiar noise. He quickly calculated the distance and figured they didn't have long.

Jack hopped off his barstool. He looked back at David Sandberg, who stared at the proceedings with complete shock on his face. The Barn had seen its share of bar fights, but nothing like this.

Sam clapped him on the back. "It's going to be okay. From now on Sunday night can be girl fight night."

"Tally up the damage and send me the bill, Dave," Jack said with a wink. "The cops are coming. I'll collect Abby. You tell Mike he needs to get Christa out of here or we'll be posting bail."

Jack walked over to their future wife and tossed an arm around her waist, hauling her off her screaming blonde opponent.

"Hey, I wasn't done with her!" Abby yelled as she was carted out like a piece of luggage.

Jack laughed. "You're done for now, warrior princess. Sam's honor has been avenged. It's time to call it a night."

Sam ran ahead. He helped Mike pull his wife off a crying

Leslie. Christa laughed when Jack caught up to them. Even though they hustled, Sam noticed Abby and Christa seemed satisfied with the chaos they had wrought.

"Abby Moore's back." Christa made the pronouncement with a hearty fist pump.

Sam opened the door.

Even from her position over Jack's shoulder, she replied with an arrogant grin. "You tell this town they ain't seen nothing yet!"

Sam couldn't wait to see what she'd come up with next.

Chapter Twelve

"**I'm** sorry, Jack, but I have to do this."

Abby sat up in the backseat of the Jeep as Jack turned onto the two-lane highway where her mother's trailer park was located. Jack had tried his hardest, but she hadn't been swayed by his arguments that she should stay the night with them. If she was going to change her whole life and make the attempt to stay here and build something, she needed to talk to her mom about it. Her mother would be impacted by this decision.

They'd been arguing for fifteen minutes, and all the while Sam had been trying to seduce her in the back of the Jeep. Sam didn't seem to be following the conversation she was having with Jack. He was intently concentrating on rubbing her nipples and nibbling on her ear.

"You're putting off the inevitable," Jack claimed.

She sighed when Sam kissed a very sensitive spot behind her earlobe. "I can't leave her alone, and I can't uproot her without any warning. It's not going to change anything. I don't think it will. She was very clear that she approved of the two of you, so it might not be as hard as I think to convince her to move."

"Looks like something's going on," Jack said, easing off the gas.

Even in the dark, she could see the smoke pouring out from somewhere up ahead. She rolled the window down and was assaulted by the acrid smell of burning wood and plastic. Up ahead, she could see a police barricade across the road. The fog of the smoke made the red and blue lights appear eerie, and Jack slowed down the car.

Abby got a horrible feeling in her gut.

"Stop, Sam. Something's wrong." Abby pushed him away.

The minute the Jeep rolled to a stop in front of the barricade, she opened the door.

Sam called out behind her, but she ran toward the lights. The rest of her neighbors were out of their homes, clutching robes around their necks and passing coffee around. She ran past them because it was obvious now where the fire was.

She hit the police line just in time to watch the volunteer fire department putting out the last of her mother's smoldering home. Fire had gutted the small trailer, and there was almost nothing left.

A cry came from her mouth. It hadn't been much, but she'd grown up in that trailer. Pure panic raced through her. What time was it? Bingo ended early in the evening. She looked around wildly for her mother. Had she been in the trailer?

Sam's firm hands came around her, holding her. He pointed to a spot a few feet away. "Baby, your mother is right there, talking to the fire chief."

Real physical relief flooded her body when she caught sight of her mother shakily talking to the fire chief. Her mother's eyes were swollen from crying, and she could see the strain on her face. Her mom looked up and held out her arms as she saw Abby walking toward her.

Sam let Abby go, and she ran the last few feet into her mother's arms.

"What happened?" Abby hugged her frail body. It struck her exactly how much her recent illness had taken out of her mother.

"I don't know." Her mom's voice was shaky. "It was already on fire when I got here. Juan and his wife kindly took me out for a late cup of coffee at the café. Oh, Abby, if they hadn't…"

The fire chief, who Abby remembered was named Eric Thompson, looked on the women with compassion. "Hello, Abigail. I'm sorry about this. Obviously, it's a total loss. Mrs. Moore, do you have insurance?"

Abby heard her mother's quiet no. She felt tears start to fall. Everything her mother had was in that trailer. It was all gone now. She shook at the thought of having to start all over again at her mother's age.

"The Red Cross has a shelter in Tyler that can take you in," Eric said.

"Don't worry about the Moore women." Jack strode up, his shoulders broad against the lights from the fire truck. "I'll take care of them. You want to explain to me what happened here?"

The fire chief looked relieved at having an unemotional man to talk to. While Jack dealt with the realities of the situation, Abby felt Sam's presence at her back. His hands found their way around her waist.

"It's going to be all right," Sam promised. "Jack will take care of the formalities. Let him take care of you. It's what he does. Don't worry about a thing. This setback just moves up our plans."

Her mother looked up at Sam. "What plans?"

Sam smiled down. He released Abby's waist and reached out to take her mother's hands in his. Abby was grateful for his abundance of charm because Sam was able to calm her mother down. "Abby agreed to marry Jack tonight. She's moving in with us, and we're moving you into the guest house. Now, we were planning on doing that before we found out about this fire, so don't you worry about it. You'll have everything you need, Mrs. Moore. We're going to make sure of it. I know we can't replace pictures or memories, but don't you worry a bit that you won't have a roof over your head. You have a home with your daughter. We will always take care of her and the people she loves."

"You're a good man, Sam Fleetwood." Her mother sniffled into a tissue. "I would be very proud to stay in the guest house."

Jack walked back over, his expression grim. "They think it was faulty wiring. We won't know for certain until the report is finished. It could be a week or so." Jack cupped Abby's face in his hands.

"Are you all right, sweetheart?"

She nodded and threw her arms around Jack's waist, loving his quiet strength. She would always be able to depend on him. "I'm fine. Can we go home now?"

He kissed the top of her head, and Sam began to help her mom toward the Jeep. "Yes, there's nothing we can do here. Let's get you home and get your mama settled in. It's going to be all right, Abigail."

She nodded, even though she wasn't so sure of that. Faulty wiring seemed too coincidental. She had a feeling there was nothing accidental about her mother's home burning to the ground.

She allowed Jack to slowly walk her toward the car, hoping all along that she was wrong.

* * * *

The next morning dawned and with it a quiet sense that, even though something terrible had happened, all was finally right with her world. Abby woke up warm and safe in bed.

The previous night, Jack had done his thing and before Sam had even gotten them all home, had made arrangements for a nurse to join Diane full time until she was completely done with therapy. Abby had been able to go to sleep knowing her mother was safe and well taken care of. She'd fallen asleep with her head on Jack's chest and Sam pressed against her back.

Sometime in the night, she came to the conclusion that she was being crazy. No one would go so far as to torch her childhood home. That would be the work of an insane person. It had to be coincidence. Or maybe, she thought as she woke up cuddled between two gorgeous men, it was just fate.

After hopping over to check in on her mom, Abby joined her fiancés for breakfast in the dining room. There was a small breakfast table in the kitchen, but Jack had been explicit in his instructions. They would use the large dining room. She wasn't sure why they went so formal for breakfast when she was dressed in one of Sam's shirts and his robe, but she went with it.

"How is your mom?" Jack asked as she walked in.

155

Abby walked over and kissed him soundly. "She's great, thanks to you." She walked around the table to Sam. "And you."

After giving him a kiss, she took her seat and a small, older woman walked in carrying a pot of coffee, a ready smile on her face.

"Abigail," Jack began, "this is our housekeeper, Benita Wells. You would have met her earlier if you hadn't stolen my truck and run away."

Abby wrinkled her nose in dismay at Jack before turning to the sixty-something woman with steel gray hair and kind eyes. She shook her head indulgently at the men, and Abby got the feeling Benita viewed herself as a mother figure.

"It's a pleasure to meet you, Ms. Wells," Abby said.

"Call me Benita, and it's good to meet you as well." Benita smoothed down her white apron. "My husband works as the foreman here on the ranch. We live in a small house out beyond the swimming pool. I think you're going to love it here. I've waited a very long time for these two to bring me a lovely woman to work with. I can't wait to show you around. It's a beautiful place, though it needs a woman's touch."

Sam was busy shoveling scrambled eggs on his plate. "Benita has been bugging us to redecorate for years."

Benita shook her head sadly as she gestured to the room around her. "I remember the seventies. They should go away."

Jack winked at his housekeeper. "I'll call a decorator. Abigail, I'm sure, will get busy shoving the age of disco right out of this house."

A light gleamed in Benita's eyes. "We should also discuss updating the kitchen. Much progress has been made in appliances in the last forty years. Were you aware, Miss Abigail, that they now have machines that wash dishes?"

She schooled herself to look properly impressed. Bringing this place into the modern age would be fun, and it looked like Benita was going to be an excellent design partner. "I had not heard. We should look into that."

Benita nodded and walked to the door that led to the kitchen. "Excellent. I'm off, then. I have some grocery shopping to do. I sent some muffins and coffee over to the guest house and asked Mrs.

Moore to join us for lunch at twelve-thirty. I'll lock up as I leave."

"Set the alarm as well." Jack took a sip of his coffee. "Thank you."

Abby poured herself some coffee and decided she might be able to get used to the idea of having a housekeeper. It was rather nice to have breakfast she hadn't prepared for herself. She did have a few questions though.

"Why are we turning on the alarm in the middle of the day? And why are all the blinds closed?"

The overhead light was on, but outside was a bright, beautiful day. She'd been happy with the gorgeous blue sky overhead as she walked the short distance from the big house to her mother's place. It was a perfect fall day in Texas. In the distance, she'd been able to see the hands already hard at work. The ranch was bustling and full of life.

"I thought you would prefer the privacy, sweetheart," Jack murmured. "I know I don't particularly want my employees to see my future wife naked. Take off the clothes, Abigail."

She looked between Jack and Sam, but neither gave any appearance that Jack had been joking. Sam was contentedly eating his breakfast and watching her with pointed fascination. Jack's long fingers drummed against the table, a sure sign of his burgeoning impatience.

"Abigail, when I give you a direct order, I expect you to comply."

"You said you were only really in charge in the bedroom." Abby repeated his words from the previous night. She was a little shocked at the idea, but it wasn't offending her, per se. The idea of eating breakfast in the buff hadn't occurred to her before.

Jack put down his coffee, and the paper beside him was forgotten. "Then let me rephrase. I'm in charge of our private life. When we're alone, I want you naked. I've done everything I can to ensure our privacy, and now I expect you to keep the promise you made to me last night."

"He's serious," Sam offered with a sigh. "You should really drop the clothes or he'll take them off you himself."

It wasn't anything they hadn't seen before and he really had made sure they were totally alone. She decided to go with it. In for a penny…in for a whole lot of naked. Her hands went to the tie of the robe, easily shrugging out of it. "I wonder how this is going to work when I'm eighty."

Jack looked at her with a very serious expression on his face. "Maybe you should think about this. I know we're demanding a lot from you. You need to understand this isn't some phase that's going to pass for me. When you're eighty, I will still think you're beautiful. I will still consider your body mine, and I will still want you naked."

Abby pulled the shirt over her head and blinked back tears. She wondered if he knew he'd said the precise thing to make her comfortable. For a man who didn't talk a lot, he always knew what to say to her. She sat back in her chair, enjoying the way both men's eyes had gone slightly glassy at the sight of her naked body.

"So when we're alone at night watching television or I'm reading a book…?"

"I'll want you naked and cuddled up with me." Jack leaned forward, touching his hand to hers. "We'll sit on the couch and you'll be between me and Sam."

Sam had his chin propped on his hand, watching her with a happy grin. "You're better than TV. I think you're really pretty naked."

"Why, Samuel Fleetwood," she teased, "I had no idea you were attracted to me."

"Besides the fact that I practically humped your leg the first time I saw you?" Sam teased right back. "I'll have to be less subtle."

"Not this morning you won't." Jack pushed his chair back slightly. "Come here, Abigail."

She got out of her chair and realized she was already getting aroused. Just being naked and having their eyes on her got her hot. She wondered when she would get used to them. She hoped never. Jack patted his lap. Abby sat down obligingly, and Jack's arm went around her waist securely, holding her to him. He offered her a warm blueberry muffin, which she took gratefully. He then proceeded to go back to reading his paper. It was all Abby could do not to laugh. Most men didn't peruse the paper while naked women ate breakfast in their laps. But it didn't seem to bother Jack in the least.

"The organic alfalfa we ordered is coming in today." Jack continued to read as he spoke to Sam. As far as she could tell, it was some article on business.

"Good thing, too," Sam replied, and then they were off on a discussion of all the work coming up later in the year.

She quickly learned that there were a whole bunch of cows having calves this spring. She didn't inject herself into the conversation, preferring to listen to the two men talk. Their easy manner with each other was obviously the result of a long, intimate friendship.

After she was satisfied with her breakfast, she let her head rest against Jack's shoulder and her hands play on his well-muscled chest. Her mind started to wander in a way it hadn't for a long while. She suspected she'd stopped daydreaming because her life had been filled with too many responsibilities and she'd had no one to share the burdens with. It had not led to hours of fanciful thoughts. It was pleasant to rediscover the joy of imagination.

She let her thoughts go where they wanted. Ideas about what she'd like to do with the house played around in her head. Mid-century modern or farmhouse chic? So many choices. She would be considerate, of course. It was obvious any money Jack and Sam made probably went back into the business, but she had a little put away, too. It would be nice to have new furniture to cuddle on. Fabric would be cozier, but she should probably go with leather given the nakedness to which she was supposed to aspire. Sure she might stick to it from time to time, but it was so much easier to keep clean.

Her eyes closed as visions of the future played out like a movie. They would snuggle on the couch, and then Jack would look down and kiss her. Sam would have to get in on that. His hands were always restless, and they would move over her, stroking her until she was crazy for them. She would spread herself out so they didn't miss an inch of what belonged to them. It was all right because the belonging went both ways. Jack would growl low in his throat right before he pounced…

"Is she asleep?" Sam's voice poked through her reverie.

She felt Jack laugh deep in his chest. "I think she's dozing. Apparently, our in-depth discussion of calving has made her sleepy."

"Was just thinking," she murmured.

"About what?" Jack's voice took on a low, sexy timbre that made Abby suspect he knew what she'd been thinking.

"You and Sam."

Jack's hand moved on her thigh, slowly climbing up. "Spread your legs." Without thinking, she complied. Jack's fingers met her warm honey and started to part her gently, stroking in and out. "What exactly were you thinking about us? Whatever it was, it seems to have inspired you. Should I take care of this?"

* * * *

Jack watched his fingers slip in and out of her pussy. She was slippery wet, and he wondered exactly what fantasies had been playing out in her head while he discussed feed schedules with Sam. His cock strained against the fly of his jeans when a fresh coat of arousal coated his fingers.

"Please." Abigail wiggled against him a little. He was playing with her, and she obviously wanted more.

"Up," Jack demanded, putting her off his lap. He tore open his pants and shoved them down to let his cock free. He pulled it out and stroked it up and down, moving from the thick base to the bulbous purple crown.

She licked her lips as she watched him. The hot look in her eyes made him all the harder.

"Sweetheart, I don't have a condom. I can have Sam go get one, but I'd rather not have anything between us." She was so hot and tight around him. It would be heaven to ride her bareback. He was a careful man and never took a woman without a condom, but Abigail was different. "I had a physical a month ago. I haven't been with anyone but you since. Are you on the pill?"

"Shots." Her voice was breathless to Jack's ears. "I take a shot every three months. We're safe."

Jack gestured her to come back. "Straddle me."

She climbed on, placing her legs on either side of his hips. Her knees wouldn't fit on the narrow chair, so Jack used his strength to lift her onto his cock. He kept his head down, watching as his cock sank into the warmth of her pussy. He moved slowly, working his way in, finally allowing gravity to seat him as she moaned and leaned into him.

Jack held her there, enjoying the depth of their connection. His hands stroked up her waist and then cupped her breasts. Her skin was silky and soft. He gently rolled her taut nipples between his thumb and forefinger before leaning over and licking the tight tip. She gasped and slanted back. Her fingers tangled in his hair and she ground herself down on him. He stopped what he was doing. It was time for some discipline.

"Be still," he demanded.

He brought his hand firmly down on her ass. She tensed slightly and then sighed. When she obeyed, he went back to teasing her nipples.

"I want to come." She was protesting, but she didn't move.

"You will, but not until I'm through with you. I want to play for a bit, and you're going to be a very good girl and let me, aren't you?"

"The answer is yes, Abby." Sam's grin was wicked as he moved his chair so he would have a better view.

"Yes." Abigail gave him the answer he wanted.

He gently bit down on her nipple and then laved it soothingly with his tongue. All the while he filled her. His cock throbbed inside her, begging to be let loose, but he had rigid control.

He sucked her nipple deeply into his mouth. Abigail moaned. She was being an awfully good girl. It made it fun to play with her, but he could tell she was reaching the limit of her control. Finally, when it seemed like she might go crazy, he leaned back.

"Ride me, Abigail." He thrust his hips up and shoved down on her hips.

She braced herself against his shoulders. Jack bit back a moan while she worked her way up and down his length.

His head fell back, and he gave himself over to the experience of making love with her. She moved, slowly and deliberately. It wasn't fast enough for him, but she seemed to be enjoying it, so he took the torture. Her sweet, tight pussy was sucking all along his dick, and he gritted his teeth at the exquisite pleasure of being inside her. Sam watching made it hotter. He was looking forward to the time when he would look over her shoulder and see the same look of passionate agony on Sam's face he was sure was on his own now.

He felt his balls draw up and knew he was getting close. He thrust his hand in between them, and his thumb found her sweet spot.

"Oh, Jack." She moaned as she picked up the pace. She ground her pussy against his thumb, and he felt the tiny contractions of her orgasm.

"Oh, fuck." His cock exploded, the orgasm flooding his every sense.

He pulled her against him, pumping his semen deep inside her welcoming body. Abigail fell boneless against him as he ground out the last of his release. A deep sense of calm satisfaction spread throughout his body as he held her against him. After a long, quiet moment, he kissed her soundly and cursed as he looked at the clock.

"What?" Her head came off his shoulder. She was deliciously disheveled.

"I have to go to work." Jack regretted the necessity. His foreman was probably wondering where the hell he was. They were riding the fences today, making sure everything was secure.

"Okay," she agreed, and then made absolutely no move to get off of him.

Jack chuckled and threw his partner a questioning glance.

"If you insist." Sam got out of his chair. He pulled Abigail off Jack and held her in his arms. She obligingly threw her arms around his neck. "She needs a shower."

"I bet you're the man to get me clean." She cuddled against Sam.

"Not until I dirty you up a bit more," Sam promised.

Jack tucked his entirely satisfied cock back into his pants and stood up, reaching for his Stetson. "You ride herd on her all day, understood?"

"Sure thing, boss," Sam said in a tone that stated he was happy with his assigned task.

"Take her shopping and get her anything she needs. Ask Diane for a list as well." His tone went lower. "And shift her up to the medium-sized plug. She can wear it while she's shopping. I want to move into the playroom tonight."

"Does that mean I'm getting tied up?" She seemed to find the energy to look up. She flashed a slightly superior grin that did all sorts of things to his insides. "I know what a playroom is. I read, you know."

He nodded. "I do, indeed. It was your highly intellectual tastes that made me believe this could work out. You have fun with Sam. I'll see you at dinner. And Abigail…"

"I won't wear any clothes," she promised as Sam turned away.

He knew he should be running to get to work, but he found himself watching them walk away, listening to them bicker playfully.

"We need to talk about those books," Sam said sternly. "Some of them are fine, but the one about the five men is perverted."

"You're one to criticize fine literature."

"Fine literature, my ass." They continued to argue as they rounded the corner.

Jack stood there for a minute in the house he'd lived in for ten years. It struck him that, while watching the two people he loved walking through it, this old house had finally become a home.

Chapter Thirteen

Abby looked up and down Main Street and wondered whether she was going to have the courage to pull this off. There were a couple of new stores, but otherwise it hadn't changed. It was still a neat slice of small-town America. She looked over at the barbershop her father used to go to. Two old men were standing outside watching her with suspicious eyes.

This wasn't going to be easy.

Sam stared at her, a worried expression on his naturally happy face. "Are you sure you want to do this? It might be easier to drive in to Tyler today. We can get everything you need there. Hell, we can get the essentials in Tyler and wait until Friday and then spend the weekend in Dallas. I assure you, we can find anything you want in Dallas. We'll go to Neiman's."

Abby shook her head. She could handle the snootiest Neiman Marcus shoe salesman, but she wasn't so sure about Greg Gunderson at the GrabItQuick. He seemed way scarier. The funny thing was the clerk at Neiman's had to bet that a customer had the cash. Millionaires in Dallas came in all eccentric types. Greg Gunderson knew for damn sure he didn't want to serve her. The trouble was Abby had to get herself served if she was going to make a go of it with Jack and Sam.

In her quest to do this, she'd made two important decisions. The first decision was to lay it all out to Sam. This morning after breakfast, she told him everything she was afraid of. She started at the beginning, when she was seventeen and had finally bagged Adam Echols. She had spared not a moment's shame, right down to leaving town in order to save her mother's job and keep Ruby away from her daughter. She started with Sam because he was the easier of the two to talk to. She'd been relatively certain that Sam would take it all with equanimity. Boy, had she been wrong. By the time she was done with her story, Sam had been in a killing mood. He'd been so angry, and not with her. After she calmed Sam down, she told him her plan. He was willing to go along with it, but he still had issues, hence the Neiman Marcus argument.

"Seriously, baby, it'll be fun," Sam continued. "We can spend the weekend at this ritzy hotel Jack and I stay at. We'll get a big old suite and only leave when we need to take you shopping. There are some stores I'd like to take you to."

She sent him a harried look. "I know what stores you're talking about, Sam. Try to tempt me another time, please. I'm still dealing with the last sex toy you shoved up my butt."

Sam had the good sense to look compassionate. The morning played out in her head. It had started with Sam tossing her on the bed, jumping on top of her, riding her until they both screamed, and ended with the pink medium-sized plug and a whole lot of lube.

"Is it terribly uncomfortable?"

She smiled and leaned over to kiss his cheek. "No. Surprisingly not. I have to do this. I have to face them down. It would be great to spend a weekend in Dallas, but I can't drive to Dallas every time we need a gallon of milk."

"They really won't sell stuff to you?" He still sounded stunned at the lengths the town would go to show her she wasn't welcome.

"Not for twenty years, although, truth be told, it started earlier than that. Once the Echols clan figured out Adam was serious, it was hard for me to buy groceries for my mom. Hell, I got an F in a class I should have gotten an A in. It was suggested that my foreign language skills weren't up to snuff. My Spanish teacher attended church with Ruby Echols."

165

He kicked at the curb with his well-worn boot, cursing under his breath. "Hell, baby, let's just tell Jack everything. He'll fix it."

That was the simple solution but it wouldn't work long term. "It isn't his job to fix my life."

"Don't you tell him that." Sam wagged a finger at her. "You're likely to find yourself over his knee getting the spanking of a lifetime. He takes this stuff seriously. He always has."

She leaned against the body of the gorgeous pearl-white Mercedes Sam was driving today. She knew she was procrastinating, but she was curious. "I know he's protective of you. The two of you met in a foster home, didn't you?"

"It was a group home for teens," he corrected. "I was almost fifteen. I guess they figured no one would want a fifteen-year-old boy. My parents and my older brother died in a car accident. I was left all alone. I was a terrified kid when I went into that home. It was basically a detention center with nice curtains. You have to understand that I'd lived a perfectly normal life up until that moment. I'd rarely left home except for school and the occasional sleepover. I went to camp once and hated it."

"Your parents took care of you." She knew a bit about what it was like to get shoved into a cold world, though even when she'd been tossed out of her home, her aunt had welcomed her. Sam had nowhere to go.

"I was sheltered. I'd never been without someone to take care of me. That made me a target for the more worldly kids. That first night, the oldest kid there decided to make an example of me after lights out. Jack stopped him. I've been with him ever since."

She reached out to run her fingers across his tense jaw. It hadn't taken long to figure out Sam was a man who needed physical affection. She planned to give him all the touches and kisses he'd missed out on. "I'm sorry you went through that, but I'm glad Jack was there."

Sam crossed his arms over his chest and stood next to her. "I don't know what would have happened without Jack, but I have a pretty good idea. I was a teenager, but Jack had been in the system since he was six. He never stayed in one place for more than a year. From what I understand, he was a difficult child. I'm pretty sure he was abused. You should know we're both pretty damaged."

Her heart swelled with love for the two men. They'd been through so much, and yet were still capable of loving a woman. She slipped her arm around his waist. He didn't fight her at all. He accepted her comfort.

"I think we're all damaged. You don't get through life without some scars. You and Jack figured out a way to make it through."

They were halves of a whole. Tragedy had ravaged both men, but together they were complete. Jack was the responsible one. Taking responsibility for Sam had given Jack an anchor in the world. Sam was the bright side. He forced Jack to have fun and connect with people. In return, Sam had someone who would never leave him.

And they both needed her. She would tie them together even more than they were now. They loved her. She was comfortable with that fact, but there was more to it. She was a conduit for them to express their love for each other. When she really thought about it, it was a beautiful thing to be. It was a unique solution, but it worked.

"All I'm trying to say is let Jack take care of you," Sam explained. "It's who he is. He needs it."

She nodded. "I understand, but this is something I have to do for myself. If I don't face these people, I'll never be comfortable here. I have to stand up for myself this time if I want to live here with you. This is about more than being able to buy a gallon of milk."

"All right, but if they get nasty with you, you can't expect me to sit back."

"If they get physical with me, you have my permission to ride in and rescue me. Otherwise, you hang back." This was something she had to try to do herself.

"Jack's gonna kill me." He pushed himself off the Benz.

Abby fondly stroked the car. "I'll be sad when he has to turn this baby in. I have to admit, driving this car gives me an ego boost the truck just can't. I feel like walking in and telling everyone I drive a Mercedes, so you better sell me a Snickers bar or my car will destroy your car's reputation."

Sam laughed. "Well, you feel free to tell everyone that."

She wrinkled her nose and shook her hair out. She was dressed in a pair of Christa's Levi's and one of Sam's too big T-shirts. She did not look like a woman who drove a Benz. "Nah, I'd feel bad when I had to turn it back into the rental agency. But it is a gorgeous car."

"It isn't a rental," Sam said slowly.

"Jack replaced his truck? Because of that tiny dent I put in it?"

"Nope. He replaced your car." Sam stood back. He gave her a charming smile and patted the car.

"He bought me a car?" She tried to process the information. In a way, she should have expected it. Jack believed in big gestures. "That's sweet, but my car is fine. It's paid off, and it still runs…most of the time."

"Abby, it has *WHORE* painted on it," he pointed out.

"So, it needs a paint job." And new tires and the alternator was tricky.

"Even with a paint job, it'll always be your whore car," Sam reasoned. "You'll never be able to look at it the same way again. You'll always see it right there on the hood of your car."

She rolled her eyes. "Don't be a drama queen. My car's honor hasn't been impugned."

"Oh, yes it has." There was a mischievous twinkle in his eyes. "It's completely ruined in the eyes of society." His hands slid across the top of the Benz lovingly. "But this baby is pure as the driven snow."

"You're insane," she declared flatly. "I want my car back."

"Not really possible. Jack thought you might want your whore car back, so he had it crushed." Sam held his hands about two feet apart. "It's this big now. It's a nice little cube."

She felt her jaw drop. "Jack cubed my car?"

"You'll find that Jack thinks ahead. He figured you might be stubborn about the whole car thing, so he took care of it for you. Now you can feel free to enjoy the pristine beauty of the Benz, since you can't exactly drive a cube."

She felt her face flush. He really had cut her off at the knees. She wasn't so stubborn as to throw the car back in Jack's face. They were getting married, and he had caused her beloved Oldsmobile to meet its sad demise. He owed her a car. She simply worried about the expense. Jack needed to understand that she wasn't some princess who had to have the best of everything. She was willing to work with them to grow the ranch. Her pointing finger came out, and Sam took a step back. "Jack and I will be having a discussion about this tonight."

"I will look forward to it." Expectation lit his blue eyes. "Please don't start in on Jack until I have a front-row seat." Abby started down the sidewalk, and Sam followed. "I think I'll pick up some popcorn because that is going to be one entertaining discussion."

She let the doors to the local grocery store swing open in front of her. She thought about getting a cart and shopping leisurely, but decided a quick guerilla assault was more likely to work this first time. She tried not to notice that everyone in the store was staring as she marched in. The girl at the register immediately picked up her phone and called for Mr. Gunderson.

Let him come. She wasn't going to be intimidated. Not this time. And she knew exactly what she wanted to be holding in her hands when that nasty Greg Gunderson showed up.

She stalked through the store until she found the aisle with the feminine hygiene products. She grabbed a big box of tampons, and when she turned around, she nearly collided with a pimple-faced kid who couldn't be much past seventeen. He dropped the box he had been carrying and packages of maxi pads went flying.

So much for a quick assault.

With a long sigh, she bent over to start helping the kid pick them up.

"You're Abigail Moore." He was staring at her. She was pretty certain he wasn't looking at her eyes.

"Yes." She was not able to keep the surly tone out of her voice. This kid hadn't even been alive when she'd left town. She wasn't putting up with his crap. "Do you have a problem with that?"

He quickly shook his head. "No, no problem, ma'am," the kid stammered. "My mom says now that you're back, you'll probably corrupt every teenage boy in town."

Teenage boys? What the hell was wrong with the women of this

169

town? "Do you listen to everything your mama says?"

He shook his head. "Not usually. I just thought…maybe I could take you out some time, Miss Abigail. I have some money left over from my birthday. We could go someplace nice."

She heard a man snort and saw Sam bent over in the aisle, laughing his ass off. No help was coming from that corner. She turned back to her boy suitor. He looked at her with the earnest expression of a young man who wanted desperately to be corrupted. "Should I expect further invitations from the town's high school boy population?"

He shrugged. "Most likely. We all decided you're the hottest thing this town has seen since Lisa Donald brought back a string bikini from her aunt's house in L.A."

Yep. Another problem for another day. She walked around the boy, completely ignoring his invitation. She narrowed her eyes at Sam as she walked by. "You're supposed to defend me from things like that, Sam Fleetwood. Some fiancé you are."

"Hell, the high school boys of Willow Fork have spoken," Sam managed to wheeze. "You are their goddess. Who am I to stand in the way? Besides, baby, he weighs all of ninety pounds. After the way you handled Melissa Paul last night, he'll be a breeze."

She frowned at him and marched straight up to the checkout stand where Greg Gunderson stood waiting. He had relieved the clerk and stood panting from the exertion of running all the way from his office in the back of the store. He was about fifteen years older than she was, and she still remembered the first time he'd told her to get out of his store. He'd put on about fifty pounds since the last time she'd seen him. He still wore the tackiest ties, though.

Slamming the box of tampons on the counter, she looked Gunderson straight in the eyes. "I would like to purchase that, please."

Unlike the last time, Gunderson looked slightly apologetic. "I can't, Miss Moore. I'm sorry. I know it seems stupid, but I can't have you in here."

A crowd of young mothers was gathering with their children in tow. Abby recognized Jan Echols among them. She'd met the woman at the diner and had been surprised someone in the Echols

170

family had the good sense to marry her. Jan and her girls seemed like genuinely nice people.

"Hey, Abby," Jan said with a wave. "How are you doing today?" Her two girls were with her and they waved as well, one of them clinging to her mama's skirt, the other trying to climb into the basket.

Normal. It was nice and normal to have an acquaintance wave her way at the grocery store.

She blinked back tears because no one had done that for her in this town. Abby nodded Jan's way. "I'm doing well, Jan. Though I am having some trouble with the management of this establishment. Thank you for asking."

She looked back at the grocery store owner with a little more strength than she'd had before. She'd come too far to walk out defeated now.

"Are you telling me I cannot buy a box of feminine necessaries in your store?"

Gunderson sighed. "You know I can't sell it to you."

"You're the only grocery store in town, Mr. Gunderson," she pointed out. "Where am I supposed to go?"

He stammered as he realized there were a whole lot of young female eyes watching him. "Well, there's always Tyler."

"You expect her to drive to Tyler for a box of tampons?" Jan asked flatly.

She looked back, noting a slightly unholy gleam in the eyes of many of the women there. It was as though the entire crowd sensed the distress of the man and was waiting eagerly to pounce.

"Obviously the man has never had a period," said a young brunette with a baby strapped to her chest. She shook her head indignantly. "Is she supposed to hold it until she can get there? Because it doesn't work like that."

"Now, this is certainly not a fit conversation for mixed company." Gunderson's eyes darted around, seeking out the first man he could find.

He wouldn't get any help from Sam. Sam looked like he was having a grand old time. He stepped back with the women. "If he can refuse to sell poor Abby Moore her much-needed tampons, what's next, ladies? He's a man on a mission to oppress the women of Willow Fork."

"That is completely untrue." The round man seemed to sense his Monday afternoon shoppers were about to turn into an unruly mob.

"We should protest," someone from the back said. "We could get signs and everything."

Jan Echols smiled. "I think, perhaps, tomorrow Mr. Gunderson might discover his store window covered in maxi pads. They stick, you know. We could line the whole storefront with them. Don't think of it as vandalism, sir. Think of it as artistic outrage."

"That'll be five dollars and ninety cents." Gunderson looked down at his cash register.

Reaching into her purse, she pulled out a ten. She took her change and held the small bag in her hand.

When she turned, the female mob burst into applause.

"About time someone stood up to that old prude," she heard another lady in the crowd mutter.

"He won't even carry hair color," another said bitterly. "He says it's for loose women."

"Maybe a protest is still called for." Jan stared at the very nervous grocery store owner.

"Maybe a new store is called for," Sam offered cheerfully. "I've been looking to invest." He took her by the hand and started to lead her away. "Baby, I take it all back. This is so much more fun than letting Jack scare the shit out of people. Let's go up and down Main Street buying stuff you don't need."

As she let Sam lead her triumphantly out of the store, she noticed the stock boy watching her. Their eyes met, and he held a single hand up to wave good-bye. The lovelorn look on his face was enough to make her giggle. It really had been worth the trouble.

The nicest salon in town was across the street.

She decided she needed conditioner.

* * * *

The stories of Abigail Moore's conquest of Main Street reached

Ruby Echols very quickly. She'd been taking tea in her sitting room when the phone was brought to her. Helen Talbot had been in the Winchester Salon when Abby had threatened a multitude of lawsuits if she was not offered the ability to purchase hair products. What was the world coming to when decent storeowners were not allowed to select their clientele?

She wanted to shake with rage as she thought about the night before. It had taken a lot out of her to start that fire. It wasn't as if the trashy trailer had put up much of a fight, but she had been obliged to walk through the woods in order to conceal her vehicle. A window had been conveniently left open, and some filmy curtains had been easy to set aflame.

It had been satisfying to stand back and watch it burn. Her only real disappointment was that Abby hadn't been caught in the trailer. She should have known the tramp would have the devil's own luck.

No, her work had been righteous and good, but ruined. It had been the sight of Adam taking care of the bitch that had infuriated her. Adam had walked up the lane and taken charge, as she had always known he would. Adam was the smart, confident one. He was a leader. He was everything she had dreamed he would become. His body was a man's body now. He wasn't a boy anymore.

But he still needed a mother's protection. He was still in that siren's clutches, and it was up to his mother to make sure things turned out differently this time.

She had another chance. She wasn't going to let the same thing happen twice.

Ruby's head began to pound. Oh, she wondered, where was that youngest boy of hers? He was supposed to bring her those pills. She hadn't taken them already, had she?

Sometimes things were very confusing.

She gathered the cashmere cardigan around her shoulders. The door chimes rang, and she heard the housekeeper hustling to the door. She sat carefully on the antique sofa as Hillary Glass, Helen Talbot, and Miranda Knight were shown into the sitting room.

"Oh, Ruby, we heard all about it," Miranda fretted as she moved to greet her.

"Did you hear the news that the tramp's trailer burned down?"

Hillary settled herself on the early-American armchair Ruby's great-grandmother had brought with her when the family moved from Atlanta after the War of Northern Aggression.

"Yes," she murmured. "I heard about it this morning. It doesn't surprise me. I'm sure someone was drunk at the time. I doubt that her mother had insurance. Are they at a shelter?"

It suited her to think of those trashy women as homeless.

"No." Helen shook her overly round head. Ruby had always thought Helen should lose some weight, but then again, her bloodlines were impeccable. One had to overlook such things at times. Now Helen's large hands fluttered. "The rumor is she's moved in with Jack Barnes and they're getting married on Thursday. Barnes called the judge this morning and got the paperwork going. Can you imagine it? Abigail Moore is going to marry the largest landholder in the county."

She flushed, her hands threatening to shake. "No, she is not."

Helen shook her head. "I don't know that you can stop this, Ruby. That Barnes fellow is quite intimidating. My son has done business with him. He says the man is tough but fair. However, when he's crossed, he can be ruthless."

"If he's decided he wants Abigail Moore, then he'll have her," Miranda pronounced.

A plan formed in Ruby's brain. She would drive Abigail out of town once and for all, and then Adam could come home. "Then we'll have to convince Abby to leave him, won't we? I do believe I would like to get a cup of coffee at the café in town. I think Abigail will more than likely show up there, don't you?"

Three hours later, Ruby smiled as a shaken Abigail Moore walked out of the café. It had been relatively simple to corner the girl. Miranda had waylaid the young man escorting Abigail around with tales of car trouble. The handsome blond man had been more than willing to help out a little old lady. Abigail had been flush with her own success. She had accepted Ruby's invitation to talk with a look of challenge in her eyes.

Abigail wasn't so arrogant now.

She had shown the tramp what real power was. Ruby had laid out a detailed plan of how she and her friends intended to destroy Jack Barnes and his business. When they were through, his business would be in ruins. Any money Abby thought she would take from the smitten man wouldn't be worth the trouble Ruby would put them all through.

She'd made it very clear that if Abby Moore didn't leave town by the end of the day, she would make Barnes's life a living hell.

She had no delusions that Abby loved her fiancé. A gold digger like Abigail Moore wasn't capable of love. She was a practical girl, however. She had learned her lesson the first time. She would move on and find easier prey.

Ruby sipped at the coffee. It wasn't up to her standards, but it tasted like victory nonetheless.

Chapter Fourteen

Jack rode in from the south field with a mounting sense of
anticipation. He gently prodded Ranger, his solid-brown gelding,
and the horse moved easily toward the barn. It had been a long day.
The south fence had several places he and Juan had been forced to
replace entirely. It was hard work, but it was best to get it all done
now while the weather was nice. The weather could be very
unpredictable this time of year. It could get cold fast, and he didn't
want to be pounding fence posts in freezing temperatures.

Tipping his Stetson as he passed one of the wives of his ranch
hands, he contemplated his current happiness. During his lunch
break, he'd made arrangements for his marriage. The thought that he
would soon have an honest-to-god wife made him smile. He'd
always thought Sam would be the one to fall in love and Jack would
allow him to have the legally recognized relationship. Loving
Abigail changed everything, and he thought it would be for the
better. He hoped Sam wasn't disappointed, but Jack wasn't letting
their wife have any name but his.

And she *would* be taking his name, he promised himself.

She'd kept her maiden name when she married her first husband
because she wanted to share her daughter's last name, but Lexi was

a grown woman. That argument would never have worked with him. He would have insisted on adopting Lexi and changing her name as well. He was a possessive man. He'd long ago stopped fighting it. He didn't get close to many people in the world, but the few he did, he considered his. Sam was his. Abby was his. He knew it was a weird relationship, but he didn't care.

Jack dismounted and walked the gelding inside the barn.

He could still remember the day he met Sam like it was yesterday. Sam Fleetwood had looked terrified. Everything the boy owned was in one suitcase and a backpack. Jack remembered thinking it was more than he'd ever had. He'd been jealous of the kid. Sam looked all wide-eyed and innocent. He had an easy charm, even through his grief. A charm Jack had never known once in his life.

Jack had been sure that Fred Hall, the biggest bully in the group, intended to initiate young Sam that first evening. After lights out, it was pretty much a free-for-all as long as it was quiet. The monitor slept pretty soundly and didn't really care what went on. Fred had tried that shit with him, but Jack was bigger than Fred and had easily handed him his ass. Jack had been vulnerable as a child, but once he'd gotten big enough to scare off people, he hadn't been vulnerable again.

He wasn't sure what made him get out of bed that night. It would have been easier to ignore it and continue the way he always had. Even at fifteen he'd been sure of himself. He knew he didn't give a shit about anyone. It didn't pay to care because people always let him down. The only foster parents who'd been kind to him had either died, like the elderly lady who'd called him son and made him dinner each night, or had sadly explained they couldn't keep him anymore. There were more people, of course, but they had other reasons beyond simple kindness for letting him into their home. He could almost forgive the ones who had beaten the crap out of him. He'd been a difficult kid. He'd certainly heard it enough. He couldn't forgive the two who had gone further than that. So his fifteen-year-old self had decided to just never care about anyone. That way he never had to be disappointed, and he never had to share his shame.

He'd lain in bed, knowing damn well that the new kid was going to get the crap kicked out of him. It happened all the time. The kid should get used to it. It wasn't Jack's place in the world to protect anyone. He didn't let anyone in, and then no one could hurt him. That had been his mantra.

It hadn't held up.

As he heard Fred walking past him, he'd gotten out of bed and followed him. When he'd attempted to assault Sam, he stopped it. He'd beaten the shit out of Fred, and the next morning everyone deferred to him. Jack found he liked being in charge. It gave him a sense of control and he desperately needed it.

That morning, while he ate his breakfast in customary silence, Sam sat down in front of him.

"What should we do today?" Sam asked.

No one had ever asked him that. He and Sam rarely spent time apart since.

At first, Sam Fleetwood had clung to him like a life raft, and he couldn't shake the kid. Later, Jack acknowledged, he didn't want to get rid of Sam. Sam was the one who convinced him to give sex another try. The woman who lived across from the group home had paid the boys to mow her lawn, and when she invited both Jack and Sam to her bed, Sam had convinced Jack they should take her up on it. It was the first hint Jack had that, maybe, he wasn't as damaged as he thought he was. He still had fond memories of Ms. Jackson. She was kind to them both, patiently teaching them what pleased a woman.

Years later, after they'd started the ranch, he had anonymously paid off the mortgage on her small house. He was a man who believed in paying his debts.

Jack forced himself to take care of his horse. He slowed down and told himself to be patient. Abby and Sam were home and waiting for him. The Benz was in the drive. He would join them for dinner, and Abigail would talk about her day. He loved listening to her talk. She was bright and funny and could make the simplest events seem interesting.

Did that woman have any idea how under her spell he was?

"Jack!"

He put down the brush he was using and walked to the front of the barn. Sam was running across the yard from the big house, a panicked expression on his face.

Something had happened to Abigail. There was no other reason for the look on Sam's face. Anxiety crushed against his chest.

"What happened?" He had no idea what he would do if she was gone. Had someone hurt her?

"She's leaving." Sam was breathless. "I don't know what happened. We were fine, and then she was quiet for a long time, and when we got back to the house, she said she was leaving."

"She's leaving?" The words felt foreign to him. "She's not hurt. She's just leaving?"

Sam nodded, and there was a dullness in his eyes. He couldn't quite meet Jack's gaze. "She says she doesn't want to live like this. She says she'd be ashamed to tell her daughter she was with us."

It was in that moment that Jack realized once and forever that the damage done to him as a child hadn't broken him. What happened had been awful, but it hadn't robbed him of his soul or his reaction to Abigail leaving would have been different. In his heart, he wondered if love wasn't really a selfish thing. Somewhere deep down he'd told himself that if Sam left for some reason, he would cut the man out of his heart and move on. Even while falling for Abigail he had told himself the same thing. If she left, he would shrug and move on. He might hurt for a while, but he'd build his wall again, stronger than ever before.

He should be marching up to the house and showing her the door. He should be righteously pissed that she'd put that look of shame on Sam's face. If she wanted to go, he'd kick her ass out. She'd never really loved them in the first place.

That should have been his reaction. His heart should be hardening, but it just softened further when he realized his love was far from a selfish thing, and if she walked out, he'd miss her for the rest of his life.

Something had happened. Abigail loved him. She loved them both. He was as sure of it as he was his next breath. He knew her deep to her soul, and he knew she wouldn't leave without a reason.

She wasn't ashamed of them. She was afraid.

So he buried any anger or fear he had because one of them had to be reasonable. One of them had to be strong and unwavering. That's what it meant to be married. They hadn't signed the paperwork, but it was time for him to be a husband to her.

Jack placed his hand securely behind Sam's neck and gave it a comforting squeeze. "She's not going anywhere, Sam."

* * * *

Her hands wouldn't stop shaking. She couldn't walk away. It was too far and now that she thought about it, where exactly was she planning on going?

Sam hadn't been an idiot. He'd taken the damn keys with him, and she had no choice but to sit here and wait for Jack. If she thought lying to Sam was hard, she couldn't imagine having to do it to Jack.

But she had to. She had to lie and she had to make him believe. She had to make him hate her.

She wouldn't be the one who brought them down. She loved them too much to cause them the kind of trouble Ruby Echols intended. It seemed that loving Adam when she was just a kid was going to cost her everything again, and this time she wasn't sure she could put the pieces together. She would be able to move through her days, but there wouldn't be any joy to them. She would spend every minute thinking of two cowboys and how happy she would have been.

The back door opened, and her whole body tensed for the coming battle. This would be an awful scene. Jack was going to be furious. He would say horrible things, and she would say horrible things right back. She had to. She had to break this relationship in a way that rendered it irretrievable.

Jack would still have Sam. She would be the one who was alone.

"Abigail." Jack's deep voice was calm, soothing almost.

That deep voice of his would haunt her forever.

She took a long breath and turned to face him, her face schooled carefully into a polite mask. "I'm sorry Sam felt the need to bother you. Look, here's the deal. It's been fun, but I have an offer to work in Austin. It's exactly what I want."

Let him think work was more important than them. She waited for Jack's eyes to narrow. He would order her to stay, and she would tell him she couldn't stand his arrogant, overbearing ways another minute.

"Is this job that important to you?" Jack stared at her.

"Yes." She was pleased with the firmness of her voice. Inside, she was shaking. Sam stood beside Jack looking so heartbroken she wanted nothing more than to walk to him and wrap her arms around him. Jack looked…curious.

"All right then," Jack agreed.

She forced herself to nod. Deep inside, she wanted to wail. She hadn't expected that he would let her go without a fight. He was letting her walk out without so much as a good-bye, and she should be thrilled. She could leave without a scene. So why did she suddenly want to slap him? Had it meant that little to him? She couldn't believe it.

It was perverse. She was getting everything she wanted and it left her utterly hollow on the inside.

"Do you need to leave right away?" Jack asked.

"Yes." A cold feeling was settling in her gut. Maybe he'd offer her a quick lay for old time's sake. She knew it wasn't fair, but she was bitter about his lack of feeling.

"Sam, pack a bag. We'll take the Benz. Call ahead and get us a hotel suite. We'll go house hunting this weekend."

"What?" She felt her jaw drop.

Jack shrugged negligently. "If this is important to you, then we'll go."

"But the ranch…"

"Juan can handle it." There was nothing about the expression on Jack's face that told her he wasn't perfectly serious. "If Austin turns out to be the place you want to stay, then we'll work something out. I like working on a ranch. I won't lie to you. I love it here. But I love you more."

"So do I," Sam said quietly.

The world seemed to stop, going silent as their words sank into her soul. Of all the reactions she'd played through her mind before this confrontation, this wasn't one of them. They were willing to leave everything she was trying to save? She couldn't let them do it. "No."

Jack didn't look surprised by her quiet denial. "No. Why not?"

"I don't want you to go with me." She was struggling to maintain her composure. Jack wasn't reacting the way she thought he would, and it was throwing her off. She decided some very tough love was required. She was going to have to get nasty. "You're going to make this hard, aren't you?"

Jack smiled gently but made no move toward her. "I'm going to make it impossible, my love."

Her heart skipped at the sight of him, but she forced herself to roll her eyes, and her voice dripped with sarcasm. She laid it on thick. "God, Jack, I really thought you were different. It was what attracted me to you. I thought you would be a man I could have some fun with, who would know the score."

"I didn't know we were playing a game, sweetheart." His eyes were almost sympathetic.

Was he not listening to her? She scrambled.

"It's always a game." She used her worldliest tone. "It's been fun. I enjoyed the whole fantasy, two men thing, but it's not something I want to spend a life doing. I'm bored now. I want to move on. You couldn't seriously think I would want to live in this pissant town. I hate it here."

"Then we'll move," Jack said plainly.

Tears of frustration welled in her eyes. "You don't get it, you idiot. I am leaving. I don't love you. I don't want you. I stayed here to help my mother, and now I'm leaving. As soon as I can get her packed up, we'll both be out of here. You and Sam there were a nice diversion, but I'm not living this freaky life with you!"

"You're embarrassed?" Jack asked the question with an almost clinical detachment.

"Yes," she hissed, thankful he was finally following the conversation. He still didn't sound pissed, though. "I'm ashamed to be seen with you."

Jack looked back at Sam. Abby realized that Jack had been

closing in on her. He had been subtly moving closer and closer. "Did she hide her head in shame earlier today when you took her shopping?"

"Hell, no." Sam frowned. "She held my hand, and she kissed me in front of town hall. When some old lady called her a tramp, she patted my ass and agreed with her."

Jack chuckled. "Now that sounds like my Abigail." He looked pointedly at her. "This does not. Are you going to tell me what happened, baby?"

"I'm tired of people calling me a tramp," she tried.

Jack shook his head. He was standing so close to her, she had to look up at him. She could feel the heat coming off his big body. God, she would miss it. "Try again."

Abby pushed him away. "I don't want you."

She wasn't able to keep the tears out of her voice. Couldn't he take a hint? If he kept this up, she was going to break. She couldn't break now.

"But I want you." Her attempt at pushing him around had done nothing to keep him away. "Abby, I'm not a fool. I know Sam fucked up somehow."

"Hey," Sam protested.

Jack never took his eyes off Abby as he replied. "Did you leave her alone?"

Sam stopped. "Well, I had to help this old woman with her car."

"That's when they got to her." Jack looked at her as though waiting for confirmation.

"No." She shook her head. She was losing control of this conversation.

"Sweetheart," Jack said quietly. "Watch what you say. You've been lying to me, and you'll have to answer for it. Now listen to me and listen well. I love you. I don't know what that old biddy said, but she can't hurt me. Even if she could, you would hurt me more by walking out."

She sighed and the tears started to fall. Her hands shook with the force of her emotion. He didn't understand. Ruby had ruined more than one person because she hadn't liked them or felt they didn't fit her idea of proper. "She can hurt you. Please, Jack, I can't take it. Let me go."

"I will," he promised. "If you can walk out the door after you've listened to everything I have to say to you, then I'll let you go."

Abby nodded. She would listen and then she would go.

"I love you." Jack forced her to look him in the eyes. "That won't change because you tell me you don't love me. My love is not dependent on yours. It's just there, and I won't do anything to cut it out of my heart. It's what I've waited for all of my life, and if you walk out that door, I'll go to my grave loving you, missing you, praying that you'll come back to me. I will never love another woman the way I love you. I will always be there for you. If you leave, know that my door is open. I will always be waiting for you to walk back through it."

She couldn't help it. The tears flowed freely now. Every emotion she'd felt since walking back into this town surged up, a well that had been sprung.

"I can't hurt you this way," she sobbed. "She said she would ruin you. She has plans, Jack. She's going to cut off your access to feed from the feed store. She has friends on the city council. She plans to pressure them to rezone the area the feed store is on. It would force them out of business."

Jack looked slightly amused. "I assume if they dropped the ranch as a customer, the pressure would be off."

Abby nodded. He finally understood her. "That's not all. She plans to try to shut down your packaging plant. She's going to have city regulators all over you. She'll bring in inspectors."

Sam laughed. "Let them in. I assure you, we can handle a visit from some inspectors. As for the feed store, we're their biggest customer. Baby, you think this town still works the way it did twenty years ago. That old biddy can talk all she likes, but the city council is more interested in the jobs we provide than pleasing a nasty old lady. She's got money but she doesn't have a business anymore. She doesn't provide the community with anything but social authority, and that's only because no one else challenges her."

Jack sighed and pulled her into his arms. "You're the only one who can ruin me, Abigail. And you can only ruin me by walking away."

"She'll hurt you." She cried against his chest.

Jack pushed her back and shook her slightly. "Would you have wanted Ben to push you away when he found out he had cancer? Would you have wanted him to spare you the pain and heartache? Is that how you view a marriage? Is it something that should work only when no one has to sacrifice?"

"No." The world was a blurry mess, and only Jack seemed real to her. Where was Sam? Then he was there at her back, as though he could read her thoughts. He pressed himself comfortingly against her. She sighed and wrapped herself around Jack. "No, I wouldn't have wanted him to do that."

"This is our fight." Jack's hands tightened on her waist. "We stand together. We face it all together. You and me and Sam."

A deep sense of relief flooded her. She knew suddenly that Jack was right. They were more important than anything else. They could make it through. Abby cried and her men held her, whispering soothing things and stroking her gently. Gradually, she calmed and felt contentment push out fear.

"Sam, I believe Abigail could use a drink," Jack suggested after a long while. "She likes vodka. I think there's some cranberry juice in the fridge. I could use some Scotch."

Sam rushed to do his bidding, and she became aware that Jack was rigid with tension. She hesitantly looked up, and his jaw was tightly clenched. It didn't take much to figure out that he was angry, and Abby didn't fool herself about what had gotten him to that state.

"I'm sorry." It wasn't enough. The words weren't going to be enough.

She'd lied to him. She had the best reasons for it, but she had lied, and he wouldn't take it well. She had forced him into a position where he was afraid and worried. He had given her two rules—submission in the bedroom, and she wasn't to try to face anything alone. She'd broken the more important of the two rules.

Jack took a step back and sat down in the big arm chair that dominated the living room. Sam rushed back in and pressed the Scotch into his hand. Jack took a long drink. She could tell he was trying to get his temper under control before he dealt with her.

"Fix him," Sam said under his breath as he handed Abby her glass.

She put it down without a single sip. If she'd broken one rule, she should really follow the other one. Without another thought, she tossed off her clothes. She noticed Jack watching her through hooded eyes. She pushed her jeans and panties off, and when she was naked, she walked to Jack and fell to her knees beside his chair. She sat with her head submissively down, waiting for him. She would stay there all night if that's what it took.

Less than a minute after she'd assumed the position, Jack's hand was curling in her hair, pulling her head into his lap. She wrapped her arms lovingly around his leg and sighed as he stroked her hair. He calmly began talking to Sam.

They spoke of completely innocuous things. Jack talked about the work on the fence and cows that were close to calving. Sam seemed to know what Jack needed, and he stayed away from anything that might remind him of what she'd put him through. Abby sat quietly, letting Jack stroke her, hoping it brought him some peace. After a long while, Benita walked in and announced that it was time for dinner. If she was shocked at Abigail's state of undress, the housekeeper didn't show it. She announced that roast chicken, potatoes au gratin, and sautéed green beans would be served.

Jack stood up and reached down to help Abby to her feet. She wanted to throw her clothes on but sensed this was a turning point. She was either in or she was out. Jack might have been willing to slowly introduce her to the lifestyle he wanted, but she had pushed him. He had shoved every bit of his pride aside to keep them together, and now she could shove aside something as ridiculous and useless as shame.

Without a word of protest, she took his hand and allowed him to lead her into the dining room. He sat her in the chair next to him and they shared a quiet meal. Jack seemed to relax when he realized she was accepting the situation. After dessert was served, Jack politely dismissed the housekeeper, thanking her for her work. When the door closed behind her, Jack held his hand out and gestured for her to come to his lap. She sat and put her arms around his neck. She leaned in and pressed a kiss to the hard line of his jaw.

"You realize all this sweet submission is not going to save you," Jack said, speaking to her for the first time in an hour.

"I don't want to be saved from you." Abby knew that she was going to get the spanking of a lifetime, and she wasn't afraid of it. Jack would need it after what he'd been through.

Jack's green eyes were filled with challenge. "You'll allow Sam to tie you down?"

"Yes," she replied.

"You'll accept my discipline?"

"Yes, Jack." She gnawed a little at her bottom lip. "Though, if it's going to be as bad as I suspect, I might need a gag to stay quiet."

Jack nodded. "When we enter that room, you will speak when spoken to. You will do exactly as I say. I am the Master in that room, do you understand?"

She nodded and didn't even try to hide the fact that she was already getting wet.

Jack looked at his partner. "Sam, I realize that up to this point I've been willing to share power."

Sam's eyes turned wary and he frowned. "I understand. You want her to yourself tonight. I can handle that."

Jack sighed. "Neither one of you lets me get a complete thought out. I wasn't throwing you out, Samuel. I was changing the rules on you. When we've used the playroom before, we shared power over our lover. I was willing to do that because, quite frankly, I didn't care enough about those women to take full responsibility for them. Now, I am willing to take that responsibility for both of you."

Sam's entire body tensed, and she sensed Sam's expectation. "What do you mean?"

Jack's smile was slow and sensual. "I mean I know what you need, Sam. Hell, you're even more submissive than Abigail is. You want discipline. I'm now willing to give it to you. I don't know how far I'll go or what I'll be comfortable with, but I'm willing to explore it."

Sam looked almost shy. "It doesn't have to change. I'm not asking anything of you."

"I know. Somehow, with Abigail here, it all seems a bit more possible, if you understand." Jack left his reflective mood, and she

187

knew he was ready to move on. "The rules apply to you too, Sam. I am Master in that room. You will obey me. You will not question me or refuse me. If I request something of you that you are not willing to give me, your safe word is 'red.' You will say your safe word and everything stops. Is that understood?"

Sam smiled slowly. "Yes, Jack."

"Excellent." Jack kissed her on the cheek. "You can start by taking her and preparing her. I want her bathed, bound, and ready for my pleasure."

Sam eagerly got up, and in a second, she was in his arms.

Jack looked at the clock. "You have half an hour. And, Samuel, she is not allowed to come, do you understand?"

"Yes," Sam replied. "You don't want me to play with her or anything."

Jack laughed. "I didn't say that. Play with her all you like. Get her soaking wet. But don't let her come."

"I think I can handle that." Sam looked down at Abby with anticipation.

Suddenly, she realized a spanking would probably be the least of her torture.

Chapter Fifteen

It didn't take Abby long to realize Jack wasn't the only one she'd hurt. Sam was distant. He'd been like this since they'd left the dining room. He'd smiled at Jack, but the minute they were away from him, Sam had turned into a robot. He had mechanically washed her in the shower and brushed out her hair after drying her off. He'd said not more than one or two words to her, and those had been orders.

Sam had taken her into the playroom from the master bath. She thought the door went to a closet, but had been surprised when Sam opened it and turned on the lights. Two of the walls were lined with floor to ceiling mirrors. There was what looked like an examination table from a doctor's office, complete with stirrups, and several places in the walls and the ceiling where a submissive could be bound.

Her first thought on entering the playroom was that it was remarkably clean and cozy for a dungeon. She couldn't hold in her second thought. "What the hell is that?"

"It's a whipping bench." Sam touched the device lightly. "Your chest goes here."

There was a padded board in the middle that formed the center of the bench. It looked like it would run from her head to just above her pelvis. It was tilted slightly at a downward angle so her head would be lower than her ass. She was sure it put her in the perfect position to receive Jack's discipline. It didn't take Sam to tell her that the four smaller padded boards were for her arms and legs. These boards were equipped with restraints that Sam would use to bind her down. She would be completely vulnerable.

Sam started to smile, showing his even white teeth, but quickly shut it down. He indicated a flat, padded bench close to a sink. It was covered with a crisp white sheet. "Go lie down, face first."

"Sam." She let the ache in her heart bleed through to her voice. "Sam, please."

His face was harsh as he turned back. "Am I not even worth obeying?"

She gasped, and her arms went around Sam's naked chest. "How can you say that?"

He stood rigid in her embrace, and she wondered how she was going to reach him. "I can say that because you're not on the table."

Reluctantly, she let him go and walked to the table. She lay down on the warmed sheet that covered the comfortable massage table and placed her head in the padded slot designed to let her breathe. She was quiet and entirely subdued as Sam poured warm oil onto her skin and began to rub his hands down her back. He started at the base of her neck and ran his thumbs on either side of her spine.

She didn't resist him in any way, but she took no pleasure from the ministrations, either. All she felt was a crushing guilt. She had screwed everything up. She thought she was doing the right thing. Protecting them had been all she could think about.

"Relax." Impatience bled into Sam's tone.

"I'm trying." It was impossible when she couldn't figure out how to heal the breach between the two of them. She was willing to do almost anything.

Suddenly, it seemed like too much. Despite her success in forcing people to let her into their stores, she knew it would be a fight to make a place for herself here. And now, with Sam angry and unwilling to speak to her, she had doubts as to putting herself between Sam and his best friend. They had been together for so much longer. It wasn't fair for her to come between them. She had been the catalyst for Jack changing the rules, and Sam was obviously not okay with that.

"You're crying." It sounded like an accusation to her ears.

"No, I'm not." As she said it, she couldn't stop a sniffle.

"Damn it, Abigail. I feel your tears hitting my feet," Sam complained.

"I'll stop."

Sam sighed, and he knelt down. His face was suddenly in view, his head at an awkward angle as he looked up at her. "Why are you crying?"

"You're mad at me, and I don't know how to make it up to you." She pushed against the table, forcing herself up. "I got you in trouble with Jack."

Sam got to his feet again. "I got me in trouble with Jack. I left you alone. He gave me explicit instructions, and I didn't follow them. I'm upset with myself."

"I'm not…" She quickly closed her mouth when she realized what she was about to say.

"If I were Jack, you would be over my knee right now." His entire body was tense.

"I'm sorry." She was pretty sure she had said those words about a hundred times today. It had been her day for fucking things up. She reached out and ran her hands along the cut plane of his chest. "I'm not used to anyone caring about me the way the two of you do. I'm used to being the one to bear the burden. It's my fault, too, you know."

"How do you figure?"

"I knew Jack didn't want me to be alone," she admitted. "I could have, should have followed you. I walked into that café. The minute I saw Ruby Echols sitting there with her cronies, I should have marched back out and stayed with you. I can't win with her. It doesn't even pay to try."

A slow smile started to cross his face. "Put like that, it does seem more like your fault than mine."

"Sam," she said, trying to pull him close. "I love you. I really

191

do, but if I'm coming between you and Jack, then I should go. I don't want to break the two of you up."

Sam's blue eyes went wide. "I was thinking the same damn thing except that I should leave."

"What do you mean?"

He glanced down for a moment, and when he finally met her eyes, he looked bleak. "I want a true threesome."

He stood there, seemingly waiting for her shock and dismay.

The truth hit her with the force of a two by four. It didn't bother her. It made sense when she thought about it. "You want Jack."

He nodded slowly, as though admitting it made it real and something they had to deal with. "I want Jack, and I want you. I know what that makes me, but I can't help what I want. It's just gotten stronger since we met you. I want the three of us together in all ways. Jack loves you like he's never loved anyone else. I'm going to freak him out and upset you. Maybe it would be better if I left and let you and Jack have a normal marriage."

"I don't want a normal marriage." She spread her legs, completely heedless of her nudity as she pulled Sam in and wouldn't take no for an answer. She wrapped her legs around his waist and her arms around his chest. "I want you and me and Jack."

He finally gave up part of the fight. He relaxed in her arms. "Baby, think about it for a minute. I want to make love with Jack. Real-live gay sex."

Yep, she searched her mind and heart and not a single word of that upset her at all. It felt right, as though there had been a tiny piece of them that was slightly out of place and now they were perfect. "Do I get to watch?"

"Abby?"

She shrugged and snuggled closer to him. He was hard, and she almost had him where she wanted him. "It's not gay if a girl watches."

All her worry had flown away now that she understood the problem. It wasn't a problem at all in her mind. It was more like wish fulfillment.

"I think most of the planet would disagree with you," he said ruefully, but she noted he was pressing himself against her now.

Abby tried to keep her breathing under control. She wiggled, and the head of his dick hit her clit. Just a bit more. A couple more strokes and she would be in a good place. "Who cares what the rest of the planet thinks? We're involved in a committed ménage à trois where, apparently, two of us are sexually submissive to the dominant male. Oh, and I spent most of the day walking around with a plug stuck up my ass. What's a little gay sex? It's practically the most normal thing we'll do."

Sam's smile was completely awestruck. "You're actually fine with this?"

She nodded quickly, wanting to soothe his fears so she could get back to her subversive plan to come before Jack got here. "As long as I get to watch."

He beamed down at her. "You are one righteous pervert, Abigail-almost-Barnes."

"I'm fine with that." There was no shame to be had. She was doing terribly dirty things with men she loved and trusted and was willing to commit herself to. She didn't see anything wrong with it. Now all she had to do was get him to stroke her one more time with that hard cock of his…

He took a forceful step back. "You're also going to get me in a shitload of trouble. I know what you're trying to do. Jack said no orgasm for you."

"But, Sam!" She had been so close.

"No," he said firmly. "And now you spent all your massage time trying to tempt me into disobeying Jack. Not happening, baby. We have exactly five minutes to get you ready. Go lay down on the bench."

She pouted but got down. It was obvious he was beyond temptation now, but at least the haunted look was off his face. She went on her tiptoes and lightly kissed his full lips. "I love you, Sam."

"I love the hell out of you, Abigail," he replied with a ready smile. "As for the rest of it, we'll see. I don't know how Jack will handle it. I don't know if that's what he wants."

"I'll handle Jack." She was looking forward to it. "We just have to take it slow."

She walked over to the whipping bench and settled herself down. The bench narrowed a bit in the middle. She discovered her breasts hung over either side and her pussy was left on the edge of the bench.

"Damn, you look so fucking hot, baby." Sam worked the leather straps over her wrists. He made sure they were tight but comfortable. He moved to her ankles, and before long, she was bound completely. It should have made her feel frightened, but instead all she felt was a hum in her pussy as she anticipated what Jack was going to do to her.

Sam stood up and ran his hand down her spine. When he got to her ass, he parted her cheeks, and she felt the cold spurt of lubricant. She sighed but made no protest. She had just gotten the plug out. Suddenly, she felt something warmer than the hard plastic of the plug. His fingers played with her anus, gently probing. He pushed against the resistance, shoving his thumb in to the first knuckle and rimming her.

She gasped at the prickles of sensation she felt all along her spine. It wasn't exactly pain, but the fine, hard edge of it was there.

"Your ass is so pretty." Sam continued to work his finger into her. "I can't wait to fuck it."

"Neither can I," a deep voice said.

She turned her head as much as the bench would allow and saw Jack standing in the doorway. He was still in his jeans, but his shirt and shoes were gone. His hair was wet from a shower, and he looked at them with deep approval in his emerald eyes. His body was tall and lean from years and years of hard physical labor, and his shoulders broad and muscular. She sighed at how beautifully masculine that body was.

"This is what every man wants, isn't it? He wants to walk in and find his best friend finger-deep in his fiancée's ass." There was a smile in his voice.

Rather than pulling out, Sam shoved his thumb in farther and rotated it. Abby groaned, not sure whether it was pain or pleasure. "She's going to be so tight."

"Yes, she is," Jack said. There was a wealth of satisfaction in his tone. He watched them for a moment. He seemed to silently enjoy the scene as Sam worked her ass, gently stretching her. Finally, he spoke again. "Has she been a good girl?"

"Nope." Sam pulled his thumb out. She felt him step away and heard the sink in the background running. "She tried her damnedest to rub herself to orgasm against me. She was like a cat in heat."

"And did she succeed?" Jack's voice was a silky threat.

"No. She only managed to work herself up."

Jack walked up behind her, admiring Sam's handiwork. Abby discovered that she could easily watch him through the mirror to her left. She was small and vulnerable, spread and bound for him. She found the picture they made extremely arousing. Jack shoved two fingers roughly up her pussy. He slid them back and forth in the warm wetness he found there.

"Nice," he said approvingly before pulling out. He didn't touch her clitoris at all. She moaned in frustration and felt a sharp slap to her ass. "I said no noise, Abigail." Jack walked around to her head and gracefully knelt beside her. His face was very serious as he looked at her. "I've decided against the gag. I want you to be able to respond when I require it. Give me your word you'll do your best to stay quiet and still while I discipline you."

"Yes." She studied the hard, beautiful planes of his face. His pitch-black hair was wavy and just long enough to start to curl. She knew he would cut it soon, but she intended to talk him out of it.

Jack's eyes widened in expectation. "Yes, what?"

"Yes, Sir." The rules seemed to be different in this room.

She breathed out as she saw a flash of anger cross Jack's face. "My name is Jack. Sir is something you call a Dom who hasn't bothered to give you his name. I am not Sir, nor am I Master. I am Jack, and I am the only Dom you'll ever get, sweetheart, so I expect you to use my name."

"Yes, Jack," she said sweetly to placate him

"I don't scare you at all, do I?"

"I love you," she said.

He leaned over and kissed her cheek before standing back up. "Remember that," he warned her. "Give me the crop, please. The narrow tip, I think, for this first time, and while you're there, Sam, you can get the leather whip as well."

She heard the closet door open.

"Do you think she can handle the whip?" Sam didn't sound like he thought she could.

"No." Jack's voice was steady. "Her skin is delicate and sensitive. I have no intention of raising welts. I want her bottom hot and pink. That's all. The whip I intend to use on you. And that's an extra stroke for questioning me."

There was a short pause, and she really wished she could see the look on Sam's face. "All right."

The closet door shut.

"You can walk out at any time," Jack offered. "I won't hold it against you, and I won't shut you out the next time we decide to play with our wife."

"I'm not leaving." It sounded like it was the farthest thing from Sam's mind.

She sighed as Jack's hands stroked her bare ass. "You are so gorgeous like this, sweetheart. You tempt me very much to forget this punishment and move on to the part of the evening when I sink my cock into you." His hand found her pussy. "Unfortunately, I cannot allow what happened today to pass."

She gasped as the crop smacked her ass. Tears blurred her vision as the pain struck her with a ferocious heat. Jack wasn't playing this time. She sank her nails in the leather-covered restraints. The crop came down again, and she swallowed the pain.

"You don't love me?" Jack threw her lies back at her. "Was that a lie, Abigail?"

"Yes, Jack." She bit her lip to keep from crying out.

Smack. She breathed through the haze of pain. Her entire backside was on fire. She caught sight of Jack in the mirror. His face was grim as he pulled the crop back again.

"You don't want me anymore?"

Smack.

"You don't want to live this freaky life?"

Smack.

Of all the things she'd said to him, that had been the one calculated to hit him where he was vulnerable.

"I do," she said shakily. "I want it so badly."

Jack thrust his fingers back into her pussy, and the pain turned into sharp pleasure.

"Your pussy sure says you do, darlin'." His thumb slid over and around, and she started to build rapidly toward a stunning peak. It was so close. He pulled out, and she stopped herself from begging him not to. She wanted him, needed him. "Your pussy doesn't lie to me. Too bad your mouth doesn't have the same sense."

Thwack.

He was alternating cheeks, never hitting the same spot twice. Each time he struck, the pain bloomed, and then Jack gave it a moment for the sensation to radiate into heat and something resembling pleasure.

"Are you ashamed of what we do?" The question was flat and calm.

She knew a wealth of fear lay behind his calm facade. She wished she could take away the doubt she'd placed in his heart.

She laughed through the pain. If there was one thing she knew, it was that she wasn't ashamed of them. "No, I am not. I love what we do."

Jack put the crop down, and his hand slapped between her legs. He smacked her pussy hard, and she screamed at the sensation. It was wicked pain and insane pleasure bound together. He smacked her sore ass again with his hand, but this was different. It was just a tap, followed by Jack rubbing her gently. Now that he was done, she felt sore but strangely peaceful. She felt his worshipful kiss on the small of her back.

Jack got back down to look at her. She could see the love shining in his eyes. "Abigail, this is the way things are going to be. You will live with us here. You will marry me legally and take my name. You will consider yourself also married to Sam, and you'll honor your vows to us. You won't lie to either of us again. You won't ever attempt to walk out again, not for any reason. You will give yourself to us, body and soul. Is that clear?"

"Yes, Jack, I promise," she agreed with a contented sigh. She felt like she was floating.

"I love you." He kissed her tenderly and then got to his feet again. "I will always take care of you. Everything you promised me,

I promise you, baby. You won't regret it."

"I know."

She wouldn't. He'd promised, and Jack kept his promises.

* * * *

"Your turn, Sam," Jack intoned darkly.

Sam nodded, the only thing he could think to do. This was new. Totally new, and he wasn't sure how he was supposed to react. Was he supposed to pretend to be scared or like this whole thing was distasteful? Because he wasn't sure he could do that.

He was naked so he couldn't hide his reaction. His cock was standing straight up. Jack had the leather whip in his hands and a small smile on his face.

At least he wasn't frowning. He could handle Jack making fun of him, but not looking at him like Sam had disappointed him.

"Do you want me to let Abby up?" He tried to figure out where he should go. Was he supposed to get on the spanking bench now? This was a turning point and he didn't want to screw it up. All of his adult life, he'd wanted to try this. He'd certainly had offers, but the truth was he'd only ever wanted one Dom in his life.

He stood behind Abby, fascinated with the pink skin of her ass. It was beautiful and he wanted to touch it, but he held back. Jack hadn't given him permission.

"No." Jack motioned for him to stay where he was. "I think she's in the perfect position for you. You'll need something to hold on to."

Sam felt his heart start to race, and lust was pounding through his system as he looked between Jack and their gorgeous, generous bride-to-be.

"Seriously, Jack? I thought this was punishment."

"It will be," he promised. "But what you did was dumb. What Abigail did was cruel and counter to everything it means to be married. She also took her punishment with incredible grace, so I find myself in a more forgiving mood when it comes to you. Assume the position now."

He moved forward, placing himself squarely between Abby's

bound and spread legs. So good. She felt so good as he pressed his cock deep into her soaking wet pussy. A deep groan stuck in his throat as he sank into her inviting warmth. He was gentle with her pinkened backside as he tunneled in, but there was no question the signs of Jack's discipline made him hard as hell. He worked his way in to his balls and held himself against her. Abby's sweet pussy clenched around him, but she was quiet. He looked at her in the mirror and could see the effort she was going through to follow Jack's instructions.

"Hold still, Sam," Jack ordered. "Let the whip direct you. Don't move on your own until I give you leave, understood?"

"Yes." Sam's voice sounded deep and a bit foreign to him.

The picture of the three of them in the mirror was one of the most erotic things he'd ever seen. He couldn't stop looking at it. Abby, beautiful Abigail, bent over accepting him and Jack…Jack was everything to Sam. He had waited so long to have this, to be in the middle.

The first lash stung and shoved him forward. He hissed instinctively at the delicate pain. Abby whimpered as her pussy tried to suck at Sam's cock to keep him there, but the motion of the whip pushed him forward and then allowed him to pull out.

"I have been indulgent," Jack was saying as he applied the lash.

Sam's hands tightened on Abby's waist as he drove in again, caught deliciously between her hot cunt and the lick of the whip. He let his head fall back, giving himself over to the mindless sensation.

"It occurs to me that if this marriage between the three of us is going to work, I have to curb some of your more impetuous tendencies." Jack cracked the whip again. "When I am not around, you're responsible for her."

"Yes, Jack." He tried to focus on anything but the pounding need to come. Abby's pussy felt like a hot furnace, and it was taking everything he had not to pour himself into her. The lash hit again and Sam groaned, allowing it to push him deeply into her channel. Sam pushed slightly against Abby's hips and pulled his cock almost all the way out, waiting for the next strike.

"You're responsible for her happiness and her safety," Jack continued. "If I am not around, I expect you to see to her needs before your own. You left her alone today, despite my instructions."

"Yes." He'd fucked up. It had weighed him down all night. Now, though, the guilt was leaving him. It seemed to float away as he was driven back into Abby's body. There wasn't room for guilt anymore. There was just sensation and passion and sweet emotion.

"You will follow my instructions to the letter from this day forward or you'll find yourself right back here," Jack promised.

Sam wasn't so sure here wasn't his favorite place in the world, but he didn't like the idea of letting Jack and Abby down. He did like the idea that he was responsible for her happiness. It made him feel worthy and that he had a place in the world. He wouldn't do anything to betray the trust these two precious people had given him.

"I promise. I promise both of you."

Jack took a step back and sighed. "Go on then, Sam."

He couldn't contain his lust any longer, and he pounded forward as Jack walked around to the front of the bench and roughly shoved his jeans down his body and onto the floor. Sam realized quickly that Jack might have been calm, but he was anything but unaffected. His cock was huge and hard as he stroked it and got it into position. Sam fucked Abby's pussy as Jack's cock found her mouth.

"Open," Jack commanded. Abby's lips parted, and Jack's cock began to disappear. "Let me use your mouth, sweetheart. You relax. This won't take long."

The thought of Jack throat-fucking their gorgeous wife made Sam crazy. He pounded into her. Jack held her head in his hands and worked his cock in and out in perfect time to Sam's thrusts.

"Breathe through your nose." Jack's voice was low and guttural. "I'm almost there. You feel so fucking good. Swallow me, Abigail. Swallow everything I give you. Don't you lose a drop of me."

Sam thrust in to his balls as Jack's head dropped back. Jack groaned, and he held her still for his orgasm. His big, strong body shook from the force of his seed jetting from it. The sight triggered Sam's orgasm, and his release shot from his balls like a rocket deep into Abby's warm, willing pussy. Every muscle he had relaxed as the orgasm left him languid and sated and blissful. He was completely satisfied until he heard a soft cry from Abigail.

Jack got to his knees, tearing at the restraints holding her arms down. He looked up at Sam.

"Get her out of this, now," Jack ordered, his voice hoarse.

He immediately got down and quickly worked the straps that held her ankles. She was free in seconds, and Jack was hauling her up. Sam was terrified because Abby had tears running down her face.

"Baby, you can cry." Jack's face was grim as he pushed back her hair and held her gently.

Abby, given permission to let go, sobbed against him, holding on to him like he was a lifeline.

Jack looked completely helpless for once. "Where does it hurt?"

She shook her head.

"Abby, please," Sam begged. Had he been too rough with her? "You have to tell us where it hurts so we can fix it."

Abby looked up at him, tears pooling in those big hazel eyes. He felt his heart seize at the thought that they had really hurt her.

"Too much," she managed to hiccup out between sobs. "Too much everything."

Jack got up, his body not straining at all under her weight. He moved swiftly to the massage table and laid her down. "Sam, get the salve and warm water. Abby, I'll run a hot bath for you. I'll take care of you."

"I know," she cried. "I'm so sorry I tried to leave. I love you so much. I never loved anyone…"

Sam handed Jack the items he'd requested. He breathed a small sigh of relief when he realized the problem had nothing to do with physical pain and everything to do with the overwhelming emotion between the three of them.

He leaned over, and his hands tangled in her hair as he held her close. "I love you, Abby. We'll take care of everything. Don't worry about the town or the Echols family or anything else. We'll take care of it."

He kissed her and stood back. She relaxed back against the plush massage table. Jack used the warm washcloth to tenderly wash between her legs.

She sniffed as she looked up at them. "Are you going to take care of me?"

There was a certain pleading heat in her voice that made Sam smile. "I don't think she's talking about a bath, Jack."

Abby wanted to come. Sam wasn't so sure her punishment was over yet.

Jack smiled down at Abby. "Just what do you need me to take care of? You did a good job, Abigail. You made up for what you did. I'm feeling indulgent. What would make you happy?"

Sam was ready to make her happy. A few orgasms should do it. He prepared himself to give it all to her.

"Kiss Sam," Abby requested, quietly looking between the two of them.

Jack's emerald eyes flared in surprise.

Whoa. He took a step back. This wasn't what he expected. He'd talked to her because he had to talk to someone. He'd never expected her to push it this way. Nope. There was no way Jack was going to do this. A fine tremble started in his hands.

What would it be like? What would it feel like to submit to Jack sexually?

"You want me to kiss Sam?" Jack's lips had quirked up slightly.

He didn't sound like a man who intended to say no. He seemed more amused than offended. Okay. Way more amused and not offended in any way. Sam swallowed.

Abby sat up. If her bottom was sore, it didn't seem to bother her. She looked between the two men and sighed, a dreamy look coming over her face. "I do. I want you to kiss Sam, and I want to watch."

Jack looked from Abby to Sam. He winked at Sam. Sam felt something deep inside him ease. Jack wasn't going to reject him.

"Will that get you hot, baby?" Jack asked.

"Yes, Jack," she replied with a happy sigh.

He looked over at Sam, serious all of the sudden. "I won't do this without your permission."

Damn it. The man couldn't just take him. Of fucking course not. "I mean, if Abby thinks it would be cool, I don't have a problem with it. I...I'm good with kissing. Girls do it all the time."

"Is that what you're going with? All right. We'll start there then." Jack shook his head with a rueful laugh. "Come here, Sam."

His cock twitched. He couldn't help it. He was sure Jack noticed it, too, but was politely refraining from commenting. Sam fought for each breath as he put one foot in front of the other. He had to think about it, otherwise he might have tripped. Awkward. He was so awkward, but there was no way he was backing down.

He was slightly shorter than Jack. This close, he had to tip his head up a little. Jack radiated authority. It practically pulsed over his skin. Jack brought his hands up to cup Sam's face and pulled him in.

Their lips met roughly. There was nothing at all feminine about the kiss. Jack was rough and masterful. It was so different than kissing a woman. There was nothing gentle about it, and that spoke to him, too. Jack's tongue plunged in, invading and conquering. Sam fought back. His tongue met Jack's in a rousing duel.

This was what sex would be like with Jack. It would be a fight to get Sam to submit on every level. He didn't think it was a fight he could win, and he wasn't sure he wanted to. Sam let his hand touch Jack's perfectly cut chest. He had never wanted a man before, but he'd always longed for Jack. He was breathless by the time Jack pulled away.

Sam noticed Abby had enjoyed the show. Her fingers were slipping in and out of her pussy.

Jack's hand shot out and slapped her hand away.

"Not on your life, sweetheart," Jack growled. "You got your wish. The rest of the night is for me and Sam. Take her to the bed."

Sam picked her up easily.

"Thank you, baby," he whispered as he carried her out of the playroom and through the master bath. She had made that moment with Jack possible.

He tossed her gently on the big, soft bed and looked forward to the rest of the night.

Chapter Sixteen

Abby shrieked when Sam threw her on the bed. He was on top of her before she'd settled onto the comforter. He had completely recovered from his first orgasm of the night and, if his dick was any indication, was ready for more.

It was perfect because she was totally ready for more.

She let her hands weave into his hair as he covered her mouth with his. Sam was voracious, and she knew that finally kissing Jack had the intended effect on his libido. He covered her body with his and forced her legs open to make a place for himself at her core. She responded to him by wrapping herself around his waist and pushing up, seeking relief from the seemingly endless stimulation.

"Are you too sore?" Sam asked when he came up for air. He tried to pull his weight off her.

"No." Abby dug her nails into the flesh of his back to keep him right where he was. "I'm fine. I'm just a little sore. It doesn't hurt."

It didn't really. She hurt a lot less than she would have imagined. What hurt was the ache in her pussy.

His tongue delved deep again, and he stopped trying to spare her his weight. She was pinned under him, and it felt wonderful.

"It was good," Sam groaned. "So good. I always knew it would be. I always knew I would like the discipline. Watching him do that over the years, especially when we were at The Club...I always wanted it but I was afraid to ask. Thank you."

Before she could grind herself against his pelvis, Sam was working his way down. He kissed her face, licked her ears, and nuzzled her neck before he got to his destination.

"Hello, you gorgeous tits." He hummed happily, letting his tongue seek the tip of one breast. He tongued the erect nipple before sucking it deeply into his mouth.

She felt the tug in her womb. She let her head fall back because there was no tempting him away now. Once he had some pink part in his mouth, Sam was like a dog with a bone. He sucked and played with her nipples, his hand molding the one he wasn't sucking. His thumb flicked across the tip, making sure the nub stayed hard and at perfect attention.

"Move over," Jack said to Sam.

She felt the bed dip under Jack's weight. When she looked down, Jack's ebony hair joined Sam's gold as each lavished affection on her breasts. Abby felt her back arch when Jack took her nipple between his teeth and gently bit down.

"Please," she begged.

"Please what, sweetheart?" Jack raised his head to look at her.

She was restless underneath him, her body twitching and rolling. He was being so stubborn. She was sure he knew what she needed, but he wanted the words.

"Please fuck me." The ache in her pussy was too much to bear.

Jack kissed her nipple one last time and then got to his knees. "Since you asked so sweetly..."

Jack's hands were suddenly on her waist, and he pulled her over until she was on top of him. His back hit the mattress. "Straddle me."

She hurried to obey. She spread her legs and reached down to guide Jack's big, hard cock to her opening. Even as wet as she was, she had to work her way onto him. She bobbed up and down, gaining ground as Jack's hips flexed up and his eyes watched her breasts bounce. Sam moved himself behind her, in between Jack's splayed legs. His hand worked around and ran the length of her torso from her breasts to the wet, silky *V* of her thighs.

"Oh, please." She flushed as Sam's fingers brushed her clit. So close. She didn't know if she could survive it if they denied her again.

"Give it to her," Jack ordered as he thrust forcefully up, using his hands to pull her hips down. He filled her fully, and she moaned at the exquisite sensation. Her head fell back onto Sam's shoulder as Sam's finger found the throbbing pearl of her clit. She went flying blissfully over the edge.

The orgasm bloomed through her body, leaving her shaking as she collapsed forward onto Jack's waiting chest. Even as she shivered with aftershocks, she could feel Jack's fullness as he pressed up into her, holding himself still. She was surprised when Sam held the cheeks of her ass apart and started to work a warm, slippery substance into her anus.

"Shh, sweetheart," Jack cajoled, pulling her head back down to rest against his chest. "He's getting you ready. Just relax. When he tells you to, push back."

She gasped as Sam slid his thumb past the ring of muscles surrounding her anus. He gently worked the lube into her super-tight passage.

"She's so small, Jack." There was no way to mistake the anticipation in Sam's voice.

"Then you have to be careful with her," Jack replied.

She felt Sam withdraw, but then something much, much larger than his finger or any of the plugs they had used before was there. The broad head of Sam's dick was pushing forward, seeking entrance.

She whimpered slightly as Sam tried to work his cock in.

"It's going to be fine," Jack promised. She could see the strain on his face. He was holding back, waiting for Sam.

"She's so fucking tight," Sam gritted out. "Push back against me, baby."

She didn't think that was such a great idea, but she tried it anyway. Sam was thrusting in short bursts, taking territory and retreating, only to thrust and gain another inch.

"It burns." She wasn't sure she liked the sensation.

"It'll get better," Jack assured her. His green eyes were dark as Abby looked deeply into them. "I can feel him."

"Can you?" She forgot about the pressure for a moment. Jack looked so pleased.

"Oh, yeah, baby. There's nothing to separate us but this tiny bit of skin. I feel his cock sliding against mine. When he thrusts in, his balls rub against mine. I love this, Abby."

Sam hissed, and she groaned in reply.

"I'm in," Sam announced as he finally slid home. "Oh, she's so fucking hot. She feels so good."

"Are you all right, Abby?" Jack asked. His face was taut with self-control.

She nodded. She'd never felt so full. It was shocking and was tinged with an edge of pain. The burn was still there, but so was a full chorus of nerve endings she never knew she had. Those nerves were singing now, begging her to go further.

"Can I fuck this sweet ass, please?" Sam begged, his hands restlessly moving across her torso. "I'm going to die if I don't move soon."

Jack thrust up into her experimentally, and she felt Sam's cock move in her ass. She shuddered at the feeling of the two men filling her up.

"She's ready," Jack said as he pulled back.

Sam pressed forward, and she gave over. When Jack pushed, Sam pulled. When Sam attacked, Jack retreated. There wasn't a single moment her body wasn't invaded and plundered deliciously. Abby cried out as Sam hit some place deep inside she hadn't known existed. Jack groaned and his hips pistoned up, fighting for his place. Sam grunted behind her, pulling his big cock almost all the way out of her ass only to tunnel his way back in. Abby rode the wave of jittery pleasure that threatened to overwhelm her.

Never had she felt so wanted and loved. Caught in between the two men she loved more than life, she gave herself completely to the experience. When Jack's hand reached between them and gently pinched down on her clitoris, Abby worried she might pass out. She bucked and screamed as everything inside her clenched and then released in a great rush of pleasure.

"Fuck," Sam cried out. His hands tightened on her hips.

Abby felt him come deep in her ass.

Sam's orgasm seemed to trigger Jack's. She watched in wonder as his gorgeous face contorted, and he moaned when his semen flooded her womb.

Sam fell on top of her, forcing her farther into Jack's arms. Abby found herself in between two adoring men. Jack's hands soothingly rubbed up and down her sides as Sam pressed his mouth into the nape of her neck.

"Never again, Abby," Sam said quietly. "Don't ever think about leaving again. I can't stand it."

She managed to shake her head against Jack's firm chest.

"She's ours," Jack vowed. "She won't leave. She belongs to us now."

She would have argued if she'd had any strength left. She would have argued with the now part. She had always belonged to them. It had just taken her a while to find them.

* * * *

An hour later, Jack rubbed his hands along Abigail's recently bathed skin. Delicious. The word rolled around in his head. She smelled delicious, looked delicious. He could eat her up and never, ever get full.

She lay face down on the massage table, her still slightly pink cheeks beautiful to his eyes. Every curve and valley of her body called to him.

"Does that feel good?" This was their quiet time, the time when he could thank her for all she did for him, when he could worship her like the goddess she was.

"Mhmm." She sighed, her whole body relaxed.

That was a good sound to his ears.

He poured more of the fragrant massage oil into his hands and soothed it onto the perfect skin of her back. He liked this part almost as much as the sex. Caring for his lover after sex seemed so intimate. Though he hadn't had many women he would truly call lovers, even the one-night stands or weekend women he'd been with, he tried to take care of.

It was a million times better with Abigail since he knew she was truly his.

He genuinely enjoyed bathing her and carefully rubbing salve into her pink buttocks. He certainly liked the intimacy of easing the muscles that had worked so hard to bring him pleasure. Her skin was soft and warm under his hands. This was the calm, loving after-time he always lavished on a submissive.

Except for Sam. He'd been willing to take care of Sam since he'd felt the lash earlier, but Sam being Sam, had fallen asleep and wasn't having anyone interrupt that. He'd grunted and pulled a pillow over his head when Jack had offered.

"You're really good at this, Jack," she groaned as he ran his thumbs under her shoulder blades.

"I've had practice." He loved the creamy perfection of her skin and how it contrasted with his own. She was a pale, gorgeous ivory, and he was a man who worked in the sun.

"At The Club?" she asked hesitantly.

Jack's hands paused before moving up to her neck. "Where did you hear about The Club?"

"Sam mentioned it. Was it there that you found out you were a Dom?"

He sighed and made the decision. She had the right to know everything about him. In the beginning, he'd been worried that his past could come between them, but knowing her as he did now, he doubted it. Still… "If I tell you the story, I should warn you, I might not come out looking like your knight in shining armor."

"I want to hear it," she said quietly. "I want to know everything about you."

"All right." He continued to move his hands over her skin, stroking her as he told his story. "I was involved with a woman shortly after I aged out of foster care. I was basically homeless, and Sam was three months from joining me. I had very little time to figure out how I was going to take care of us. I was responsible for him, you see. At first, I spent my nights trying to make cash playing pool. Despite the fact that I was eighteen, I looked older and could get into most bars. I met this woman at one. She took me home with her and she taught me what she liked. She liked to be dominated, and I enjoyed doing it. She was impressed with my control. Apparently, some men play at being a Dom when what they really want is to abuse a woman. The trust a submissive places in a Dom is a gift. It should be treasured. I was careful with her. She introduced me to a man named Julian Lodge. He owned an underground club in Dallas that catered to men and women in the lifestyle. It still does. I lived at The Club for several years. I made a living there."

Abigail's head came up, and he waited for her judgment. He should have known better, because there was just a wicked smile on her face. "Really? People paid you to spank them?"

There wasn't a bit of condemnation in her big hazel eyes, and he relaxed. That was his woman. She would be far more interested in hearing stories about his time at The Club than she would waste worrying how it affected her.

"Yes," Jack said, returning her grin. "I worked for clients. I acted out scenes and scenarios with them. You have to understand that what I did mostly involved discipline. I got a lot of clients off, but I didn't have sex with them, not the way you would think. I only had sex outside of work. I wanted to keep it separate."

She frowned and looked like a disappointed kitten. "They don't have sex at The Club? That kills a lot of fantasies."

He leaned over and kissed her, a light joy lifting his heart. She was beyond perfect. "They have plenty of sex at The Club, baby. Not all Doms work the way I did. I preferred to keep sex private and off the clock. It seemed too much like prostitution the other way."

"What did Sam do while you spanked the regulars?"

"Sam tended bar," he explained. She'd turned over and he walked down to the end of the bench and took one of her pretty feet in his hands. He kissed the arch and started to work it over with his thumbs. He was satisfied by the happy purr that came out of his sweet sex kitten. "We worked there until we were ready to buy the ranch."

Her eyes narrowed curiously again. "You made enough money at The Club to buy this spread?"

She didn't sound like she believed it, and it wasn't true. He decided to lay all his cards on the table. She would find out sooner or later. Sam had a big mouth and no ability to keep it shut. "No. I got that money the old-fashioned way."

"You stole it?" The question came out on a gasp, as though he'd finally managed to shock her.

Lucky for him, that wasn't the truth. "I blackmailed my politician father for it. Over the years, I became close to my boss at The Club. Julian was only a couple of years older than me, but he had so much more experience that he became a bit of a mentor to me. Julian believes in doing deep background checks on all of his employees and clients. He considers it essential to covering his ass. When he checked into my background, he found out some things I didn't even know about my past. I'd always assumed my father was some guy my mom hooked up with who fled the scene. My mom was sweet and she loved me, but she wasn't smart when it came to men. She was working as an assistant to a politician when she became pregnant with me. Shortly after, she left the job and she didn't work again. Julian found it odd that she managed to raise me with no visible means of support."

"She had an affair with that politician, and he paid her hush money," she surmised. "I've read enough tabloids to know how that story goes."

"Yes," he confirmed. "My biological father took care of her financially until she died, and then it was easy to let me go into foster care. She was alone in the world. No one would have known or cared what happened to me."

"Bastard." Her hands had fisted at her sides. She was a ferocious one.

"After Julian confirmed I was, indeed, his biological son, we cooked up a plan. I went to him and explained the situation and offered my complete silence in exchange for five million dollars," Jack stated. "Baby, you should know my biological father is Senator Allen Cameron, but I've signed a bunch of documents claiming it isn't true."

"Holy shit. He's talking about running for the presidency."

He nodded. "Yes. So you can imagine how having a love child who worked at an underground sex club could have put a wrench into his aspirations. He was more than happy to pay me off and get me out of his house. Funny thing is, now the bastard's people call me trying to get me to contribute to his campaign." He put her foot down and held his hand out to pull her to him. "So, you're marrying a bastard son who used to work in a profession most people would consider prostitution. You still all right with marrying me?"

She hugged him close to her. "I am going to be so proud to be your wife. I love you. I love Sam." Her smile was radiant. "Though I still don't see a ring on my finger."

He chuckled and held her close. "I will have to do something about that first thing in the morning. I wouldn't want your finger to be ringless."

She bit at her bottom lip. He was beginning to see it as a nervous habit. He could always tell when she was worried. "I was kidding about the ring. We can get a band. They don't cost very much. And you have to take the Benz back. I can make do with a cheaper car. I'm not a princess."

"You're my princess." He'd thought, maybe, she was under a few mistaken impressions, but this confirmed it. It just made him love her more.

"Well, I can be an economical princess," she stated firmly. "I will not have you hurting the business to dazzle me. I'm dazzled enough. I love you. I want to help out. I realize that every bit of that five million went into building your ranch. It'll be years before it really starts to pay off, and I'll help. I can get a job. Nurses make good money."

"Whoa." He pushed her hair back, luxuriating in the soft feel. "I'll take care of you. First, the ranch pays quite nicely. Second, seven years ago we found out that the ranch is built on top of roughly half a billion dollars' worth of natural gas."

Her mouth dropped open. "You're filthy rich, aren't you?"

"I am intensely dirty, baby," Jack acknowledged. "I signed half of everything over to Sam. When you marry me, he intends to make you his beneficiary and so do I. If anything happens to us, you'll be well taken care of."

Suddenly, there were tears in her eyes. "They can't hurt you, can they?"

"No." He kissed her mouth. He would never get enough of this woman. "They can't hurt me or Sam, and they can't hurt you. I can't promise that they'll all be kind, but no one can force you out again. I can promise you that Sam and I will be by your side for everything that happens."

She clutched him to her body.

The door opened. Sam's eyes were sleepy as he watched them.

"Did she figure out we're rich and nobody's going to mess with us?" Sam asked, scratching his naked belly as he yawned.

"Yes, as a matter of fact she did," he replied with an indulgent smile. "I thought you were asleep."

He still appeared to be. "Can't sleep alone. Cold. Lonely. Come to bed."

He shuffled back through the bathroom, and Jack picked her up to follow. Abigail yawned, too, cuddling against him.

"Jack?" She sounded sleepy and happy.

"Yes, baby?"

"I did tell you I loved you before I found out you were a multimillionaire, right?"

Jack stifled his laugh. "Yes, you did. I believe you told a struggling rancher you loved him and would work hard to make his business successful."

Abby nuzzled his neck. "I rock."

He did nothing to contain his amusement this time. "You do, love, you certainly do."

* * * *

Later, after he'd settled her into bed and Sam was curled against her, Jack rose and got dressed. It wasn't late. There was still time for what he needed to do. He took the Benz, and it wasn't even nine o'clock when he rang the doorbell at the stately home that had housed the Echols family for years.

A weary butler opened the door.

"Tell Mrs. Echols that Jack Barnes is here," he said. "We have something to discuss."

Chapter Seventeen

Ruby Echols watched as the door closed. Adam was walking out the door once more. It was all happening again. At least she'd had her husband by her side that night twenty years before. She hadn't been forced to face ensuing tragedy alone. This time she didn't know where Hal had gotten off to. He should have been here. He could have made Adam listen to reason.

"Ma'am?" The maid's voice cut through her dark thoughts. "I have your medication."

She looked up and her eyes focused on the young woman in her black uniform. It was too tight. She would have to say something to the housekeeper about the help she was hiring. They weren't up to the Echols's standards. The brunette maid held a glass of water and a familiar bottle of pills. Which one was this? There were so many pills these days.

"I don't want it," she snapped. "Get my son."

The young woman looked slightly confused, but Ruby had long since decided that all young people were confused. The public education system was in shambles. They weren't even allowed to spank the children anymore. How would they learn anything?

"Ma'am, Walter moved out a couple of days ago. He left a number to call." The young woman stood by the phone. "Would you

214

like me to call him for you?"

"How can Walter move out?" she asked irritably. "He's fourteen years old."

The idiot simply looked at her. Ruby huffed. Good help was impossible to find these days. She pointed out the window where she could hear a door closing and the engine to a car purr to life. "Go and stop Adam from leaving. He just walked out the door. Tell him his brother is missing. That should stop him."

Yes, she could use that. If Walter was in trouble then Adam would take time out of chasing that tramp to help him. They were brothers. A much stronger connection. Why hadn't she thought of that before? The stupid girl stood there doing nothing.

"Well, what are you waiting for?"

"Ma'am," the girl chirped in her irritatingly young voice, "the only person who walked out of here was Jack Barnes. He's a rancher. He owns the Barnes-Fleetwood Ranch outside town."

Ruby's head hurt. She put a hand to her temple to rub the throbbing there. So much pain. It was better when the fog came over her.

Yes, Jack Barnes had come by and threatened her. He'd been calm about it, so she knew he was serious. She understood that a man like Barnes was infinitely more dangerous when he was calm. He'd told her he could ruin her socially and financially and that he'd do it without a second's remorse if she hurt Abigail Moore again.

He was marrying Abigail Moore on Thursday. He was giving that slut his name and his protection.

Or had it been Adam who said that?

"Ma'am, please take your medication." The girl's voice grated on her nerves.

Without thought, she downed the pill and took a drink of the water. She needed to rest. She had to plan. It was obvious Adam wasn't going to see reason, and neither her husband nor her younger son could see how it all would end. They would tell her she was overreacting, but she would not have that tramp in her family. Sometimes Ruby felt like Cassandra from the old Greek stories. She told them all what would happen, and no one would listen to her.

Ruby heard the door close softly and settled back against the plush cushions of the couch. She had to think, and this time she wasn't going to bring anyone else into it. That had been her mistake. She let others influence her. She was Adam's mother, and she was the only one who knew what he needed.

This time would be different. She would take care of that siren and save Adam. Could a mother do any less for her son?

* * * *

Jack growled at the reflection in the mirror. Well, he was really growling at the tie he couldn't seem to get right. Damn tie.

Sam shook his head and turned him around. There was a slight smile on his face, indulgent and knowing. "You never learn."

The sound echoed against the walls. The men's bathroom at the Hamilton County Courthouse was empty save for Sam and Jack. It was a good thing, too. He didn't need a bunch of men watching him screw up menswear. Damn, but he was nervous. Trying to fix his tie was a nearly impossible task. Sam sighed and took over.

"Well, I don't have occasion to wear them very often," Jack admitted.

He allowed Sam to pull the silk tie off and stood quietly as his partner efficiently began to retie the knot.

Sam worked the silk with an easy hand. "You should be glad one of us listened to Julian's numerous lectures on proper dress. I have to admit, it's fun to see you so nervous."

"I'm not nervous," he lied.

Sam finished and looked over the pristine pinstriped suit Jack was wearing. "You look perfect."

He felt awkward. It was there between them. He could remember the way Sam felt underneath his hands, his mouth moving. Sam had been submissive and giving.

Sam stepped back, worry lines forming around his eyes. "Is there something wrong? Besides the tie?"

He thought about it for a moment. The truth was Sam had felt good under his hands. It had felt right to have them both under his control in that room.

He put a hand on Sam's shoulder and gave him a smile. "There

216

is nothing else wrong and everything right."

The words brought the smile back to Sam's sunny face.

This new relationship with Sam was something they could explore. The possibilities suddenly seemed endless. But first, he had some formalities to get through.

"Do you think we should have driven into Tyler and gotten her roses?" He looked down at the store-bought bouquet of lilies on the counter. It was wrapped in green tissue paper and covered with plastic.

"No," Sam replied. "Abby loves lilies. She'll like the flowers, Jack. They're the best we can get in Willow Fork. Now, I believe you'll find that when we get to Hawaii, we'll have to upgrade. Don't worry. I planned everything out. We have the best suite, the finest hotel, first-class tickets to everything."

He nodded. "Good. I want that…for both of you."

Sam grinned. "Yes, you made that plain when you gave Abby the go-ahead to redecorate. I saw the check you wrote to the contractor. That was a lot of zeroes. I write the next one, okay?"

He wanted to argue but shrugged instead. "All right. She's your wife, too. Well, she will be in twenty minutes."

Jack turned and looked at himself in the mirror, praying he didn't look like an idiot. Everything seemed to be in the right place. He needed a haircut, but when he'd mentioned it, Abigail had sweetly pleaded with him not to. She'd told him she liked his hair longer.

Damn. He pushed the thick black stuff back. The things he was willing to do for that woman.

There were, however, some things he was not willing to do. "You talk to Kyle Morgan about what's wrong with his football players? You tell the coach that it is not my responsibility to give his players work. Ranching is not a part-time business."

For the last several days, the ranch had been inundated with high school boys looking for part-time work.

"I don't think they really want to learn the business. Besides, a couple of them offered to mow the lawn or clean the pool…for free."

"Why the hell would they do that for free?" he asked, letting

217

irritation tinge his tone. "Why are they trying to do me favors?"

Sam shook his head and readjusted his own tie. "I don't think they give a damn about you. If you haven't noticed, it's Abby they ask for." Sam looked down at his watch. "We have to go. It's time"

He didn't really care about the time in that moment. "Are you telling me we've got twenty horny high school boys sniffing around our wife?"

"Get used to it." Sam slapped him on the back. "She's one hell of a woman. That's the good news. She loves us. I doubt she'll be running off with the high school quarterback. He's the one who offered to wash her Benz." Sam guided him out of the bathroom and into the corridor that led to the justice of the peace's office. "The running back has written a few lines of poetry to welcome Abby back into town."

He heard Sam, but his words didn't really register. His attention was wholly on the woman in front of him. The rest of the world fell away the minute he caught sight of her.

Abigail sat on a bench outside the office. She was talking to Christa and her mother. Mike stood in his best Sunday suit. He murmured something to the women, who looked up. Abby stood and smiled.

She wore a form-fitting, cream-colored suit with black heels. Her glorious hair was in an elegant bun tied at the nape of her neck. A small hat sat dashingly on her head. She looked every inch the gracious lady, and he had no idea why a woman as beautiful as Abigail wanted to marry the two of them.

"You still nervous?" Sam's voice was full of emotion.

"I was never nervous, Sam," he replied, his own voice thick. "I'm anxious. We need to get her to sign those papers before she comes to her senses."

She walked toward them, glowing with happiness.

"She's never coming to her senses," Sam vowed. "She's going to love us forever."

"Thank god," Jack breathed.

"I was beginning to wonder if I was getting stood up," Abigail complained good-naturedly.

"Never," the men managed to say in complete synchronicity.

They each took a hand and led her into the office.

* * * *

The justice of the peace had never actually married a couple where the woman held hands with two men. He supposed sometimes the bride held hands with her father before he gave the bride away, but Fred Johnson didn't think the other man in this scenario had any intentions of giving the bride away on a permanent basis.

All in all, it was one for the record books.

Abigail Moore said her vows with a steady voice, but the judge saw her squeezing Sam Fleetwood's hand, though she was legally becoming Jack Barnes's wife. It was an odd but emotional ceremony. Barnes didn't seem to have a problem with Fleetwood kissing the bride after the ceremony. It wasn't a friendly peck, either. It was quite the passionate kiss, but the new groom merely smiled indulgently before taking another kiss for himself. The small wedding party congratulated the bride, the groom, and Sam Fleetwood.

And there had been a nice tip for him. Yes, it was clear that things were changing around Willow Fork.

With a simple signature, the former outcast of Willow Fork became its queen. One simple "I do" and Abigail Barnes became the richest woman in the county, so the judge wasn't about to say a thing about the odd, apparently true rumors about the ranchers' habits. Money turned perversity into eccentricity, and the judge was smart enough to know it. He simply signed all the paperwork and wished the happy couple a good marriage.

Or should he say threesome? He wasn't sure, but as long as everyone was happy, it was all in a good day's work.

* * * *

Abby held her new husbands' hands as they walked out of the judge's office and toward the exit of the courthouse. A sense of satisfaction flowed through her. It was going to be all right. It would be more than all right. It was going to be good. She would build a life with Jack and Sam, a life filled with love and joy.

Sam dropped her hand and hurried ahead to open the door for her.

"I know that the three of you are anxious to get on with the honeymoon," Christa announced as the small party began to march out of the courthouse. "Still, I put together a lunch reception at the café. Some of your friends and neighbors would like to celebrate. You aren't flying out until tomorrow, so come by and do your duty."

Jack frowned as they walked into the brilliant fall day. "Are there going to be any high school boys there?"

Christa's laughter had more than one head turning. She'd hoped Jack hadn't noticed the mob of high school boys plaguing their door.

"No, Jack. They're all in school. Abby is safe," Christa assured him.

"Then let's go have lunch," Jack offered magnanimously. "Now that I have a wife, I should get used to doing more social things."

Abby grinned. He didn't sound like he was looking forward to it.

He would get used to being social because she intended to fit in, even if it killed her. It had occurred to her that this town needed a few things. Willow Fork lacked a free healthcare clinic. Young girls, like she'd been, had nowhere to go for healthcare. Abby felt a crusade beginning and knew Jack and Sam would have to put in face time with the county politicians if she wanted to turn her clinic idea into something real.

Jack offered to bring the truck around when she caught sight of trouble.

"Damn that woman," Diane Moore cursed.

Ruby Echols strode toward them, dressed in a pale blue suit and elegant pumps. She'd had her hair done and carried a large designer bag. It looked far too big for such a small woman to carry, but Ruby managed with her usual flair. The older woman looked all around with great disdain for the ordinary men and women walking in and out of the courthouse. Her steely-eyed gaze moved around the park in front of the courthouse, and Abby had no doubt who she was looking for. Abby sighed. She wasn't about to let that old biddy ruin her wedding day.

"I'll call Walter," Mike offered, pulling his cell phone out.

Sam tugged on her hand, but she resisted. Ruby had backed her down a couple of days ago. It wasn't going to happen again. That woman needed to understand that Abigail Moore...*Barnes* wasn't going anywhere.

"No, Sam. It's long past time for me to stand up to that bat. I'm not letting her push me around anymore."

"Mrs. Echols." Jack greeted her with a low warning as she stepped tentatively onto the courthouse stairs.

Ruby had the strangest expression on her face as she walked up to the group. There was an odd affection in her gaze as she looked at Jack. Her eyes went slightly watery, and her hand disappeared into her bag, searching for something.

"Hello, dear," Ruby said, her voice warmer than Abby could ever remember it. "You look so manly in a suit. I always knew you would be a handsome man."

Jack and Sam exchanged a nervous look. Mike seemed to have gotten in touch with Walter. He was explaining the situation in low tones.

There was something wrong with Ruby Echols and her son needed to take care of it.

"Mrs. Echols," Mike said gently as he slipped his phone back into his pocket. "Your son is on his way. Why don't we go sit down and wait for him?"

Ruby's silver head shook. "Silly boy, my son is right here." She looked at Jack with a maternal smile. "He's here making the biggest mistake of his life. Luckily, he has his mama to correct it."

Abby gasped as Ruby pulled a revolver out of her bag.

The world seemed to shift into slow motion, the moment elongating, horror drawing out. Her heart threatened to stop as Ruby held the gun up with surprising strength. It would hit her in the head. She was going to die. The sound of the gun firing split the air around her. She felt Sam jerk on her hand, but it didn't do any good.

And then she was on the ground, covered completely by Jack's big body. She hit the concrete steps with a resounding thud and felt the wind knocked out of her body.

She couldn't breathe. Where was she hit? Pain wracked her

body, but she didn't think it was from a bullet. Her body ached from being thrown to the concrete. Had Ruby missed?

The keening sound of someone wailing cut through the pain of slamming into the ground.

"Jack?"

Everything around her was chaos. Mike was rushing forward to do something. Someone was crying and screaming about her baby. Was that Ruby? Christa was down on her knees beside Abby, tears streaking down her face.

Through it all she heard her mother talking on a cell phone.

"Yes, there's been a shooting," her mother was saying.

But she was okay. She opened her mouth to speak, but couldn't find the air in her lungs.

"Yes, we have a man down," her mother said.

Oh, god. Something worse than pain struck her. If she wasn't hit…

Sam was suddenly staring down at her, his face a ghostly white. "I'm going to move Jack. I'll get you out in a second."

Panic welled inside her. "He's been shot?"

"Yeah," Sam replied, his voice grim.

"You can't move him. Moving him could cause more damage," she insisted.

But Sam had already shifted Jack's heavy body. "I don't think I can do any more damage."

How bad was it? This couldn't be happening. Not now. Not today. She'd just found them. She couldn't lose one of them. Abby looked down at him, at the man she'd married. Ten minutes before her world had been open and full of hope.

Jack had promised to protect her, and Jack never went back on his word. He'd leapt in front of the bullet meant to end her life. His dress shirt was covered with blood. He'd been shot in the chest.

Shot in the chest. Calm down. He was breathing. It was shallow but he wasn't gone yet. She could panic or she could use decades of training and experience to do everything she could to pull him through this.

It had been worth it. All the pain had been worth it if she could do this one thing. One thing was going to go right. She hadn't fought, sacrificed, raised a child while going to school, worked her way to the top of her trauma unit to let the love of her life die in front of her eyes.

She glanced up because the first thing she needed to do was take control of the scene. Sam looked like he was going to be sick. Christa was weeping. Mike had Ruby's gun in his hand and was holding her back. She could do what she needed to.

Abby got to her knees, slapping at Sam's hands when he tried to pull her to her feet.

"He isn't dead," she barked in a voice that would have let any intern know to back off. "Don't move him any more than we have to."

She quickly took the phone out of her mother's hand. "My name is Abigail Barnes. I am a trauma nurse. We have one man down with a GSW to what looks like his left lung." She listened to the 911 operator as she felt for a pulse. "It missed the heart, but the victim is unconscious and…I've got air bubbles in the blood. I'm passing you off to someone else, but we need a care flight. He needs surgery and possibly life support. He needs to get to Tyler as soon as possible."

She handed the phone back to her mom. Suddenly, Jack's green eyes opened. She felt a flood of relief that she didn't allow to slow her down one bit.

"You okay?" He struggled to get the question out.

She looked around for something suitable to use. Jack's lung was punctured, and he was losing air out of the hole in his chest. It was what they called a "sucking chest wound" in her field. She had to get it covered. The big bouquet of lilies caught her eye. "Sam, tear the cellophane off those flowers."

While Sam went to do her bidding, she stared down at her patient. "I'm fine, Jack. And so are you."

He looked like he wanted to say something but couldn't. The pain was evident on his face. It was pinched and stark white.

"I bet it hurts like hell, baby," she said sternly. "That's what you get for jumping in front of a bullet, Jack Barnes. Listen here, husband of mine, there's no eternal rest for you today, got that?"

Sam handed her the piece of plastic, and she gingerly covered the wound. Jack groaned when she pressed down, but his breathing eased immediately.

"Better," he managed. "I'm not allowed to see a white light?"

She let a small smile tug on her lips. He still had a sense of humor, and as a nurse, she knew the value of that. "You can see it all you like, but don't you dare walk into it."

Abby felt Sam at her side. His hands were shaking.

"I love you," Jack said, a weariness taking over. His body went slack.

In the distance, she heard the thud of a helicopter coming to take Jack. Abby held her hand against his chest and prayed they would make it in time.

Chapter Eighteen

Six Weeks Later

Abby stood beside her daughter, looking out over the expanse of land that made up her new home.

"Should he even be on a horse six weeks after chest surgery?" Lexi stared out the window.

She followed her daughter's line of sight. Jack was by the barn. He carefully dismounted his horse.

Abby was more than happy to have her daughter in Willow Fork. Having Lexi in the house she shared with Jack and Sam made it seem more like home than ever.

"He's made a remarkable recovery," she murmured with a grin.

"You know your mama's taking excellent care of him." Abby's mother joined them at the family room window. She hugged her granddaughter.

"I hear she's the reason he's alive," Lexi said with a proud glance at her mother.

Lexi had the Echols's coloring. Her black hair and dark eyes gave her a slightly exotic look. Her hair was up in a high ponytail. To Abby, she looked younger than her twenty years.

She would always be her mama's baby.

"The way Jack and Sam tell it, Mama was practically a superhero," Lexi continued. "She managed to bandage up Jack so well the paramedics didn't have to do anything but load him onto the helicopter when they got there."

"The doctors said she made the difference," Abby's mom commented. "Then, when Ruby collapsed, Abigail gave her CPR."

"That didn't make a difference," she said briskly.

She didn't like to think about that day at all. It only led to her thinking about the interminable hours she and Sam had spent huddled together in the waiting room praying that Jack would make it through. It was so much nicer to look forward, but Lexi deserved to know.

Lexi turned and enveloped her in a hug. "You did everything you could, Mom. You did way more than anyone could have asked. She shot your husband and you still tried to save her life."

"Well, I was hoping she'd spend the rest of it in jail," Abby allowed.

There were tears in Lexi's dark eyes as she ignored the joke. "Uncle Walter really appreciated it. He and Aunt Jan think the world of you."

Lexi had been visiting with Adam's brother and his family quite a bit while she spent time in her father's hometown. Walter had shown her around and told her all kinds of stories about Adam. Abby had been worried, but Lexi seemed to be enjoying learning about the dad she'd never met and getting to know her little cousins.

"Oh, there's Sam," Lexi pointed out, shaking her head. "I'm going to have to get used to that."

"Used to what?" She stared out the window, trying to see what her daughter was talking about.

Sam dismounted and went to help Jack, who slapped him across the chest. They bickered back and forth for a moment and then smiled as they walked into the barn to put up the horses.

"How hot my dads are," Lexi admitted with a groan. "I'll never be able to bring friends here. They'll drool over my dads."

Abby slanted her daughter a cautious glance. She had been pleased with how well Lexi had taken everything up to this point.

Abby had to suffer through a few "Moms Gone Wild" jokes, but her daughter had seemed thrilled with the arrangement. "It's all right to be embarrassed. I know that this new marriage of mine is…odd."

Lexi grinned at her. "I believe the word you're searching for is bigamy, Mom. Polyandry is a good one, too. Don't worry. I'm going to be a writer so it doesn't bug me at all. My friends will think it's eccentric and cool. Besides, threesomes are all the rage on campus."

"I don't think I wanted to hear that," Jack said as he walked in. He took his new stepfather role seriously. He'd groaned when he heard his daughter was dating a musician.

"It sounds perfectly normal to me." Sam followed Jack. Abby had noted how carefully Sam watched Jack since he left the hospital. He was always close, waiting to lend a hand if he needed it. "Now, when we start getting into foursomes or fivesomes, one has to start questioning the morality of the woman involved."

Abby rolled her eyes. He was still on her about that one little book.

Sam had purchased a bookcase and placed it in their bedroom. He'd lovingly stored her entire collection of erotica, even the really filthy stuff.

Benita walked in and, with a huge smile, announced that lunch was ready. Jack winked at Abby as he turned and started for the dining room. Sam was talking to Lexi and Diane about the renovations they were doing to the house, and Abby hung back for a moment, watching her family walking in for a meal together.

She felt love surge through her heart as Sam said something that made Jack's laugh boom through the house. He'd proven to be a perfect patient. He'd followed her every order. He seemed to bask in her attention and genuinely appreciated the love she lavished on him. Sam had stepped up and kept the ranch running in perfect order. Any worries he'd had about taking care of things were a distant memory now. Sam seemed surer of himself than ever before, and Jack was more peaceful. Her daughter and her mother loved her new husbands and had accepted them without a qualm.

"Are you coming, sweetheart?" Jack asked, looking back into the living room.

"The roast is going to get cold," Sam pointed out.

"I'm coming." Abby brushed away the happy tears in her eyes.

She couldn't help but cry when she thought of it. It had taken twenty years.

No, it had taken a lifetime, but she was home. She was finally and forever home.

* * * *

Jack, Sam, and Abby will return in *Siren in the City*, coming January 23, 2017.

Author's Note

I'm often asked by generous readers how they can help get the word out about a book they enjoyed. There are so many ways to help an author you like. Leave a review. If your e-reader allows you to lend a book to a friend, please share it. Go to Goodreads and connect with others. Recommend the books you love because stories are meant to be shared. Thank you so much for reading this book and for supporting all the authors you love!

Sign up for Lexi Blake's newsletter
and be entered to win a $25 gift certificate
to the bookseller of your choice.

Join us for news, fun, and exclusive content
including free short stories.

There's a new contest every month!

Go to www.LexiBlake.net to subscribe.

Siren in the City
Texas Sirens Book 2
By Lexi Blake writing as Sophie Oak
Coming January 23, 2018

Re-released in a second edition with new scenes.

Jack and Sam married Abby. It was supposed to be for forever, but lately Abby wonders where her alpha male has gone. Jack has retreated and life has become decidedly vanilla. It isn't the true marriage she and Sam wanted. Sam and Abby know the time has come to fight for what they need.

A call from his mentor forces Jack to revisit the club where he discovered his sexuality. Jack's half-brother is in the city and interested in a little blackmail. Can Jack handle two defiant subs and a brother in need of some tough love?

Sometimes all it takes to find the way home is a little love and a lot of mischief.

Come back to the beginning and revisit some of your favorite old characters or find new ones to love. Siren in the City has been revised and new scenes added. And if you look closely, you'll find not only the beginnings of the Sophie Oak world, but also the seeds of how McKay-Taggart began…

* * * *

"Are we done, Julian? I would like to take my subs upstairs. It's time I had a long talk with them."

She held her breath as Leo stepped forward. "I'm not done." He stood in front of Jack, going toe-to-toe with him. "I'm the Dom in residence now, Master Jack. I know that used to be your job, but you're a guest now. Had two subs caused the trouble yours did tonight, what would you have requested then?"

Jack's jaw tightened. "I would have immediately requested

punishment. Julian would have wanted punishment for disrupting the scenes, but I would have requested punishment for the insult to me."

Leo nodded. "They both will pay for abusing Master Julian's trust. I want her to pay for the insult to me."

The hand on the back of her neck tightened almost painfully, and Abby decided not to argue.

"What insult?" Jack asked.

Leo's eyes skimmed over her. She watched from beneath her lashes. "She started everything. I was attempting to watch over Master Julian's possession. She questioned my authority over Sally in public. She proceeded to ignore direct orders given to her for her own protection. Though the male is the one who fought, I understand and forgive his actions. He was protecting her. He's your partner?"

There was not an ounce of condemnation in the Dom's question. He was merely attempting to outline the relationship.

"We share our wife. But I am the head of the household."

"Well, your wife is topping from the bottom," Leo accused. "I can't let the rest of the subs see her get away with it. Twenty tonight, over my knee, right now."

The hand came off her neck and she heard a sigh. His voice was low, and she couldn't stand the defeated sound of his reply. "We'll be out of here in an hour. Julian, I'm sorry. Consider my membership revoked. Come along, Abigail. Sam, I expect you to pack whatever you need and meet us in the lobby."

"No!" She reached for his hand. Jack did business with the members of this club. It meant something to him. It was the whole reason she wanted to come here. She wanted to see this side of him. It had been the first place he'd called home. Now she would be the reason he lost it. Jack growled at her. She kept her head down, but she couldn't keep quiet. "Please, Jack. Please don't. I couldn't live with it. I'll do whatever he asks. I can handle it. Please don't let this happen."

His hand found her chin again, and his expression was softer now. "Abigail, he could hurt you."

"Nothing will hurt me more than knowing I did this to you."

232

She could feel the tears streaming down her face. "Please?"

He forced her to look him straight in the eyes, his gaze steady. "I will never allow another man to put his hands on you like that. Do you understand me? I don't care what you've done or what their rules are. I only trust Sam. This relationship is between the three of us. I won't let anyone else in, not even for a moment, no matter what it costs me. All right?"

Though it hurt her heart, she knew he wouldn't move. She nodded.

"Leo, I wonder if you would indulge me." Julian's voice cut through her misery. "If Jackson administers the punishment, will you be satisfied? He's serious. He will leave and not come back rather than allow you to touch her. It will more than likely cost me a friendship I would prefer not to lose."

The slight incline of the dungeon master's head indicated his assent. "But I expect him to take this seriously. It's obvious to me he has no control over his subs. He needs to reestablish control or allow them their freedom so they can find more appropriate Masters."

"How about you let me worry about my wife and my partner and you keep your hands off of her." Jack took a threatening step toward the other man. "Don't think I don't see the way you look at her. You don't want to punish her. You want to get your hands on her. It's not going to happen while I'm still breathing. Get me a chair."

Jack hauled her up and she let him. If this was what it took, she could handle it. Hell, a part of her was already soft and wet. Deep down it was what she had hoped for. She glanced around at the crowd of people watching while Jack was brought a chair. They were going to watch him spank her. She hadn't really hoped for this part. She felt her skin flush as they watched her.

Julian and Leo seemed particularly interested, but Sally's head was up, too. There was a strangely familiar face in the back. He had black, fashionably tousled hair and wore trendy clothes. He was young, but he watched the scene before him with a fascination that was hard to miss. An older man in a suit, however, stood right behind the young man, and his disdain shone on his pinched face. It took her back to a time when she saw that look on a lot of people's faces. She felt seventeen again, with the contempt of her hometown all around her. She'd been young and pregnant, and they'd called her a whore.

"Abigail." Jack's voice brought her back to reality. He sat on one of the office chairs from the horny ad execs scene. "Come here."

She turned away from the man with the disgusted expression. The rest of the room didn't seem shocked at what was about to happen. They were excited. A thrill went through her. Screw the guy in the back. She wasn't going to let people like that affect her anymore. She walked to Jack and let him pull her over his lap.

Her pussy throbbed in anticipation. Her mouth went dry as Jack's big hands stroked up her legs and began to push her skirt up. She was suddenly glad she'd fought Sam on her choice of underwear. He'd pushed for a thong, but she was eager to wear the cute silk bikinis that matched her corset. Now it would give her a bit of modesty.

"What the fuck?" Jack fingered the underwear. "Since when do I allow you to wear panties? Get me a knife."

So much for modesty. She felt a touch of metal as Jack cut the super-expensive underwear off her body. She watched them fall to the side.

"You're just running wild aren't you, baby?

Nobody Does It Better

Masters and Mercenaries 15
By Lexi Blake
Coming February 20, 2018

A spy who specializes in seduction

Kayla Summers was an elite CIA double agent, working inside China's deadly MSS. Now, she works for McKay-Taggart London, but the Agency isn't quite done with her. Spy master Ezra Fain needs her help on a mission that would send her into Hollywood's glamorous and dangerous party scene. Intrigued by the mission and the movie star hunk she will be shadowing, she eagerly agrees. When she finds herself in his bed, she realizes she's not only risking her life, but her heart.

A leading man who doesn't do romance

Joshua Hunt is a legend of the silver screen. As Hollywood's highest paid actor, he's the man everyone wants to be, or be with, but something is missing. After being betrayed more than once, the only romance Josh believes in anymore is on the pages of his scripts. He keeps his relationships transactional, and that's how he likes it, until he meets his new bodyguard. She was supposed to keep him safe, and satisfied when necessary, but now he's realizing he may never be able to get enough of her.

An ending neither could have expected

Protecting Joshua started off as a mission, until it suddenly felt like her calling. When the true reason the CIA wanted her for this assignment is revealed, Kayla will have to choose between serving her country or saving the love of her life.

* * * *

"Kayla?"

Her eyes came up, a flash of recognition there. "Yes?"

"Are you going to sign the contract or do you have more questions?"

She picked up the pen sitting on top of the contracts that would bind the two of them together for the next six months. They would reevaluate the relationship at that point in time, but for the next six months, she was his. His bodyguard. His submissive.

Bought and properly paid for. He would take care of her and she would give him what he needed.

She signed with a flourish and sat back, a gleam of curiosity in her eyes.

He was curious, too, and there was zero reason to not satisfy their curiosity. Hard and soft limits had been gone over. They would find their communication style as they went along. But first she should understand that he was in control.

"Come sit on my lap."

She didn't hesitate. She stood and turned, shifting so she could maneuver her way onto his lap.

Her weight came down on him and he wrapped an arm around her waist. Damn but she made him feel big. He'd seen her take out a man twice her size, but sitting here in his lap she felt small and vulnerable, and fuck him but that did it for him.

He slid a hand along her knee, letting himself indulge in the silky smooth feel of her skin against his palm. "Did you do as I asked?"

He was well aware his voice had gone husky, deeper than normal.

"Yes, Joshua." She squirmed the tiniest bit, as though trying to find a comfortable position. It might be difficult for her because she was sitting right on his cock, and it was harder and thicker than he could ever remember it being.

"How can I trust you?" This was all part of the game he loved so much. Here he could let go and play out the darker of his impulses—to control, to take, to possess. See. Want. Have.

"You'll have to check," she replied. "Though shouldn't we go inside?"

He reached out and picked up his cell with his free hand, pushing one number and connecting to the security room. He put them on speaker. She needed to understand what she was up against in order for the game to be fair. "Landon?"

"This is Burke," the deep voice replied. "Shane's on patrol. What can I do for you?"

"Burke, I would like to fuck my submissive on the third-floor balcony. Is anyone watching us? Can you see any cameras pointed our way?"

A low, masculine chuckle came across the line. "No, Mr. Hunt. And given the angle relative to the beach, you should enjoy your evening without worry. The only peepers I would worry about would be your next door neighbor, and Jared is out for the night."

"I wouldn't care if he wasn't. Keep up the good work." He hung up and his hand tightened. "I would prefer when we're playing that you don't question me like that. I know where I want to fuck you. I know when I want to fuck you, and I'm in charge. If I want you in the middle of a crowded freeway, your only response is a yes or a no. Not to question me."

She seemed to relax back against him, as though she was giving up the struggle and choosing to submit. "Yes, Joshua. Yes, I understand, and yes to the sex. Please."

He liked the breathy little *please* and loved how she squirmed. Still, he wasn't absolutely sure she'd obeyed him, and he was a man who required proof. He slid his hand up her thigh. "Spread your legs for me."

About Lexi Blake

Lexi Blake lives in North Texas with her husband, three kids, and the laziest rescue dog in the world. She began writing at a young age, concentrating on plays and journalism. It wasn't until she started writing romance that she found success. She likes to find humor in the strangest places. Lexi believes in happy endings no matter how odd the couple, threesome or foursome may seem. She also writes contemporary Western ménage as Sophie Oak.

Connect with Lexi online:

Facebook:
https://www.facebook.com/pages/Lexi-Blake/342089475809965
Twitter: https://twitter.com/authorlexiblake
Website: www.LexiBlake.net

Sign up for Lexi's free newsletter at www.LexiBlake.net.

Made in the USA
Middletown, DE
03 May 2018